S0-APO-807

Instead of stepping back as she expected, her rescuer placed his hands on her waist and drew her against his chest.

"I claim my reward," he said, tipping back the flamboyant bonnet, and the next minute Miss Beringer was being thoroughly kissed.

Emma had been kissed before, hurried affairs delivered by callow youths, but this was far different. This man obviously knew what he was about, and it was quite clear that he had practiced the art to perfection. Clasped against him, bent backward at the waist, Emma hung in his arms, aware of his strength, and for one wild moment savored the sensation before shocked rage came to her rescue.

# THE
# BERINGER
# HEIRESS

## Jan Constant

FAWCETT CREST • NEW YORK

A Fawcett Crest Book
Published by Ballantine Books
Copyright © 1992 by Janis Dawson

All rights reserved under International and Pan-American Copyright Conventions. Published in the United States by Ballantine Books, a division of Random House, Inc., New York, and simultaneously in Canada by Random House of Canada Limited, Toronto.

Library of Congress Catalog Card Number: 91-92401

ISBN 0-449-22137-7

Manufactured in the United States of America

First Edition: July 1992

# Chapter One

"*O*h, it does feel so good to be back in England!" exclaimed Emma, leaning her elbows on the windowsill and propping her chin on her hands as she surveyed the scene beyond the confines of the inn.

The street below bustled with townsfolk, intermingled with blue-clad sailors and marines in their scarlet tunics and tall, black hats. By craning her neck, Miss Beringer could see clusters of tall masts rising like forests as ships rode at anchor in the harbor. A salt breeze wafted in at the open window, bringing with it the faint tang of tar and newly cut wood from the nearby dockyard and spice and other exotic commodities imported by the many merchant ships busy discharging their cargoes at the quays on "Spice Island," just off the High Street.

Emma found the invitation of sun and new surroundings too much to bear and turned round from the window, saying impulsively: "Let's go out, Peggy. I'm sure you would like to explore Portsmouth as much as I."

"I don't know as we should, miss," demurred the older woman, pausing in the task of shaking the creases out of a pale green crepe dinner gown.

Emma bit back an impatient sigh, telling herself for the hundredth time that she must make allowances for Peggy Jones, who had lost her husband at the storming of Badajoz, where Emma's own father had died. The sergeant's widow had agreed to accompany Emma home and act as lady's maid in return for the passage home from the Peninsula.

"It would do you good, Peggy," Emma Beringer insisted. "You know the sergeant wouldn't want you to mourn forever."

"It's only been two months," the other protested, but, sensing a softening in her voice as she glanced out at the busy street, Emma picked up her straw bonnet and tied the strings under her chin.

"It will do us both good," she declared firmly.

"What about Sir Julian?" queried Peggy. "He did say as how he'd meet you here."

"Pooh! The *Hera* was two days late in making port, and we've been here all day. If my guardian can't be bothered to call—then I certainly do not intend to wait for him."

"What's he like, miss, this guardian of yours?" asked the older woman as they left the old inn behind and began to walk along the crowded thoroughfare.

"I've no idea—I've never met him. It was arranged by my father years ago when my mother died. I daresay Papa forgot all about it, for at my age the idea is quite ridiculous. A girl of twelve may need a guardian, but an intelligent female of nearly twenty is a different matter entirely—as I intend to tell Sir Julian Leyton."

"He'll be an old gentleman, then?"

"Good Heavens, as old as Methusula at least, rheumatic, bald, and toothless, to be sure!" Miss Beringer answered cheerfully, and in no doubt as to her ability to manage such a decrepit figure, passed on oblivious to the possibility of any thwarting of her plans. "I shall explain how it is," she went on and, having reached a row of interesting shops, walked on slowly, studying the goods displayed in their bow windows, "and tell him that he has no need to bother himself with me. I have no intention of troubling him and, being quite capable of looking after myself, shall take myself off to Haslemere, where my dearest friend lives—I propose to become a governess, you know. At his age Sir Julian will, no doubt, be grateful to escape the responsibility of a ward."

By mutual consent they both paused in front of a milliner's shop, gazing with undisguised pleasure at the hats and bonnets arranged invitingly in the little bay window. Emma was pleased to see that Mrs. Jones stared as avidly as herself, glad to have found something that aroused the other from her apathy.

"You've been very kind to me," she said. "I'd like to give you some token—will you let me buy you a bonnet?"

Peggy Jones looked startled. "Oh, miss, that's ever so kind of you," she said, while her face colored uncomfortably, "but I've already had my fare home paid, and I'm grateful for that—"

Emma smiled gently. "That blond straw with the pink rose would suit you," she suggested and, seeing from her companion's expression that she had aquiesced, led the way into the shop.

A thin, modishly dressed woman came forward as the bell above the door jangled and smiled invitingly. "Can I help you, miss?" she inquired pleasantly.

"We'd like to see the straw with the rose from the window," Emma said, seating herself beside a table laden with headgear of various shapes and styles.

The woman produced the bonnet and, removing her old brown velvet affair, Peggy allowed the new hat to be placed on her head. The broad pink ribbons were tied beneath her chin and, to her surprise, Emma saw her companion transformed into an attractive woman. Peggy turned this way and that, admiring herself blissfully in the mirror, and Emma realized that for the first time in their acquaintance the older woman looked happy.

"You must have it," she urged involuntarily. "It suits you so well—you'll be the village belle when you get to your destination."

Peggy's face crumpled. "Do you think I should—me being a widow and all?"

"The sergeant would have loved you in it," Emma assured her positively, and Peggy turned back to the mirror, nodding at her reflection.

"Thank you, miss," she said. "Charlie always did like me in pink." Her eyes grew red and, dragging a handkerchief from her reticule, she blew her nose vigorously. "No," she said as the milliner reached up to remove the new purchase. "I'll wear it."

The thin woman smiled understandingly and turned her attention to Emma. "And, miss—can I show you anything?"

It was so long since she had seen anything to compare with the elegant frivolity of the array in the shop that Emma had been quite dazzled at first. Since then, she had been fighting temptation, having fallen in love with a delightful creation as soon as she had sat down. Following her longing gaze, the milliner tweaked it off the stand, swiftly removed Emma's old chip straw, and placed the new bonnet on the blond curls with practiced ease, knowing that most ladies, of whatever age, could not resist a new hat once it was on their head.

An extravagantly curved brim of pleated red silk framed Emma's face, two white ostrich feathers curled and waved over the high crown, while opulent white roses attached the wide red ribbon bows on either side in a final touch.

"Oh—it's *beautiful*!" Emma breathed, bewitched, as she gazed wide-eyed at her reflection. "I'll have it," she heard herself declaring, refusing to think of her light purse.

"Do you think it's . . . quite—?" Peggy began doubtfully, eyeing the elaborate edifice with misgiving. More worldly than her mistress, she was aware that the hat was not entirely suitable for a lady and certainly not for a girl of Emma's years.

"It becomes you, if I may say so," put in the milliner quickly.

Emma knew that she was speaking the truth. The bonnet *did* become her; the bright color brought out the delicate tints of her skin and hair, while her dark blue eyes sparkled with pleasure at the prospect of owning such a work of art.

"How much is it?" she asked, her face falling as she heard a sum above anything she could afford.

"Of course, there will be a discount, as you are purchasing two items," the milliner continued smoothly, recognizing the possibility of losing the sale. The bonnet had been in stock all season, and soon she knew the Portsmouth ladies and demimonde would be looking for winter fashions. A cheap sale was better than being left with last year's model. She named a price that was judged to be within her customer's range, and Emma, who had seen her desire snatched out of her hands, sighed in relief.

"I'll take it," she cried, ignoring her conscience which told her not to fritter away her small store of cash.

Peggy touched her arm. "You could leave mine," she suggested quietly. "My brown velvet will do for a while yet."

Emma was touched and gave the other a quick hug. "No," she whispered. "I won't hear of it."

Well pleased with each other and their purchases, they sallied forth. Determined upon stringent economies, Emma was thoughtful as they continued along the High Street, but once having viewed the Sally Port and having remarked upon the circumstance of Admiral Nelson having passed that way on his last journey to the Victory, she put aside her worries and walked along the esplanade with enjoyment.

Leaning her arms on the high seawall, she shaded her eyes and studied the vast array of ships, rising and falling on the swell, which was being driven up the Solent by the rising wind. "Do you think we can see the *Hera*?" she wondered. "I should like to see the outside of her, having come to know the inside so intimately during our crossing."

"All boats look alike to me," answered Mrs. Jones indifferently, hugging the ends of her shawl closer about her plump person. "I miss the heat—strange, isn't it? All those years in Spain hating it and wanting to be home again, and, now that I am, all I can think of is the cold."

Emma looked at her sympathetically. "Where are you going?" she asked. "Do you have something planned?"

"Oh, yes. Charlie had saved a bit and sent it home. His brother has an inn Fareham way. I'm to go there—it's all been arranged for years. Charlie was a good man, thoughtful-like. He had it all worked out. He made me promise not to go from man to man if he was taken. Not like some women do. Not decent, he said."

Emma nodded, knowing that some of the army wives had been obliged to take as many as three or four husbands in the course of the Peninsular War, as each spouse was killed in turn.

For a while she fell silent, her thoughts returning to the country and life they had left behind. Despite the discomforts and dangers, she had enjoyed "following the drum" and knew that she would find the return to conventional society irksome, to say the least. Never one for formality or accepting the subservient role of compliant female, she had grown used to a free reign. Her father had curbed her headstrong tendency with the lightest of leads, and Emma had come to believe in her own strength of mind, disliking strongly anything that threatened her wishes.

She viewed the idea of a guardian with misgiving, wondering how her father could have left such an arrangement, which he could not but know must fill her with antipathy. He had praised her for a sensible female on the very day on which he had died, and here Emma blinked sharply and whisked a tear away from her eye. A chill caught during the cold nights had been the death of Major Beringer, and she had nursed him devotedly. In those last few days she felt that they had come to know each other better than in the two years since finishing school, in which she had traveled the Peninsula with his regiment. . . . Already those hot days and freezing nights seemed an age away.

"Look, miss—that child . . . !" Peggy touched her arm, indicating where the shingle beach shelved steeply to the sea, which was breaking on the shore with a force that sent the spray flying. Almost at once the water was sucked out again, leaving a trough in the stones, which was quickly filled by the crashing arrival of the next wave. Following her finger, Emma saw a small boy in nankeen pantaloons and smock jumping in the curling edges of the waves, oblivious of his danger, as he wandered nearer the breakers.

Both women had the same intention, but, being younger and lighter, Emma was first away and well ahead of her maid as they raced over the uneven, soft shingle. Praying that she would not fall, Emma knew that she would have only one chance to save the child; once the waves had seized him, he would be sucked beyond the help of all but the strongest of swimmers.

Even as she stretched out her hand to grasp him, the undertow sucked away his footing, and only by flinging herself full length could Emma catch the hem of his full smock. Scrambling to her knees she held onto the material, hoping that it would not tear, and at last she felt the sea release its hold on him as it rolled out and paused at the zenith of its retreat before returning in greater force.

Scooping him under one arm, she turned and ran, the waves seeming to tower over her as she fought her way up the wet, shifting beach. Time slowed, and, as in a dream, each footstep took an age to accomplish. Knowing that almost certain death was behind her spurred her on, and at last she reached the top of the shelf. At that moment, as if in a final effort to claim a victim, the sea pounded down, falling behind her in a rage of spray, which smothered her in salt water and small particles of stone.

"Oh, miss—oh, miss!" gasped Peggy, arriving at that moment and reaching out her plump arms to drag her further up the beach. "Oh, *miss*, I thought you were gone! You saved this young scamp's life—I'll swear to it!"

But far from grateful, the boy turned a look of fury on his rescuer and struggled to be set down.

"Nasty lady," he yelled, kicking enthusiastically with his chubby legs. "You did push me in the wet!"

Emma burst out laughing and put him on the ground, keeping a careful hold of his collar. "What an ingrate!" she exclaimed, as he wriggled to be free.

"What do we do with him?" Peggy asked doubtfully, watching his squirms and spirited jiggling. "Folk'll think we're ill-treating him," she warned, as his face turned bright red with rage and he opened his mouth, preparatory to bawling with all the power of his lungs.

"Quick—quick, look at that funny bird!" cried Emma with great presence of mind and, pointing to a solitary seagull flying overhead, successfully distracted the child.

Holding onto him with one hand and delving into her reticule with the other, Emma produced a penny, which she held up invitingly.

"If you're a good boy and tell me where you live, I'll give you this penny," she promised.

Closing his mouth, he eyed the coin with a covetous gaze. "Dere," he announced, waving an arm in the direction of the esplanade.

"Yes, sweetheart, but where over there?"

"*Dere*," he cried impatiently and, heedless of the arm that still held him, set off up the beach.

Arriving back on the stone walk, the child pointed at a row of terraced houses, neat and clean in the sunlight. "Dere," he repeated triumphantly, holding out his hand.

Dropping the money into his palm, Emma was made suddenly aware of her disheveled dress as the wind moulded her damp clothes to her body.

"I can't possibly take him home like this," she said, trying to pull the clinging folds away from her legs. "You'll have to take him, Peggy, while I go back to the inn."

Peggy looked prim. "Let's hope no one sees you, miss," she remarked. "It's not for me to say, but you don't look at all ladylike. You'll catch your death, miss."

Suddenly aware that the only part of her attire that had escaped a soaking was her new hat, Emma laughed at the picture she must present. "Thank Heavens it's my old muslin and the year before last's spencer," she said and, leaving Mrs. Jones to her task, set off in the direction of the High Street.

Once away from the sea, the wind lost its gale force and became merely playful, tugging at her skirt and endeavoring to whisk her new bonnet from her head. Clasping the brim with both hands, Emma tucked her head down and fought her way along the street, keeping close to the walls for the protection they afforded. This was her undoing; crossing a garden bound by an ornate iron railing, she suddenly found herself held fast. Taken by surprise, she at first tried to pull herself free, before craning her neck and seeing that the strings which tied the bodice of her high-waisted dress were caught round one of the iron spikes. Try how she would, she could not reach them and knew that she was in the ridiculous position of being a prisoner until someone chanced along and released her.

Unfortunately the street was deserted, and she had to stand in growing impatience until a tall gentleman rounded the corner and advanced toward her. Far from the kind, elderly person Emma had hoped would arrive to rescue her from her predicament, this gentleman was fashionable and broad shouldered and, while not in the first flush of youth, was of an age to be interesting to any unmarried female. He strolled toward her, his tall hat at a dashing angle on his black curls, a gold pin gleaming in the snowy folds of his cravat, his buckskins and blue jacket fitting without a hint of a wrinkle, and his black boots gleaming with all the loving care that a valet could bestow.

So grand was his appearance and so self-confident his manner, that Emma's nerve nearly failed, and she would have let him pass without asking his aid, but her manner had obviously caught his attention, and he turned his gaze upon her as he drew level.

One black eyebrow rose in a quizzical manner and, pausing in his long stride, he made her a half bow.

"Madam?" he inquired, taking in the enchanting picture she presented, cheeks flushed with effort, blue eyes sparkling with enthusiasm for the adventure she had just enjoyed. Golden curls were escaping from the outrageous hat, and the length of her slim figure was clearly outlined by the clinging folds of her damp gown.

"*Could* you be so kind?" she asked. "I am afraid that I am caught fast—"

For a moment he eyed her appreciatively, then peered over her indicated shoulder, saw the trouble, and smiled in a way that was unfamiliar to Miss Beringer.

"Of course. I'll have you free in a trice, my dear," he drawled and, standing closer than she cared for, reached both hands round her shoulders to untie the tangled strings.

Made unduly nervous by his nearness, Emma tried to appear unconcerned as his fingers brushed her back and his breath fanned her cheek. He seemed to take an inordinate length of time to free her, and at last she glanced up to find his gaze fixed on her face.

Black eyes smiled warmly down at her, and, not at all discomfited by the fact that she had caught his steady gaze, he allowed his obvious admiration to show.

"Are you looking for a protector, my dear?" she was surprised to hear him ask easily.

"We—ll—I have a guardian," she answered cautiously, wondering what he could mean.

"And are you in need of a new one?"

"I haven't met this one yet," she was astonished into admitting and saw his eyebrows shoot skyward.

"Your attitude is refreshingly practical," he told her, and she was almost sure that a suppressed laugh shook his shoulders.

Beginning to suspect that all was not as it should be, Emma was about to suggest that she should be grateful if he would go in search of her maid, when she felt the strings of her dress freed. Instead of stepping back as she expected, her rescuer placed his hands on her waist and drew her against his chest.

"I claim my reward," he said, tipping back the flamboyant bonnet, and the next minute Miss Beringer was being thoroughly kissed.

Emma had been kissed before, hurried affairs delivered by callow youths, but this was far different. This man obviously knew what he was about, and it was quite clear that he had practiced the art to perfection. Clasped against him, bent backward at the waist, Emma hung in his arms, aware of his strength, and for one wild moment she savored the sensation before shocked rage came to her rescue. Freeing her hand, she hit her assailant soundly above one ear with all the force of her young arm, the slap seeming to echo around the empty street.

"H—how dare you!" she cried, pleased to see that she had drastically altered the rakish angle of his hat.

Before he could recover from his astonishment, Emma pushed past and, back stiff with outrage, walked hurriedly away, careless of the direction.

Luckily, when a short while later her temper had cooled enough for her to take in her surroundings, she found that by good fortune she was marching along the High Street and that the George Inn was only a short distance ahead.

Rushing upstairs, she burst open the door of her room and, running past the surprised Peggy, threw herself on the bed.

"I'll kill him—I'd like to stab him through his black heart! Ooh, how I *hate* him. The brute, the beast—how *dare* he!"

Peggy closed her open mouth and then took breath to say: "Oh, miss, what do you mean? Whatever happened? Not in broad daylight—you don't mean to say . . . you weren't, were you?"

"Of course not," was Emma's withering reply. "The creature k—kissed me! I just asked for his help, and he kissed me."

"It's that hat, miss," stated Mrs. Jones phlegmatically, relieved that nothing worse had happened. "I knew you shouldn't wear it. It's more suited to a kept woman, if you don't mind my saying so, than an innocent young lady."

Sitting up, Emma pulled at the red ribbons and, tearing the offending hat from her head, flung it into a corner. "Do I *look* like a demimonde?" she demanded.

"In that hat you do—especially with your dress all wet like that," was the response, and Miss Beringer could only grit her teeth and snarl with rage.

"If I knew who he was, I'd make him sorry," she muttered darkly, drumming her heels in frustrated anger. "I'd like to puncture his arrogant pride. I'd enjoy making him grovel!"

She fell silent, imagining the enjoyable scene as the elegant gentleman lost his sangfroid and knelt at her feet, begging forgiveness.

"A kiss isn't so bad!" commented Mrs. Jones knowledgeably, a reminiscent smile playing around her mouth before she changed the subject. "A message came for you, miss, just before you came in. Sir Julian has arrived and will call on you this evening after dinner. I put your green crepe out earlier—if I give it a good press it will pass muster."

Emma nodded, her bluster suddenly deflated at the prospect of meeting her unknown guardian. "Why can't the old man stay at home and let me mind my own affairs?" she asked crossly.

"I don't know, I'm sure, miss," returned Peggy Jones, not attending. "I'm sure as you want to look your best, so I've asked for hot water and a bathtub to be sent up. You'd best get out of those damp clothes anyway. Come along, miss, it would never do to keep the old gentleman waiting. I daresay he keeps early hours."

The warm water and delicately perfumed soap soothed Emma's ruffled feelings, and by the time she was wearing her pale green gown and was seated in front of her dressing table, she could smile at her reflection as she recalled the look of total astonishment on the handsome face.

Peggy was willing, but had had no training or aptitude for being a lady's maid, and Emma had quickly discovered that she was better dressing her own hair. Luckily her honey blond hair curled naturally, and she had only to arrange her long plaits in a coronet high on her head and fluff out her fringe and side curls. The green crepe was sadly washed out but, consoling herself that the old gentleman's eyesight could not be good enough to notice such details, she clasped her mother's short strand of pearls around her neck, slipped earbobs into her lobes, and declared herself ready.

She picked at the cold colation that she had asked to be sent up to her room, finding that the prospect of confronting her guardian and making her point understood quite spoiled her appetite.

"Send it away, Peggy," she said, leaving the table and going to stare down into the street. "I shan't need you again— I'm sure there is something that you wish to do."

Mrs. Jones bobbed a rare curtsy. "Thank you, miss," she said, "but are you sure? Is it right for you to be alone with an unknown gentleman?"

"Of course. I *am* his ward, and he *is* elderly. One can't be too formal with one's guardian, you know. He stands in place of a parent."

"Hmm—" Peggy was doubtful. "Well—I'll be in my room, if you should want me."

Once alone, Emma picked up a book and went to sit in the window, but the printed page did not hold her attention, and she found herself watching the scene below. Dusk had begun to fall, and candles were being lit in the houses and taverns. Men and women strolled along the road, sailors with their rolling gait and an arm around the waists of their female companions, officers with their ladies on their arms. Now and again a coach or carriage clattered over the cobbles, affording a brief glimpse of rich or aristocratic passengers on their way to some social event. It was all so different to that which she had been accustomed for the last two years that Emma watched in fascinated interest, not noticing the time, until the room grew dark behind her and a maid entered to light the candles. She had hardly retired before she was back again, announcing Emma's expected visitor with as much pride as if the Prince Regent himself were arriving.

Emma stared at the tall unmistakable figure, eyes wide with shock. *"You!"* she exclaimed with loathing in her voice.

"Good God!" ejaculated Sir Julian in similar tones. "The kitten with claws!"

# Chapter Two

*For* a moment they eyed each other, surprise and outrage warring in Emma's expressive countenance, a hint of amusement in Sir Julian's black gaze.

"You *can't* be my guardian," Emma stated positively at last.

Julian Leyton bowed impassively. "I am afraid that I do, indeed, have that somewhat dubious pleasure," he told her blandly. "Unless, of course, you are not Miss Beringer?"

To her mortification, he allowed the merest touch of hope to appear in his voice. Aware that she was not being treated with the respect which she thought proper, Emma eyed him stonily.

"Are you in the habit of kissing any helpless, unaccompanied female you happen to meet?" she demanded frostily.

"Helpless?" he queried, touching his cheek reminiscently before replying. "The answer, Miss Beringer, is no, I am not—unless they happen to be wearing outrageous hats and artfully dampened clothes, which to the unwary would suggest ladies of a particular profession. Good God, woman, what do you expect me to think when I am accosted by a young female in such attire asking me for help in a carefully contrived situation?"

Emma had flushed scarlet during this diatribe. "I was wet because a wave had soaked me, and, despite whatever you may think, the wind had twisted my strings round the railings," she cried, and was instantly annoyed with herself for attempting an explanation. "You, sir, are a touch above yourself! Why in the world should I wish to make your acquaintance in such a manner?"

Julian Leyton took a breath but, struck by the impropriety of what he had been about to say, remained silent. Reading his thoughts, Emma's eyes opened wide, and her lips formed an almost perfect O.

"I do believe that you thought I was a demimonde looking for a new protector!" she exclaimed ingenuously, things which had puzzled her falling into place.

Somewhat startled by her frankness, Sir Julian's eyebrows rose, and Emma eyed him, her head a little on one side.

"You don't care for frank speech," she commented, pleased to see him a little disconcerted.

"I—own to a little surprise," he told her gravely. "Perhaps it would be best if we were to begin our acquaintance anew." Bowing elegantly, he said, "Julian Leyton—at your service, Marm."

Accepting this way out of an impossible situation, Emma held out her hand. "How do you do," she said politely, offering him the tips of her fingers and wishing that she did not have to look quite so high to meet his gaze.

Her hand was taken in a deliberate grip. "Pleased to make your acquaintance, Miss Beringer," said Sir Julian.

Leading her to the curved sofa against one wall, he obliged her to be seated and, while she settled herself with what composure she could manage, poured them both a glass of claret from a decanter left on a side table.

Returning, he handed her a glass and seated himself beside her. Rather discomposed by his nearness, which brought back memories of his lips on hers, Emma sipped her wine, covertly aware of his masculine presence, the length of his long legs, and the breadth of his broad shoulders.

"We have a great deal to talk about," she was told and raised her eyes to search his face.

"I have a friend in Haslemere," she said quickly. "I thought to go there—"

Sir Julian shook his head. "I think not," he said gently. "Perhaps a visit later, when I am sure of her suitability, but until then you will come to my house in London."

Torn between the lure of the capital city and her wish to go her own way, Miss Beringer could not resist murmuring softly, "Is that quite proper?"

"Perfectly," was the curt answer. "Both my sister and an aunt live with me. We will leave tomorrow."

Annoyed by his high-handed assumption that she would comply with his orders, Emma made a show of considering, her head to one side. "I would still prefer Haslemere," she said.

"My dear child, do you really expect me to pack you off to stay with someone I've never met and have no knowledge of? Believe me, I take my guardianship more seriously than that. Until you are twenty, you are in my care—as your father wished."

Emma lifted her chin and stared down her nose. "You know as well as I that he had no wish for me to be kept on leading reins. The papers were drawn up years ago when I was a child and had need of a guardian—"

"And were never revoked," pointed out her companion provokingly.

Miss Beringer ignored the interruption. "Now, I am a woman grown," she went on grandly, only to be interrupted again.

"So I had noticed," Julian Leyton said meaningly. "And for that reason alone, I have no intention of allowing you to besport yourself in a manner likely to provoke gossip."

"Provoke gossip!" gasped Emma. "If anyone was to do such a thing, let me tell you, sir, it was yourself," she cried, quite forgetting the proposal to begin anew.

"I daresay you are right," drawled Sir Julian slowly, leaning back to regard her lazily. "Remember, though, that men may be gossiped about, but it does them no great harm—in fact, it may even enhance their reputations. A female, however, who causes gossip will soon find herself in sad shape. Would you like a rumor to go ahead of you and to find your reputation in tatters when you arrive in London?''

He waited for his words to sink in and, when he felt they had, went on, ''My dear ward, only a foolish girl would be uncareful of her name. In your situation it is better by far to be above reproach.''

''But—what shall I do in London?'' queried Emma who, despite her anger, had been pondering this point.

''My sister has need of a companion. You are older and, I hope, wiser. To say that she has formed an unsuitable friendship would be charitable. You, as my ward, should make an ideal companion for Elvira, who has been left too much to her own devices.''

Appearing to think that all was settled, he stood up. ''Tomorrow, then. My carriage will call about midmorning. I take it you will be ready?''

''Oh, yes. I'll be ready,'' promised Miss Beringer meekly. Anyone who knew her would have been worried by such mildness, but Sir Julian merely allowed a hint of relief to cross his handsome face.

''Good girl,'' he said kindly and appeared about to pat her head. ''You'll like the city, you know. There really is no need to be shy; Lady Beauvale will be delighted to have another young lady to launch into Society, and Elvira, if a trifle spoiled, is still the kindest of girls.''

''I am most grateful,'' simpered Emma, swallowing her chagrin as Julian Leyton bestowed a brilliant smile on her and bowed elegantly.

''Until tomorrow, then,'' he repeated and, pleased to find her so amenable, went on his way, congratulating himself upon the ease with which he had dealt with an awkward situation.

As he walked downstairs a crash in the room he had left

made him pause, but as no outcry followed, he decided it was not his concern and went on his way.

Behind him, Miss Beringer retrieved her book only to hurl it to the ground again and then kick it into the furthest corner.

"Arrogant pipsqueak!" she cried, ignoring the fact that Sir Julian was much too large to be termed a pipsqueak. "Shy!" she snarled, and kicked the unoffending volume again. "Make me a companion to his odious sister, would he? I suppose he plans that I should hold his aunt's wool for her—in between toadying to dear Elvira."

In her rage she fell to pacing across the room, until, by chance, her eye fell on a bill advertising a theater, which was posted on the wall across the street. Suddenly her eyes narrowed, and, regardless of her safety, she leaned out of the window, the better to read the large, crudely printed writing.

"Rourk!" She exclaimed, repeating the name with growing excitement. "Rourk!"

Her mind shot back two years to the dapper, little sergeant, who had been the life and soul of the regiment, until he had been shot in the foot and invalided out of the army. Preparing to leave for home, not a particle abashed by fate's treatment, he had declared his intention of running a theater in Portsmouth, and, remembering with pleasure the theatricals and concerts which he had arranged, no one had doubted his ability to do so.

The night was too far advanced to take action at once, but Emma determined to seek out "Rourk's Theater" first thing the next morning, and, a plan simmering in her mind, she spent a sleepless night, leaping from her bed at first light, impatient to put her plan into action.

"You've not forgotten that I'm off to Fareham this morning?" Peggy reminded her, when she found her mistress already up and dressed. "The arrangement was to last only until we arrived and Sir Julian made contact."

"Yes, I know," Emma assured her; knowing Mrs. Jones would disapprove of her proposed idea, she was eager for her to be gone. "I'm very grateful for your company and hope that you will enjoy life in your brother's inn."

"Well, there's no knowing about that—one thing, it will be as different to life on the Peninsula as chalk is from cheese! However, I intend to make the best of it, though I can't say but as how I'll miss Charlie."

She looked at Emma's baggage piled in the middle of the room and tightened a strap. "So, you're all ready, miss? If there's nothing you want me to do, I'll be off. I hope as you are happy with Sir Julian. The Red Lion will always find me, miss, if you've a mind to."

The two women smiled at each other and nodded, both a little anxious at the parting, which symbolized a new life for each, and then Peggy Jones left the room, determination in every inch of her sturdy figure.

As soon as she was alone, Emma rang the bell for attention and was answered almost immediately by the familiar diminutive figure in drab gown and large mob cap.

"I wish to leave my luggage to be called for," Emma told her, holding a shilling between her forefinger and thumb. "Can that be arranged?"

"Yes'm," replied the girl, her eyes on the coin.

"And I wish to settle my bill."

"Sir Julian said to put it with his—"

"Do you mean that he is staying here?" cried Emma, shaken by the revelation.

"Oh, yes'm—he's in the dining room now eating mutton chops."

"Indeed!" Emma thought deeply for a few minutes, wondering how best to enlist the aid of the little inn servant. "Can you keep a secret?" she asked thrillingly, at last.

"Yes'm," answered the child promptly, laying a finger alongside her nose. "Eyes open, mouth shut, says Old Beerbelly."

Recognizing the landlord without difficulty from his nickname, Emma smiled encouragingly and decided to embroider the truth only a little, just enough to rouse the sympathy of her listener.

"Sir Julian is taking me away to London against my will," she declared theatrically. "He is about to carry me off and keep me a prisoner."

"Ooh, miss," squeaked the little maid. "It's like one of Rourk's plays! And Sir Julian looks such a bang-up, proper gentleman. Is he really kidnapping you?"

Emma hesitated only a second, fighting with her conscience. "Yes," she said emphatically, abandoning the truth. "I pleaded with him last night, but he said that I was in his power and nothing would prevent him having his way!"

"Well, I never did! Who'd have thought it? Does Old Beerbelly know as you've been ravished in his inn?"

"R-ravished!" Looking down into the intent gaze of the younger girl, Emma closed her mouth over the indignant denial, realizing that sympathy was her only means of enlisting the help she needed. "N-no, I shouldn't think so."

"He could be in the plot, you know," the other said, confidentially. "He's a wily old devil. You can count on me'm. I'll get your things hid away, never fear."

Emma dropped the shilling into her palm. "If anyone asks you, you haven't seen me."

"Mum's the word," she was assured, and, entering wholeheartedly into the intrigue, the maid led her down the back stairway and through various dim passages until she opened a narrow door onto a squalid street, much different to that on which the inn fronted.

Seeing Emma hesitate, the girl patted her arm encouragingly. "I daren't leave the inn, miss, but I'll stay here till you're at the corner if you like."

"You're very kind," Emma told her. "What's your name? I'll need to know it when I come for my baggage."

"Maria, 'm."

"Well, thank you, Maria." The older girl smiled before

squaring her shoulders, then stepping off briskly in the direction of the High Street.

"Rourk's Theater" was not hard to find. In a side street just off the main road and near to the Cathedral, Emma found a tall, narrow building with a shallow flight of steps leading up to a pair of dark red doors. Above them "Rourk's Theater" was proudly picked out in gold, and on either side bills advertising the week's performances were prominently displayed.

As she was hesitating, unsure whether to knock at the imposing doors or seek a side entrance, the doors opened and a small, smartly dressed man appeared, pausing on the top step to take snuff and survey the street below.

"Sergeant Rourk," Emma cried, recognizing him at once.

Hearing his name and old rank, he turned his head, taking an unwary amount of snuff at the unexpected sight of Emma and sneezed several times before he could gather himself enough to blow his nose and hasten down the remaining steps to her side.

"Miss Beringer, by all the gods!" he exclaimed, seizing her hand and pumping it up and down enthusiastically. "What thoughts—what memories! You're a joy to behold, if I may be so bold. What brings you here—is the major with you?"

Emma's smile faded, and she could only shake her head. Used to what such silences portended, Tom Rourk patted her hand sympathetically and, without more ado, contrived to whisk her up the steps and into his office.

Considerably to her surprise, Emma found herself seated in a shabby, but comfortable, armchair, sipping sherry and nibbling ratafia biscuits, while Sergeant Rourk surveyed her benignly.

"Oh, Sergeant Rourk, can you help me?" she asked, and launched at once into her tale, finishing: "So you see, I *cannot* be beholden to such a horrid man. You *know* that my father would never have left me ward to such a person. . . .

I am sure that Sir Julian is not at all suitable for such a position."

"It beats me why he should have acted in such a way," observed the actor-manager, eyeing her worn, demure bonnet and serviceable gown in a puzzled way. Remembering the red bonnet, which now appeared odious in her eyes, and the clinging, damp folds of her dress, Emma had the grace to blush and, mistaking the cause of her embarrassment, Tom Rourk made haste to put her at ease. "You mustn't take on, Miss B, if you'll allow me to say so. Some men only have to see a pretty girl to feel frisky. Don't go thinking anyone will imagine that you led him on. Tell me how I can help you."

Turning the full force of her pleading blue eyes upon him, Emma clasped her hands and leaned forward. "Do you remember our camp theatricals?" she asked eagerly.

"To be sure I do. They were what started all this," he jerked his head at their surroundings.

"And I was good, wasn't I? They all said that I was the best Desdemona they'd ever seen."

Following her line of reasoning, Tom Rourk looked at her warily.

"Please, please, dear Sergeant Rourk, give me a part in your theater."

"It's not for the likes of you. You're a lady, Miss Beringer," he protested.

"Pooh! Who could be more ladylike than Mrs. Siddons?" she pointed out. "Just a little part," she coaxed, "to see how I do."

The actor began to shake his head, and she hurried on: "You can't turn me away. Think of old times . . . for my father's sake. I need the money, Sergeant. I'm destitute . . . and have only my bad guardian to go back to—and you know what that means."

Tom Rourk looked harassed, running his fingers through his thinning hair. "As it happens, an actress has left me in the lurch—but it's a breeches part," he said, thinking to deter her.

"I'll take it," Emma cried, not too sure what was meant but determined to gain her desire. Jumping up, she bestowed a quick hug on the gratified actor. "You *are* kind, Sergeant. I knew I could depend on you. When do I begin?"

"Tonight. We're doing 'The Sultan's Slave.' It's one I wrote myself—a jolly Tar is captured by the Sultan of Morocco—it's very popular. You'd take the part of the Princess of Morocco's page—you don't say much, just 'Yes, oh mistress' and 'I obey, Your Highness' and so on." He paused, adding delicately, "You'd have to show your legs in satin breeches—and the audience doesn't care for a shy actress!"

"Pooh," said the aspiring actress, who had never been shy in her life. "I've worn breeches for riding since I first climbed on a horse, so *that* won't bother me."

Tom Rourk refrained from pointing out that the circumstances would be decidedly different, instead taking her to view the stage and get some idea of what was expected of her.

"Here's the book," he said, giving her a motley collection of pages. "Read it, and you'll understand the plot. How are you fixed about lodgings? Do you have somewhere to stay?"

Emma shook her head. "No—my bags are at the George, but I can't stay there."

"My wife and I have a room to spare—we usually take a lodger. You can stay with us, if you want. Bed and board and half a crown a week is what I'll offer you."

Emma was so relieved that she readily agreed to his suggestion without any real idea as to whether she was being offered a paltry sum or real wealth.

"Right!" The actor nodded. "Curtain's up at eight o'clock. You be here an hour earlier—"

"I'd sooner stay here now and read your play," Emma put in, remembering that Sir Julian would no doubt be touring the streets looking for his errant ward.

Sergeant Rourk was indifferent. "As you will," he said, preparing to leave himself. Tapping his hat into a rakish angle, he straightened his somewhat frayed cravat and shot out his shirt cuffs from the sleeves of his jacket, which Emma now saw was rather threadbare. Concluding that acting was not well paid, she looked round with new eyes, noting the many signs of lack of cash.

"I'll leave you to the Green Room," Tom Rourk told her, making a jaunty bow. "My good lady will show you how to apply your greasepaint. She, of course, plays the princess."

After he had left and she had time to realize how empty was the building in which she waited, Emma half wished that she had not elected to stay in the theater. Curling up on a well-worn chaise longue, she studied the closely written pages given to her by the actor and, after some time, decided that the convoluted plot was impossible to follow. Sam Bowling, the hero, appeared much given to heroic speeches and cries of "Have at thee, sir," and "Take that, you villain," while the Princess of Morocco took every opportunity of swooning. Nevertheless, she decided, if the many stage directions to "fight" were anything to go by, it was a very thrilling play.

Growing tired of inactivity, she decided to explore the theater and, wandering backstage, was amazed to discover the gaudily painted backdrops representing various scenes suspended from the roof. Ropes and pulleys supplied their maneuverability, while heaps of furniture and props were waiting in the wings. A stormy seascape was already in place, a few judiciously placed spars and suitable flotsam were obviously intended to suggest a shipwreck.

Advancing to the front of the stage, Emma stared out at the rows of empty seats, trying to imagine what it would be like facing an audience other than one made up of friends, which was all her previous experience had been.

Her toe caught a little metal shield, and, looking down, she saw that she had knocked against a short but stout candle speared to a heavy iron saucer. A thrill shot through her as she realized that these must be the famed "footlights" which all aspiring actresses had heard about. Feeling very professional, she returned happily to the Green Room, her head full of notions of the fame and fortune which would undoubtedly be hers.

Sometime later, when she had been obliged to assuage the pangs of hunger by dipping into Mr. Rourk's jar of ratafia biscuits, she heard the front door open and the sound of approaching footsteps.

Tom Rourk led a large, florid lady into the room. Holding her fingers in the manner of a courtier, he presented her to Emma.

"This is Miss Beringer, who I was telling you of, my love," he said. "Miss Beringer—my good lady and principal actress of this company of mine."

The two women exchanged genteel bows, Molly Rourk taking a quick assessment of Emma as their fingers touched.

"Mr. R tells me that you are wishful of a stage career," she declaimed thrillingly, every syllable carefully enunciated. "Of course, you must realize that, as yet, you are a mere novice on the stage of life, as it were."

"I am sure that you can teach me a great deal," replied Emma diplomatically.

"I was never one to stint myself. Talent is given to a few to give pleasure to many, I always say. Yes, my dear child, I shall give you advice and teaching—and in return, I shall expect you to realize that Rome wasn't built in a day and that all comes to he who waits."

"In other words, Miss Beringer, don't expect to run before you can walk," put in Sergeant Rourk.

Emma, who had been entranced by this flood of clichés, could not resist joining in. "I shall be as good as gold, I promise, and am truly grateful for the opportunity to sit in your shadow!"

For a moment she thought that she had gone too far, but

Mrs. Rourk smiled benignly. "Very prettily put," she approved. "Now, dear child, come with me, and I will arrange your costume and show you how to apply your greasepaint and powder."

When at last Emma waited in the wings to make her entrance, she was clothed in a blue satin suit in the fashion of fifty years ago with tight breeches, silk stockings, and a fitted jacket, her sole concession to Arabia being a pink silk turban with a large blue glass jewel set in the shining folds. Under the layer of makeup her face was stiff and uncomfortable, and she felt it was a good thing that she had little to say, as she was uncertain whether she could open her mouth or not.

Molly Rourk was attired in the height of fashion in a high-waisted gauze gown of shimmering pink, a fine veil covered half her face, and pink pantaloons, gathered at the ankles, completed her ensemble. Mrs. Rourk was a decidedly ample woman, and she reminded Emma vividly of a large pink cloud hovering in the wings. She dwarfed her slim husband, who had blacked his face, added a pointed black beard and mustachios, and arrayed himself in yellow turban and emerald green jacket to his knees—beside his splendor, the hero in a sailor's blue jacket and white trousers looked very ordinary.

Dazzled by noise, lights, and excitement and the overpowering smell of greasepaint and old perfume, Emma could remember none of her instructions and was almost surprised when Molly Rourk dragged her onto the stage, towing her in her wake like a ship in full sail with an attendant rowing boat.

Their entrance was greeted with sighs and whistles, which the Princess of Morocco accepted as her due, but which her page, unhappily conscious of her revealing costume, found decidedly embarrassing. Pushed and pulled, thrust here and there, Emma abruptly began to have doubts about the desirability of a stage career and greeted the fall of the curtain at the end of the first act with relief.

Seeing that she had no rival in the newcomer, Molly Rourk looked at Emma more kindly. "Well done, child," she entoned. "In time you may well play a leading role, but now—the next act is more important, so follow me closely. The aristocracy, having dined, will arrive."

"But they won't know what has happened," Emma pointed out. "How will they understand the plot?"

"Tush, child." Her mentor smiled. "They come to be amused not instructed. Pretty sights and fine gestures will please them more. In all modesty, I can say that I am a great favorite—regard how I move and speak, nothing can teach you quicker how to go on."

Taking her advice literally, Emma followed close behind, mimicking each larger than life, theatrical gesture and suddenly found herself enjoying the experience. Emboldened by a ripple of amusement which greeted a particular sweep of her arm, she attempted a little swagger in keeping with her breeches. Encouraged by the enthusiasm which this was accorded, she assayed a saucy wink and suddenly was aware that the audience was hers—unfortunately the intoxicating experience went straight to her head, and she began to play to the audience with all the abandon of youth.

Becoming aware that something was not as it should be, Mrs. Rourk turned to find the cause, when one of her dramatic speeches was greeted with laughter, and found Emma in full, but silent, mimicry. Quivering with outrage, the actress rounded on her page, who at that moment flung her arm wide as she made a particularly fine theatrical gesture. The large button on her wide cuff attached itself to Molly Rourk's veil, which in turn was fastened to her pink satin turban. With one sweep of her arm, Emma dislodged the yashmak, pulling the headdress firmly down over the Princess of Morocco's eyes, who gave a howl of rage and staggered blindly backward into her diminutive page's arms. Emma tried bravely to support her, but despite her efforts, weight finally won, and they both slowly, but inevitably, toppled over.

As Mr. Rourk signaled frantically for the curtain to be lowered, his wife emerged from the turban and dealt Emma, who had managed to struggle free from the enveloping folds of pink gauze and rosy flesh, a resounding box on the ear, which promptly laid her low again. The curtain finally fell to the chagrin of a delighted audience, who had not expected to enjoy the play so much.

Tom Rourk rushed onto the stage and freed Emma from the grip of his enraged leading lady, who, deprived of her prey, took refuge in a noisy fit of hysterics.

"I always s—said, Mr. R, that you couldn't make an ear out of a s—sow's purse," she screamed, as he thrust Emma into the wings.

Taking his unspoken advice, Emma ran to the dressing room and, having reached her refuge, slammed the door shut and leaned against it.

"Well done, Miss Beringer—I think even you have surpassed yourself tonight!" said a horridly familiar voice, and the tall figure of Sir Julian Leyton emerged from the shadows.

# *Chapter Three*

*E*mma turned to run, but before she could make her escape a long arm reached out, and Sir Julian's fingers hooked firmly into the back of her blue satin collar.

"Oh no, my dear," he said. "I've spent all day hunting for you—I don't intend to waste the night in the same way!"

Wisking the turban from her head, he turned her to face him, and Emma was surprised to recognize a glimmer of amusement at the back of his dark eyes. Deliberately, he let his gaze slide over her, taking in the formfitting jacket and tight satin breeches, while she grew hot with embarrassment.

Shuffling uneasily, she wriggled in his grasp. "I'll go and change," she said gruffly.

"No need for that," Sir Julian surprised her by saying. "Tom Rourk has lent me a cloak." With the words, a long black cloak was tossed over her shoulders, and, enveloped in its smothering folds, Emma was lead relentlessly to the door.

"I can't walk the streets like this," she protested, digging in her heels.

"Oh, yes you can," she was told softly.

Looking up, she found her guardian smiling in a way she could not like, his satanic face in shadow, but his teeth gleaming in the candlelight. Abruptly deciding not to argue, she gathered the cloak about her with what dignity she could muster and, chin high, swept toward the door.

The damp night air was pleasant on her hot cheeks at first, but after a few minutes Emma began to feel as if the grease and powder were setting like a mask. Hoping desperately that no one would see them, she attempted to hurry along the deserted pavement, but Julian Leyton set a deliberately slow pace, strolling along as if oblivious to her discomfort.

"Pray walk a little faster," she urged at last.

"Don't you find the night air enjoyable?" he asked blandly.

"You know I do not—not in these clothes and with this stuff on my face!" Emma was goaded into replying.

"Then, my dear girl, you should not have put them on in the first place," he replied silkily.

His companion gritted her teeth and walked on in silence, asking after a thoughtful pause, "Did Sergeant Rourk tell you I was at the theater?"

Sir Julian looked down at his charge. "Only in the most innocent way. Tom is an old friend of mine. . . . We often meet. He was full of the news of his old major's daughter. He did not betray you, have no fear of that." A sound suspiciously like a suppressed chuckle escaped him. "I fear, in my eagerness to intercept you, that I missed the best of your performance, but I own to a suspicion that your talents lie on the comic stage."

"I only did what I was told," said Emma crossly. "All would have been well if the princess had not fallen on me!"

Sir Julian's shoulders shook, but when he spoke his voice was suitably grave. "F-fell on you! Well, indeed that *would* tend to spoil anyone's performance!"

Miss Beringer shot him a dark look. "Let me tell you, sir, that it is not to be laughed at."

"That, I can believe," agreed her guardian in reflective tones. "Few would wish for such a fate, and your own dismay is perfectly understandable."

Entering the George Inn, Emma turned to look up at him. "Are you teasing me?" she demanded, eyebrows drawing together in a frown.

Before Sir Julian could reply, a movement behind made

them both look round to find that a gentleman on the staircase was surveying them through a quizzing glass.

" 'Pon my soul, Sir Julian,'' he drawled, and turned his gaze upon the shrouded form of Emma. "And . . . companion, I see.''

"Your servant, Devern,'' said Sir Julian curtly, placing himself squarely in front of his ward. "I had not expected to find you here.''

The slim figure on the stairs bowed elegantly. "Your servant, Ma'am. Aren't you going to introduce us, Leyton?''

"No,'' was the bald answer, and a hand on Emma's shoulder restrained her, when she would have curtsied in return.

"How selfish,'' drawled the other man. "But then you always were a dog.'' His gaze traveled over as much of the muffled figure as he could see, lingering with interest on the slim pair of ankles which were revealed beneath the cloak. "Another of your Cyprians, Ju?'' he inquired softly.

"Go to hell,'' advised Julian Leyton evenly and marched his ward firmly past the man on the stairs, whose eyes lit with interest as Emma's honey-colored hair glimmered in the candlelight, and her satin suit was revealed briefly as the enveloping cloak fell open. Gathering it about her, Emma ran up the stairs and, bidding her guardian the briefest of 'good nights,' fled into the room which she had occupied previously.

Something in the encounter had shaken her, ruffling her already disturbed feelings in a way which she could not understand. There had been a certain air about the stranger which she had found attractive, his obvious admiration had made her very aware of being female and the appreciative gleam in his pale eyes had made her spine prickle in an unfamiliar but totally delightful way.

She could not help but compare him to Sir Julian and found her guardian wanting. *He* may have stolen a kiss, but he had never looked at her with open admiration and a blatant invitation in his expression.

Dropping the cloak into a chair, Emma went through into the bedroom and, seating herself at the dressing table, gazed with dismay at her reflection; heat and emotion had made the paint and powder run together, the lurid colors doing nothing to enhance her delicate coloring. The cold air had set the grease into a mask, which resembled a child's painting—or the visage presented to the world by a woman of the streets to proclaim her trade.

Emma gasped in dismay, agonizing over what the strange man must have thought and then, seizing a handkerchief, attempted desperately to remove the stage makeup applied so hopefully a few hours previously. Her frantic efforts had no result apart from smudging the thick substance in a rainbow-colored mess across her face.

When after a timid knock Maria entered, it was to find Miss Beringer slumped over the table, her shoulders heaving with smothered sobs.

"Lawks!" exclaimed the child, hurrying forward. "Don't take on so, 'm—I'm as sorry as I can be that Sir Julian found your things, but he has a way with him, and I couldn't hold out no longer. He's ever so charming, as you know 'm."

Emma shuddered. "He's horrid!" she cried emphatically. "Anyway, it's not that that is bothering me—look at my face! What am I to do?"

Examining her garish appearance, Maria was hard put to hide a grin but exclaimed in a suitably sympathetic way, "I know how to get that off." She added, more usefully, "Lard is what you need. I'll nip down to the kitchen and get a dollop."

As good as her word, she was quickly back with a basin of clarified dripping. For a moment all was silence as the two girls worked, rubbing the grease into Emma's face and wiping the resulting mess off. At last she emerged, recognizable, if shining and slippery.

"What *have* you been doing?" the younger girl inquired, covertly studying Emma's blue satin suit.

"I went on the stage—" said Emma with casual pride.

"You never!" There was every admiration in Maria's tones. "Well, I never did—and you a lady, too."

"I *wish* everyone would not keep saying that," observed Emma peevishly. "Anyway, I've given up the idea. Now I shall go to London and make a grand marriage," she announced.

"There's a lord here now," Maria told her, as if she might wish to make a start that instant. "He's ever so nice—gave me a guinea."

Emma looked away to hide her interest. "What is his name?" she asked casually.

"Lord Devern—but I heard his friends call him Viv—funny name, ain't it?"

"Vivian, I expect," Emma told her. "Do you know where he lives?"

Maria shook her head. "But, I can tell you that he and Sir Julian don't care for each other," she went on. "My Lord was trying to chivy him about some doxy, excuse my French, 'm, in a friendly way, and Sir Julian was very stiff—give him a proper set down, I can tell you. If you don't mind me saying so, 'm—he'll make a stern guardian, and no mistake."

Having a good idea who was the female under discussion, Emma was not surprised at her guardian's response but had to agree with Maria's pronouncement and faced the coming months with foreboding.

She was awoken early next morning with the information that Sir Julian wanted to take the road by nine o'clock. Maria's voice sounded muffled, and her downcast eyes were suspiciously pink. Sitting up in bed, Emma noticed a fiery red mark on the side of the girl's face and exclaimed in shocked surprise, demanding who had struck her.

"Old Beerbelly, 'm. He's a bad'un, I can tell you. Proper heavy-handed, he is." Maria sniffed, rubbing her cheek reflectively. "And I hadn't done nothing—not really. I'd overslept a bit, and the stove wasn't hot when he came down."

Jumping out of bed, Emma soaked a handkerchief in the washbasin and gently dabbed the inflamed cheek.

"No need for you to do that, 'm," said the girl, backing away. "I've had worse—I nearly lost a tooth last time."

She sounded surprisingly cheerful, almost proud, seeming to accept violence as a normal part of life, and as she scurried about the room she appeared to have forgotten the incident. Emma felt helpless; filled with sympathy for the other girl yet unhappily aware that, without an establishment of her own, Emma thought there was nothing she could offer in the way of practical help. She was still pondering the problem and had just decided that, much as she disliked the idea, she would apply to Sir Julian in the hope that his better nature would emerge to solve her difficulty, when Emma's guardian entered the room.

He was already dressed in a green riding jacket and tight-fitting yellow buckskins. Gold tassels dangled from his shiny black Hessian boots, and a spotless linen cravat had replaced the fine muslin one of the previous evening. He carried a black beaver hat with a curly brim and a pair of kid gloves. Even Emma had to admit that he made a handsome picture as he stood in the doorway, the epitome of masculinity.

"Good—I see you are ready," he said, coming into the room. "Now, Miss Beringer, I have a proposition to make to you. You are in need of a female companion, and Maria, here, is in need of a position."

Emma wondered briefly if he could have been reading her thoughts as she turned to Maria to see how she was taking this suggestion. Exchanging glances, the girls knew without speaking that the idea was agreeable to both. Hope flared across Maria's thin features, before the joy died away and her shoulders slumped.

Shaking her head, she said, "Old Beerbelly'ud never agree."

"I have . . . persuaded him," Sir Julian told her gently, surprising Emma with the unexpected kindness he showed.

"You are free to accompany Miss Beringer, if you wish. No one will force you, and Old—er, Beerbelly will keep you on, if that's what you prefer."

The child looked up into his face. "Really?" she asked. "Really and truly?"

Sir Julian smiled down at her. "Really and truly," he repeated. "Trust me."

A wide grin broke over the little face, and Maria did a jig of joy. "Coo, ta ever so," she cried. "Fancy me, a lady's maid!"

Looking up, Julian Leyton met his ward's eyes. "Go and pack, Maria," he said. "You have ten minutes."

"Shan't need two!" she retorted, and ran from the room.

"She is not what I would have chosen for you, if I had had the choice," said Sir Julian, when they were alone. "However, you have need of a companion on the journey, and that child obviously has need of a home. She is young, wise in the worst way, and . . . vulnerable. I shall expect you to have a care to her until we get to London, then she can be put in the hands of my housekeeper, who will find a suitable situation for her."

"Cannot she stay with me?"

Sir Julian looked surprised. "I had not considered it. . . . Someone older and stolidly respectable would be more the thing."

"I would prefer Maria," Emma said obstinately.

"I daresay," said her guardian, a knowledgeable smile lurking at the back of his black gaze. "I've known many a maid to keep her young mistress in order, and I'm persuaded that you have, too. Forgive me if I'm blunt, Miss Beringer, but, from what I have seen, you have need of an older, wiser companion."

Emma fought her lower lip, which had developed a determination to stick out. "I thought you wanted me to play companion to your naughty little sister. You are being inconsistent," she pointed out.

"Heaven forgive me, I did have such a thought in mind!" Julian Leyton murmured. "But now, I wonder if a finishing school would not be more suitable for you both."

"I am too old," Emma told him with satisfaction.

"I know, my dear. I'm afraid there is nothing for it but the cellars and bread and water when you misbehave."

Emma stared at him, shock on her face, before her eyebrows drew together. For the second time she had the uneasy feeling that her guardian was teasing her, and she did not know how to respond.

Amused that he had silenced her, he picked up his hat and gloves. Tucking his riding whip under his arm, he strode to the door and held it open, saying with a slight bow, "The carriage is at the door, Miss Beringer."

Emma was joined on the front steps by an excited Maria, clutching a large checked bundle which contained all her belongings. They were both gratified to find an elegant equipage awaiting them, a coat of arms displayed on its black-painted door. Two handsome horses chewed their bits patiently, while a coachman waited with an impassive face for the groom to load the luggage behind. Miss Beringer managed to hide the fact that she was impressed by the outfit, but her newly acquired maid did not even try.

Mouth and eyes agape, she stared, before crying loudly, "Ooh, miss, he ain't half doing us proud! He must be ever so rich!"

"Hush, Maria," chided Emma quietly. "Pretend you are used to such magnificence."

The girl did her best, accepting the groom's helping hand to follow her mistress up the folding steps with chin high and her small nose tilted skyward. Only her genteel, "Ta, my good man," spoiled the effect.

Emma covertly admired her guardian's black gelding as Sir Julian and his valet trotted ahead through the narrow streets. Soon they were clear of the town and driving along country lanes until they reached the little village of Cosham at the end of the bridge that joined Portsea Island to the mainland. Topping Portsdown Hill, Emma stole a quick look backward at the panorama laid out behind her; the whole of Portsea, surrounded by sea, ships riding at anchor in the Solent and beyond, the Isle of Wight half hidden in a misty haze. Then the horses plunged down past the inn and gathered speed on the well-kept road which was the main thoroughfare to London.

Maria's head was turning in all directions as she tried to watch everything which flashed past the windows. "I ain't never been in the country before," she explained, catching Emma's eye.

"Do you like it?"

Maria was doubtful. "It's ever so big," she murmured. "You could easy get lost."

Emma pointed out a windmill, its sails turning slowly on a hill near the road and then nodded toward a much larger hill on their left. "That's called Butser," she said, "and it is only a few feet off being a mountain."

Maria appeared suitably impressed, but spoiled it by asking innocently if a mountain was bigger than a hill. Settling back in her corner, Emma fell silent, idly watching the scenery and wondering what life in London would be like. They flashed through Petersfield and then Haslemere. Here she roused herself, staring out of the window in the unlikely hope of catching a glimpse of her friend.

Turning right onto the Guildford Road, they settled into a steady trot that devoured the miles and set the well-sprung carriage into a soporific sway. Both girls fell asleep, to be awakened by the sudden cessation of motion, to find that they had arrived in the yard of an inn and that the steps of the coach were being let down.

A meal was procured for them in a private room, somewhat to Miss Beringer's disappointment, for she rather liked the idea of eating in a busy, public room, gazing out at the shops and passersby as she did so. However, she had to be content with what little she could glimpse of Guildford as they set out again, toiling slowly up the steep main street, passing under overhanging upper floors of medieval buildings, by mullioned windows and more modern bays, and even past the ruined gate of what could only once have been a castle.

"It's a long way, in'it, miss?" commented Maria, sighing heavily and shuffling around on the seat in an endeavor to find a more comfortable spot.

"I believe that we still have some way to go," Emma agreed, wishing herself that the long journey was over. "I take it, Maria," she went on, pursuing a question which had been bothering her, "that your parents know of your move to London? You *did* ask your mother's permission?"

"Ain't got no mother—nor no father neither," was the cheerful answer. "I'm a foundling, 'm."

"I think that if we are to be better acquainted, you must call me Miss Emma," said Emma diplomatically. "If you are to be a lady's maid, you must start as you mean to go on."

"Yes'm—Miss Emma," agreed the child. "I was found in the porch of St. Thomas's—that's why I'm called Maria Thomas. Maria was the woman who found me. I suppose if I'd been a boy, they'd have called me Thomas Thomas!"

"What a romantic tale—like a novel."

"Romantic or not, miss. I'd sooner have had a Ma and Pa. The orphanage was something horrible, and Old Beerbelly weren't too nice neither." She paused and looked across the enclosed space, her expression anxious. "Do you think Sir J will turn me off once we get to London?"

"I'm sure not," comforted the older girl. "Why would he have bothered to take you so far, if he was going to do that?"

"You will put in a word for me, Miss Emma, when we get there? I'll be ever so good as your maid. I'm used to hard work—no one can scrub a floor cleaner than me."

Emma smiled. "A lady's maid doesn't do things like that.

They look after clothes and learn how to do hair. Some maids are even grander than their mistresses! When I was in Portugal, Lady Pultney, General Sir Timothy Pultney's wife, came out, and *her* maid wore silk dresses and had her own maid. She kept her nose in the air and was much too grand to speak to anyone except her mistress!''

"Well, I never! Tell me about your travels, miss. Was it hot, and were all the folk blackamoors?''

Emma laughed and began to recount her adventures in the Peninsula. With only a little embroidery, the tales became distracting and made the miles pass quickly. The afternoon gave way to evening without them noticing, and dusk had fallen by the time the equipage rounded Hampton Court and began the last part of the journey into the city.

Looking out of the window, Maria became uneasy. "Do you suppose there are highwaymen around here?'' she inquired fearfully.

"No one will attack us with two outriders," Emma assured her. "Besides which, I have a pistol myself, so you are quite safe.''

Maria peered into Emma's reticule, gazing at the tiny, pearl-handled pistol, which reposed there without much enthusiasm. "Is it safe, m-miss? Can you work it?'' she inquired doubtfully.

"Of course I can," she was told bracingly. "My father taught me to load and fire it years ago. But I am sure we shan't need it.''

To Maria's relief and Emma's slight chagrin, for she would have liked the opportunity of being a heroine, the last few miles were traveled without incident. When they arrived in Cumberland Square, the hour was so late that a fitful moon pierced the blackness of the night and lighted windows shone like stage sets, fascinating the girls with the diversity of interiors that met their dazzled eyes.

The coach stopped outside a large house, the last of an imposing terrace that faced a square garden of which Emma could only see the silhouette of wide spreading trees and the gleam of iron railings. The folding steps were let down and Sir Julian appeared, his hand upraised to help her descend.

After so long a journey Emma was stiff and glad of his aid. Stepping down onto the pavement, she took a breath of damp night air and, for the first time in weeks, missed the smell of salt. Behind her, her guardian helped Maria down and then led them up the steps to the front door, which had been opened wide by a butler.

"Welcome, Sir Julian," he said, bowing. "And Miss Beringer," he added, bowing again.

"How do you do, Frobisher," said the baronet pleasantly, pulling off his gloves. "I hope we haven't kept you up."

"Not at all, sir. Her ladyship is in the withdrawing room."

"Announce us then," commanded Sir Julian. "This is Maria Thomas," he went on, drawing the girl forward. "Take her to Mrs. Frobisher, and ask her to take care of her."

"Very good, sir," answered the butler impassively, appearing to accept the arrival of a forlorn little figure, clutching a shawl-wrapped bundle, as an everyday occurrence.

Crossing the hall ahead of them, he flung a pair of double doors open and announced them in sonorous tones that reminded Emma forcibly of her brief sojourn with Molly Rourk.

A plump, fashionably dressed lady looked up from a small table where she had been playing patience, a smile lighting her face.

"Julian, my dear," she exclaimed, holding out her hand.

"Aunt Di," he murmured, touching her hand to his lips. "Pray let me present my ward, Miss Beringer—Lady Beauvale."

Coming forward, Emma curtsied and raised her eyes to find herself receiving a surprisingly shrewd gaze. "Your servant, Ma'am," she said.

"A pleasure to receive you, my dear," said the older

woman. "My sympathies on the circumstances which bring you here, but be sure that Elvira and I, indeed the whole household, will do our best to make you feel that this is your home now."

She smiled pleasantly, and Emma began to feel that perhaps her sojourn in Cumberland Square would not be so bad after all.

Seeing her weariness beginning to show, Lady Beauvale went on kindly, "I'm sure you are tired after your journey. I know from experience that Julian travels as if the devil were on his heels! Being so healthy himself, it never occurs to him that others may feel tired or wish to rest. So, my dear, your bedchamber is ready to receive you, and a supper will be brought up to you. For tonight, I have asked my maid to wait on you—I'm certain that her services will be welcome."

"That's very kind of you, Lady Beauvale," said Emma, grateful for the thoughtfulness of the older woman.

Lady Beauvale rang a bell. "Then, my dear, I'll look forward to seeing you tomorrow, when you are rested."

The bedroom to which Emma was shown was light and airy with elegant furniture in the fashionable style. Pale green and white paper covered the walls, a dark green carpet was thick and luxurious underfoot, and the half-tester bed was a froth of white muslin curtains, looped back with green velvet ties.

"Oh, how pretty!" she could not help exclaiming, and won a glance of approval from the thin, dour-faced maid waiting for her. "How do you do?" she went on ingenuously, holding out her hand in a friendly manner. "You must be Lady Beauvale's maid. I'm very grateful for your offer to help me tonight."

The other sniffed, not to be won over so easily. "The name's Hill, miss," she said. "I wouldn't be here—it's really more Hetty's place than mine—but Miss Elvira wouldn't hear of losing her, even for a night. And, things being the way they are, of course I agreed."

Although filled with curiosity by this speech, Emma felt unable to ask the obvious question and had to wonder silently "how things were" with Sir Julian's little sister. Too sleepy to care for long, she allowed the maid to help her undress and then slipped gratefully between the cool sheets of the high bed. Sitting up against the pillows to partake of a dish of tea and some chicken sandwiches before sliding down into the warm softness, she fell asleep to the comfortable sounds of Hill moving softly about the room.

# Chapter Four

$\mathcal{D}$isturbed by unfamiliar sounds and surroundings, Emma woke early next morning and lay for a moment listening to the calls from the street below, as traders offered "fine milk," "sweet lavender," or "fresh meat" to the occupants of Cumberland Square.

Sitting up with a sudden thrill of excitement, she could not help wondering what the future would hold for her. Climbing out of bed, she padded across the room and drew back the curtains to find that her bedchamber was on the corner of the house. To her right she could see the communal garden in the center of the square, and by opening the window and leaning out at a perilous angle, she could see that to her left the long garden belonging to the house was a riot of color with a stable-block at the far end.

Having expected that a town house would be without a garden, she was pleased with her surroundings and, eager to explore, washed and dressed quickly in a drab cotton morning gown that had done stirling service on the Peninsula. As she was arranging her hair there was a smart tap at the door, and a maid entered bearing a tray, accompanied by a young lady of about Emma's age.

"Oh, good!" she exclaimed. "I hoped that you'd be awake. I'm Elvira," she added, holding out her hand. Small and plump, with a pink ribbon threaded artlessly through curls as dark as those of her brother, she smiled at Emma, who, having expected a child, was trying to hide her surprise.

"I'm very pleased to have you stay, you know," she went on, her big black eyes sparkling with delight. "I am badly in need of a friend."

"Indeed?" was all Emma could find to say, unhappily aware of the maid, who was setting down the tray and seemed to be lingering longer than was strictly necessary.

Catching her meaning, Elvira waved her hand airily. "Take no notice of Hetty—I assure you that she is the soul of discretion and totally in my confidence." Pouring two cups of chocolate, she handed one to Emma and sipped from the other herself. "I must tell you at once, lest there be some misunderstanding, that there is tragedy in my life. My heart is broken!"

She sighed dolefully and neatly demolished a thin slice of bread and butter, her expression sad and thoughtful.

"I'm . . . very sorry to hear that," said Emma. "A bereavement, you mean? Forgive me, I did not know."

Elvira shook her head impatiently. "My brother, whose name shall never pass my lips, has blighted my life," she announced dramatically. "He has refused to allow me to become betrothed to the only man I shall ever love—and even worse, he has made sure that I shall never see my dear Bevis again, by sending him to his death!"

"Dear me!" exclaimed her listener, blinking. "Surely not. I mean, Sir Julian does seem rather high-handed, I admit, but how could he send someone to death?"

"Bevis is of a delicate disposition—to be forced to live in servitude in the depths of despair would be his death!" said Elvira, in tragic tones.

"Well, I can see that that would not be to anyone's liking," agreed Emma sympathetically. "But surely he must have done some wrong to be sent to prison?"

Elvira shook her head impatiently. "Not to *prison*. Bevis is a poet!" she announced, tears sparkling on her black eyelashes. "And—that wretch, would send him to be a—a *secretary* with one of his cronies in N-Norfolk which, let me tell you, is just as bad as prison to one of Bevis's sensibility!"

Having expected much worse, Emma nibbled a piece of bread thoughtfully. "Cannot he refuse to go?" she asked practically.

"My love is poor . . . penniless, in fact. He relies on Ju—that wretch, for support, and *he* has withdrawn his aid, having found out our affection. He insists that poor, dear Bevis needs must earn his own living!"

"Many must, you know," Emma pointed out.

"But Bevis was left to my brother's care—"

Emma looked up quickly. "His ward, you mean?"

"Not exactly. Bevis is a distant kinsman, and when he was left an orphan, *Julian*—" having given up the attempt never to use her brother's name again, she pronounced it with a fine note of loathing—"took him under his wing—and now when we have need of it, he has cut off his allowance and sent him to work like a common clerk. Just because he has never fallen in love himself, he has no feelings for those who have!"

"To be sure, I thought him rather overbearing," Emma agreed, and proceeded to tell her own tale of ill treatment.

"Well, to be sure, I call that mean!" declared Miss Leyton at the end of the account. "To deny you the chance of being another Mrs. Siddons is just like Julian. He thinks of nothing but his own desires. I'm sure you looked very attractive in your blue breeches. Oh, I do envy you such an experience—though, I must admit that I would feel a little discomforted in male costume."

"So did I," confessed her new friend with feeling. "My legs seemed twice as long as normal, and I was horridly conscious of their shape. To be honest, I don't think that I would care for a career on the stage."

"I don't think Ju would allow it," Elvira told her. "He's a stick in the mud. Why, when I wanted to go to Vauxhall

Gardens with a friend from school, who was in town visiting, he would not hear of it. And, what harm could there be in that? I told him that we all intended to wear masks, but it made no difference. *And* Aunt agreed with him—she usually does.''

"Lady Beauvale seemed very pleasant when I met her last night.''

"Oh, Aunt Diana is the kindest person. Unfortunately she dotes on Julian and will almost always take his part.''

"What does she think of his treatment of Bevis?'' asked Emma curiously.

Elvira's lower lip protruded, and her black eyebrows drew together. "In that she is utterly unfeeling—she says it's time he learned to stand on his own feet.'' She leaned closer to say confidingly in Emma's ear, "I intend to invite the Prince Regent to be his patron. All poets have patrons, don't they? Even Shakespeare. I did ask Julian, but he was very rude.''

Her new friend had no difficulty in imagining Sir Julian's response to such a request. "What does Bevis—I really should know his surname,'' she pointed out. "It seems very familiar to be using his first name, when I haven't even met him.''

"Browne—with an E. I don't think that there has been a poet with that name before.''

"No,'' agreed Emma, and continued with her question. "What does Mr. Browne write?''

"Oh, such romantic, beautiful poems. One I liked particularly was 'Upon the First Wagtail' . . . *quite* different from Keats's 'Upon the First Skylark,' I do assure you. Just now he is working upon one about me. It begins 'To the mole upon my love's alabaster cheek.' It sounds well, don't you think?''

"Extremely so,'' said her companion, forebearing to point out that Miss Leyton's healthy complexion in no way resembled the poet's description. "*Do* you have a mole?'' she asked, leaning closer.

"Well, no," confessed Elvira, "but Bevis says it is poetic license."

"I—see," murmured Emma, nonplussed. "But then, how do you know it's about you?"

"Bevis told me so," answered Miss Leyton with beautiful simplicity. She looked at Emma with huge, artless eyes. "I must confess that when I heard that you were coming, I was not at all pleased, but now I am sure we shall be great friends. I shall call you Emma, and you must call me Elvira, we shall not be formal and term each other Miss Beringer and Miss Leyton. Do you not agree?"

"Agreed!" cried Emma, holding out her hand and feeling happier than she had felt for some time.

Her hand was clasped warmly and then, jumping up, Elvira dragged her to her feet. "We have so much to do today, I declare that we shall be exhausted well before dinner. My horrible brother has promised me a purse to go shopping with this morning, but first we must go and pay our respects to Aunt Diana."

Emma hung back as the other hurried to the door. "I brought a little girl with me. Sir Julian said she could be my maid—I really ought to see her before I do anything."

"Maria, you mean? I've heard all about her from Hetty. Her tale is vastly romantic. Perhaps she is a lost heiress. Let Hetty bring her up here while we see Aunt Diana."

Satisfied with the suggestion, Emma followed her friend down the stairs and into the breakfast room, where they found Lady Beauvale perusing her mail as she sipped her tea.

"Good morning, my dears." She smiled, looking up, and Emma thought that she had never seen so becoming a morning cap as adorned Lady Beauvale's soft curls. "You are looking refreshed, Emma. I trust that you slept well?"

The door behind her opened before she could reply, and Sir Julian entered, dressed for riding, and Emma could not but admit that the habit became his tall, broad-shouldered figure.

"Good morning, ladies," he said, bowing. "I had not expected to see you up so early, Elvira. You may not believe it, Miss Beringer, on this evidence, but my sister is usually a slug-a-bed."

He spoke teasingly, but Elvira had assumed the expression of a martyr and would not allow herself to be wooed.

"As you can see, Emma, my brother is set upon being disagreeable."

"Nothing of the kind, Elf—and well you know it. Let us be friends and forget what has gone before."

Elvira turned a shoulder upon his winning voice and stared moodily out of the window. Her brother sighed, his face clouding.

"Knowing the usual state of your finances, I take it that you intend to accept my gift to enable you to buy some fripperies this morning?" His mouth was tight as he held out a purse, making no effort to hand it to his sister but forcing her to come to him.

Elvira hesitated, wanting the money but not wishing to accept largess from her brother.

"Elvira," put in Lady Beauvale softly. "We have a guest. Such squabbling is unseemly. If you wish the money, pray take it with good grace."

Abruptly, the dark girl turned back from her contemplation of the railed garden below, tears glittering on her black eyelashes, looking so miserable that Julian relented, tossing the net purse to her before she reached him and then, to her surprise, crossed to Emma and dropped a similar receptacle into her lap.

"A guardian's privilege," he said, as she looked up, startled.

"Oh, no," she cried. "I really don't think—"

"Of course you can, Emma," put in Lady Beauvale. "It would be perfectly proper to accept, indeed it would be churlish to refuse."

Emma's cheeks flared hotly with embarrassment. "It is very k—kind of you," she began uncertainly, "but . . ."

"Nonsense!" was the robust reply. "You must know that I am trying to make amends to my sibling, here. She has filled the house successfully with misery and gloom for the last three weeks. If you go shopping with her and she forgets her personal tragedy—even for a few hours—the entire household will be extremely grateful to you, Miss Beringer. So take it, child, you'll be doing us all a favor."

Without waiting for her reply, he bowed to the ladies in general and left the room. His footsteps could be heard crossing the marble tiles of the hall, before the front door closed smartly and a few seconds later the sound of horse hooves announced his departure.

"The brute!" cried Miss Leyton feelingly.

"Elvira! I grow tired of your dramatics," announced her aunt. "Julian has your welfare in mind. You may think that you would like life in a garret, but, believe me, you would not. You do not need me to remind you of your manners—you are forgetting Emma. Pray calm yourself, and remember the courtesy due to a guest."

Elvira pouted but made an effort to obey her aunt, turning to Emma to say in a bright, social voice, "I daresay it is nothing new to you, Emma dear, to shop in London."

"Now there you are wrong," answered Emma candidly. "To own the truth, I have never been in London before. After my mother died, I was at school in Hampshire, and after that I was with my father in the Peninsula. Shops, to me, are a new luxury, and I'm afraid that I have already made one blunder—!"

Elvira was interested. "How?" she demanded, and even Lady Beauvale appeared interested.

Emma hesitated teasingly. "It was a hat," she said at last. "A totally unsuitable but devastatingly beautiful bonnet, lined with red silk and bewitchingly trimmed with voluptuous white roses. I fell in love with it, and when I wore it . . .

was taken to be other than quite a lady!'' As she had hoped the others laughed, lightening the atmosphere. ''However, I have learned my lesson and shall only purchase the most demure of headgear in the future.''

''A wise lesson, Emma, which it is as well to learn early in life,'' commented Lady Beauvale. ''I may add that some females of my acquaintance have yet to benefit from their mistakes. Now, run along girls, I have ordered the landau to be at the door at eleven.''

Arriving back in her room, Emma was pleased to find Maria there and gave her an impulsive hug.

''How have you fared?'' she asked.

''Oh, miss, ain't this house big? It's bigger than the George, and that was an inn. And look at my dress! Isn't it *beautiful*?'' She smoothed her long white lawn apron and spun round to show off her gown of lavender print. ''All the maids wear them—and I've got new shoes and stockings, too!''

''You look very pretty,'' Emma told her, which was true; freshly bathed and dressed in new clothes, rather than secondhand rags of any size or style, Maria was revealed as an attractive young girl.

Smiling broadly, she executed a spirited jig around the room. ''I ain't half going to like it here,'' she said, coming to a breathless halt in front of her mistress and assuming a more sober demeanor.

''Now, Miss Emma, Mrs. Hill said as I was to get you ready to go out with milady—'' She bit her lip, looking confused. ''What do I do?'' she asked, suddenly a child again.

Emma laughed. ''Find my hat and blue spencer jacket,'' she told her, ''which should not be difficult, as I saw Hill put them away in the clothes press last night.''

She was quickly ready and was not aware of her own shabbiness until she encountered Elvira, a vision of fashion and style in a pale pink gown and clover velvet spencer and bonnet. Suddenly realizing her need of new clothes, she understood that her guardian's gesture had not been merely one of condescension and, despite certain misgivings about accepting his gift, felt a wave of excitement at the prospect of shopping.

Lady Beauvale and her maid were already taking their places in the open carriage as the girls crossed the hall, and they hurried to join them; Elvira insisting that they should share the back-facing seat, while her aunt had the pleasure of seeing where they were going.

The coachman quickly took the carriage out into the traffic, leaving the quiet of the square behind as they joined the stream of vehicles and horses that filled London's main thoroughfares. The sun was warm enough to cause Lady Beauvale to shield her complexion under a parasol, but Emma and Elvira trusted to the shade of their bonnet brims, eager to see and, in Elvira's case, to be seen.

At first Emma was unhappily aware of her drab attire, sinking back in the corner of the seat and making herself as effacing as possible, but after a while she forgot her embarrassment and lost her self-consciousness in looking at the buildings and people as Elvira pointed out anything of interest.

Almost too soon, they arrived in Oxford Street, and, bidding the coachman to return in an hour, Lady Beauvale led the way into the first of many shops. Three made-up morning dresses and the same number of afternoon gowns in various muslins and lawns were quickly chosen, with a new spencer jacket in cream silk and a long, patterned shawl to go with them; then the ladies turned to the more exciting business of choosing the material and style of two evening gowns.

Elvira was much taken with a shimmering gold silk, but, remembering the hat disaster, Emma settled instead for a white silk gauze and an aquamarine satin, both of which Lady Beauvale declared to be charming. Having been measured, Emma and her companions left the dressmaker's establishment and went happily in search of accessories to go with the new ensembles.

The somber-faced Hill, following behind, was soon laden with boxes and packages, which she clutched to her bosom with a righteous air, despite the best endeavors of the girls to carry their own purchases. Emma soon lost count of the gloves, ribbons, fans, feathers, and lace which they bought but was aware with total satisfaction that she now owned two hats, both of which had enough style and fashion to throw the red silk creation bought in Portsmouth quite into the shade.

Sated, she followed Lady Beauvale and Elvira into the landau, and her joy was overflowing when she discovered that they were to drive through Hyde Park on the way home. She was recalled from the happy reverie of her numerous new possessions by the sight of a gentleman standing on the side of the path, bowing as they passed. Acknowledging this courtesy with the briefest of civilities, Lady Beauvale began at once to discuss a dinner-dance that she proposed to hold for the girls, leaving Emma with the distinct impression that she had wished to ignore the incident.

Certain that she had recognized the man who had been on the stairs at Portsmouth, Emma looked back to see that he was watching the landau out of sight, making no attempt to hide his interest.

Waiting until they were alone in the sitting room that had been assigned to them, she asked Elvira casually for his name and had her suspicions confirmed.

"But do not mention him to my aunt," she was adjourned. "For he is the most dreadful man—we only acknowledge him in the slightest way, you know. I am not precisely sure of the circumstances, but I believe that he called Julian out. Of course, it was years ago and all hushed up, but we do not choose to mix with him."

Curious but feeling it would be unmannerly to ask further, Emma hid her disappointment, for she had found Lord Devern attractive and even more so on this second meeting. As the carriage had driven away, their eyes had met for an instant, and she was almost sure that she had seen a flare of recognition in his pale gaze. Her heart beat quicker with excitement at the thought, and she wondered if he would contrive to make her acquaintance during the coming months.

"Did he and Sir Julian actually fight a duel?" she could not resist asking.

"Well . . . Ju was the injured party, so he had the choice of weapons." Elvira seemed reluctant to go on, and Emma gave her a sharp look, discovering something like chagrin on the other's face. "Would it not have been romantic to have one's brother fight a duel?" Elvira asked abruptly. "Of course I was in the schoolroom at the time, but you can imagine my mortification when I heard what the wretch had chosen!"

"I can't, for I have no idea what weapons he favors," put in Emma, impatient to learn the end of the story.

*"Fisticuffs!"* declared her friend in tones of disgust. "What must the ton have thought? And Ju is a bang up shot, too."

Emma considered. "That really was remarkably clever," she said at last, reluctant admiration in her voice. *"That* choice would certainly have made sure of the affair being kept secret. Think how foolish Lord Devern must have felt, if it got about."

"Well, yes, I daresay he would," was Elvira's reluctant agreement. "But I still think Ju was sadly lacking in high ideals."

"Romance is all very well, but sometimes practicality is not to be sneezed at," said Emma, for once in accord with her guardian.

"Pooh!" remarked the other, tossing her black curls. "Soon you will be telling me that my brother is in the right to be mistreating me so."

Emma hastened to reassure her on this issue, so effectively

that, having made certain that they were alone with no one in earshot, Elvira bent closer with a confiding air.

"I am in touch with my dearest Bevis," she announced triumphantly, her eyes sparkling. "By good fortune, Hetty's brother works at the 'Angel,' an inn near here. Bevis has taken the direction with the intention of sending letters there, and Hetty will collect them when she visits her brother. Is not that well arranged?"

"Sir Julian would not like it!" proclaimed Emma solemnly, her eyes bright with amusement.

"No, indeed. And that's one of the joys of the whole thing," declared the baronet's undutiful sister. "Ju is too busy by far interfering in other's affairs."

Emma could not but agree with this sentiment, and the two girls smiled impishly at each other, pleased with the thought of outwitting Sir Julian.

"And when do you know if this postal system of yours will work?" Emma inquired.

Elvira could not restrain a little twitch of excitement. "Today!" she cried. "Hetty is calling on her brother this very afternoon."

"Now, what could be more romantic than that?" asked Miss Beringer with satisfaction, and, for the moment, well content with their prospects, the girls fell to the pleasant task of examining their morning purchases in the minutest detail.

# Chapter Five

To Miss Leyton's joy, the longed-for letter spoke of a sooner than anticipated return to London, as Mr. Browne's employer had business needing attention. This so pleased Elvira that when Lady Beauvale proposed a walk in the park for the next afternoon, an event which was usually viewed with less than favor, she agreed without protest.

The ladies were taken to the park gates in the landau, which drove away with instructions to return in an hour. Hill and Lady Beauvale deposited themselves on chairs near the entrance, and the girls were encouraged to stroll along the paths under their benevolent eyes.

"This will be very dull," discoursed Elvira, taking Emma's arm, "unless we have the good fortune to meet up with an acquaintance."

For a while Emma was content to air her new bonnet and view the members of fashionable Society, who had come to see and be seen. However, after a time this occupation palled, and she began to think kindly of her stay on the Peninsula where she was known to everyone and had forgotten what it was like to be a stranger.

"I do declare that is Clarissa Melvin waving to us!" observed her companion suddenly, and, following her gaze, Emma saw a tall girl among a group of young people gesturing toward them. "I am sure I do not know why she should be so enthusiastic, for we were never particular friends at school," Elvira went on as the group approached.

"Elvira, *dearest*," gushed Miss Melvin the moment that they were in earshot of each other. "How delightful this is, to be sure. I vow it's an age since last we met."

"How do you do, Clarissa," replied Elvira. "Are you in town for the Season?"

"My mama has taken rooms for the next two months. You are the first of my friends we've met. Pray let me introduce my brother, Freddie—this is Miss Leyton of whom you have heard me speak."

She pushed forward a rather shy-looking youth, who seemed on the point of growing out of his obviously new clothes. Blushing, he bowed, dropped his top hat, picked it up, and muttered something inarticulate as he shook Elvira's hand.

"This is my brother's ward, Miss Emma Beringer," she returned, indicating her companion, which announcement caused obvious interest among the newcomers, who turned a concerted gaze upon Emma.

"I say—not the Beringer Heiress?" asked one youth, more brash than the others.

"Dash it all, Henry old fellow, mind your manners," put in Freddie, blushing for his friend. "Not the kind of thing to say, y'know."

"Only asked a civil question," muttered the brash one, melting away to the back of the group.

"My apologies, Miss Beringer," said Freddie Melvin, seeing her puzzled embarrassment. "Pray forgive the impudent fellow."

To her surprise Emma found that she rather liked the gangling young man, who reminded her of some of the youthful officers she had known, and she offered him her hand. "My name *is* Beringer," she allowed, "but I assure you that I would know if I was an heiress," she told him, laughing at the ridiculous suggestion.

"Of course you would. Only a rumor—no one knows precisely how . . . Sounds like a play, doesn't it?" Freddie went on somewhat incoherently and, abruptly abandoning the subject, bowed and offered his arm. "May I have the honor of escorting you back to Lady Beauvale?" he asked.

The group of young people opened to receive Emma and Elvira, and by mutual accord proceeded toward the main gate. Lady Beauvale looked questioningly at their approach until her niece took introductions upon herself, and then the older woman nodded and smiled.

"I believe that I was at school with your mama," she commented. "Pray give Mrs. Melvin my compliments, and tell her that I should be very happy to receive her card. Perhaps we could arrange a picnic for you young folk. . . . But now, I see the landau is at the gate, so make your farewells, Elvira and Emma. We must not keep the horses waiting."

"I wonder why Clarissa was so friendly?" mused Elvira after dinner that evening as the girls amused themselves with a pack of cards. "We were not in each other's 'set' at school. In fact I thought her a dead bore. She was always giggling and flirting with the music master!"

"I thought that her brother seemed quite sensible—he reminded me of some of the young officers I knew—all bony wrist, freckles, and blushes!"

Elvira laughed. "He *was* rather endearing, wasn't he? Like a half-grown colt. They must be a horsey family—*skittish* would describe Clarissa," she observed darkly, before going on, "Oh well, I suppose it is pleasant to know someone of our own age. I *do* wish I had been one of a large family, don't you?"

"I've often longed for a big brother."

Elvira shuddered. "You are welcome to mine," she offered, and then fell silent, nibbling her finger and obviously thinking deeply, while gazing thoughtfully at Emma. "Surely," she said at last, "Julian being your guardian must make us almost related?"

Emma considered. "W—ell . . . a guardian is in place of a parent—but that would make you my aunt!"

"Pooh! What nonsense!" cried Elvira. "We shall have to be just special friends. I do hope that Aunt Diana really intends to arrange an outing," she went on, her eyes sparkling at the thought. "And perhaps she will invite them to our dinner-dance. How fortunate that she knows Mrs. Melvin. We only have to wait for that lady to call on her, and all will be settled."

The girls' anxiety was put at rest the next day, when Hetty informed them that Mrs. Melvin was at that moment in the act of making a morning call upon Lady Beauvale. Her daughter accompanied her and soon was escorted upstairs to the young lady's sitting room.

"My dears," trilled Clarissa, pausing in the doorway, "is not this delightful? To find two friends so unexpectedly—and just when one was resigning oneself to the dullest of stays, for you must know that brothers and their friends are dead bores."

Elvira found herself so in agreement with this sentiment that the next few moments were taken up by extolling the annoying natures of brothers.

"And to think that all my life I have thought myself hard done by in lacking one," Emma remarked into a pause in the conversation. "Only think from what I have been saved! I must own that I had no idea that the breed behaved so shabbily."

Elvira looked closely at her, suspecting that she was being teased, but Clarissa accepted the statement and at once began to list Freddie's faults.

A tray of coffee and pastries was brought in, and as the cups were filled and passed round Clarissa turned confidingly to Emma.

"Now, tell me, my dearest Miss Beringer—of course I only mention it as we are such friends and I promise you that my lips are sealed—is the tale true?"

Emma was amused. "I have no idea what you mean," she said.

"Oh, come now. There is no need to be secretive with me. I assure you that the story only appeals to my romantic nature—that you are an heiress can mean nothing to me. I view money as of very little importance, I can tell you."

Emma set down her cup and sat up straight. "You are mistaken," she declared firmly. "Far from being an heiress, I am as poor as the proverbial church mouse."

Miss Melvin's eyes opened wide, and she took a breath preparatory to making another remark, but, catching Emma's austere gaze, she closed her parted lips and smiled in an understanding way. Favoring her with a knowing nod, she turned to Elvira, who, seeing her friend's annoyance, had turned the conversation by reminding Clarissa of the music master at their mutual school.

"Of course I remember Senor Conti," she cried, losing interest in the "Beringer Heiress." "He joined the army when he was dismissed so unfairly and now is teaching drill, wearing a vastly fetching uniform. I happen to know, for I saw him last month at my little brother's school. He positively goggled when he saw me, but I behaved very correctly and refused to meet his eye . . . until just before we left, when I gave the poor man a *little* encouragement with the tiniest smile. Mama, of course, did not recognize him."

Emma and Elvira found very little to reply to this and shortly after, Miss Melvin left, called to rejoin her mother and continue their round of morning calls.

"Well, did you ever meet such a henbrain?" asked Elvira in disgust. "She obviously only came to quiz you about the rumors she had heard."

"What is this about an heiress with the same name as me?" wondered Emma. "Have you heard the story?"

Elvira shook her head. "But then, I've only recently come up from the country," she pointed out reasonably, "and, to be honest, I've had other thoughts on my mind. When one is in love, the rest of the world is at a distance, you know.'' For the first time she gave the matter her attention. ''It *is* odd—Beringer is an unusual name.'' She looked closely at her friend. ''You don't have an elderly, extremely wealthy relative, do you?''

Emma shook her head. ''Not that I've heard of,'' she replied. ''Both my parents were only children—I suppose that I must have cousins somewhere, but I've never heard of them.''


The mystery was explained the next day; she was crossing the hall and encountered Sir Julian, who begged for a moment of her time, ushering her into his study.

''I understand that you have heard of the 'Beringer Heiress,' '' he began, without preamble. ''I had hoped that you would have been spared gossip, but now that rumor is about, it is only right that you should be made aware of the truth.''

Emma sat down slowly, aware of her heart beginning a steady thump against her ribs. ''Pray go on,'' she said as her guardian paused, swinging away to stare out of the window, his hands clasped behind his back.

''You may have wondered why your father appointed me as your guardian,'' he said suddenly. ''He told me that it was because I was the most wealthy of his acquaintances.''

Emma stared at him in disbelief. ''I had not thought the matter would weigh with him,'' she said stiffly. ''My father was the least material of men.''

Sir Julian turned back into the room. ''My position meant nothing to him—but he wished to safeguard *you* against the unwelcome effects riches can bestow, and he knew that your wealth would hold no interest for me.''

''My *wealth*? I fear that you are mistaken—I have no money nor prospects of any,'' Emma assured him spiritedly.

Julian Leyton regarded her intently before replying. ''Now there, Miss Beringer, you are the one to be mistaken!'' he informed her.

Emma returned his gaze blankly, still disinclined to believe the unlikely story but aware that her guardian was serious. "H—how . . . why . . . w—who?" she stuttered.

A faint smile crossed Sir Julian's face. "You sound like an owl," he remarked before continuing, "Have you never heard of an aged great aunt of your mother, Emma Hodge? Your grandmother's sister married a city merchant against her father's will and was immediately disowned by her family—save for your grandmother. Mrs. Hodge had no children, and now rumor has it that she has named you as her heir."

"How absurd!" exclaimed Emma. "I have never heard such fudge in all my life!"

Sir Julian was amused. "How so?" he demanded, lifting one black eyebrow.

"I've never heard of such a person. Surely my father would have told me. He often worried over how I would manage if anything s-should happen to him, which is why I had determined upon some means of earning my living."

"He told me that he preferred you not to know. . . . I imagine that he planned on telling you in his own time. Possibly your mother wanted it that way. She may have thought that the idea of being an heiress would have altered your outlook on life."

Emma studied his face, realizing from his tone that he was serious. "You're not bamming me?" she asked in a voice that shook a little.

Shaking his head, her guardian seated himself beside her. "No. In fact as soon as I heard the rumor, I took it upon myself to ascertain the facts. My man of business has been in touch with Mrs. Hodge, who has indicated that she has named you as her main beneficiary." For a moment he watched the play of emotions crossing Emma's face. "Most would be pleased," he pointed out.

"I have been brought up to be poor. I find that to suddenly have prospects is somewhat unnerving," Emma admitted.

"I am afraid that you will find yourself the object of fortune hunters. Good fortune is not an entirely unmixed blessing."

He spoke harshly, and Emma wondered what experience had embittered him. "Do Lady Beauvale and Elvira know?" she asked.

"My aunt, of course, was informed, but I leave you to tell Elvira. I have written to your great aunt, asking if she wishes you to visit her. If she does, of course I shall take you."

Emma studied her hands lying in her lap. "Does not that seem rather mercenary?" she wondered quietly.

"Not at all," was the bracing reply. "If the old lady has chosen to leave her wealth to you, it is only right and proper that you should be in contact. Not to do so would seem lacking in duty." Sir Julian paused, looking down at her reflective figure. "Do you ride?" he asked abruptly.

"Oh, *yes*." Emma was surprised into saying, a sudden smile breaking across her downcast face. "In the Peninsula, you know, one had to."

"So I had supposed. I ride most mornings. I've a mount that would suit you. If you care to breakfast with me about eight, I'll take you to the park."

"What?" exclaimed Elvira, when told of the prospective outing. "You must be in high favor. Ju utterly refuses to accompany me. He says I only have to look at a horse to fall off! And to own the truth, I do prefer to sit at comfort in a carriage."

"They are certainly more difficult to fall off," teased Emma, privately pleased at the thought of her first ride for several months.

"Oh, miss, you don't half look smart!" Maria said the next morning, having helped her mistress to array herself in the riding habit her father had had made by the regimental tailor. "You'll put all the other ladies in the shade."

Emma smiled happily at her reflection, admiring the green, heavily frogged jacket which was a replica of the Rifle Brigades' uniform, and adjusted the long green apron which covered her tightly fitting riding breeches. Throwing the folds of the skirt over one arm, she caught up the shako which completed the ensemble and ran downstairs.

Sir Julian stood up as she entered the breakfast room, his expression altering at the sight of her dashing outfit.

"Is it not beautiful?" cried Emma, enjoying the effect. "Papa said that as I'd kept up with the regiment, I had every right to wear the uniform. The men loved it."

"I daresay."

A tiny frown appeared. "You don't care for it," she remarked challengingly. "I had not supposed you overly conventional, sir."

"Nor decidedly unconventional." As her chin came up, he suddenly relaxed and held a chair for her. "You may very well start a new fashion," he told her. "I own only to a little surprise—not disapproval, Miss Beringer. May I express the hope that your performance matches your outfit."

"You will not find me lacking in horsemanship," Emma told him serenely, and set about the business of making a hearty breakfast.

Within the hour they arrived at the gates to the park, having trotted sedately through the half-empty London streets. Emma had been pleased to see that the mount provided by her guardian was a small but spirited mare, not the placid animal she had half-suspected him of offering. Sir Julian had ridden close by her side, obviously prepared to intervene should it be necessary, and once inside the park, she turned to him.

"I really am no novice, you know," she assured him kindly.

"I daresay—but until I know your ability, it would be both foolish and dangerous to give you free rein."

Lifting her brows, Emma laughed and, throwing caution aside, kicked her heels into her mount. She had intended only to gallop a short distance, just to show off her horsemanship, but the feel of the fresh morning air against her cheeks and the excitement of being on horseback again after so long proved too much for her self-restraint, and, heedless of the consequences, she settled into a headlong gallop. The mare was fresh and eager to stretch her legs, and for a while she and Emma enjoyed each other's efforts, Emma concentrating on the merely physical demands of controlling an unknown animal and flexing muscles unused for many months.

She had just decided that the mare was entirely suited to her weight and strength, when she became aware of someone quickly catching up with her and, snatching a look over her shoulder, saw that Sir Julian was fast approaching. That one glance was enough to tell her that he was not challenging her to a race, and, as he drew level and seized her mount's bridle, she allowed the pace to slacken.

"What the devil do you think you are doing?" exploded her guardian, having ascertained that she was not hurt, as he brought both horses to a halt.

Emma lifted her chin. "I could ask you the same thing, sir," she returned evenly. "My actions must have told you that I was not being run away with, so I cannot imagine why you should feel able to take the management of my horse into your hands!"

Sir Julian had, indeed, suspected a runaway, but, having realized that his ward had her mount under control, his anger was directed at behavior which would draw attention to himself and his companion.

"May I remind you, Miss Beringer, that this is a royal park, where some degree of decorum is expected. A full gallop is neither sensible nor accepted."

"No? Well, then I shall not do it again. It was just that I have not been on a horse for so long. . . ."

Sir Julian was not to be mollified. "Reputations are easily

lost—in that outfit and with unbridled behavior you could become noted as fast.''

Emma opened her eyes. *"Fast!"* she repeated. ''You sound like a maiden aunt! I had not supposed you to have a care for gossip.''

Her guardian ground his teeth. ''It is *your* reputation of which we talk,'' he pointed out.

Emma considered him, turning in the saddle the better to see his face, her eyes dancing with mischief. ''I know what it is—'' she said suddenly. ''You do not care for my habit. You cannot take exception to my riding, for I was taught by my father, who was noted for his horsemanship.''

''I do not question your clothes or riding ability. It is your wild behavior which I find outrageous and will not tolerate.''

Ignoring this challenging statement, Emma, who had been staring over his shoulder, said, ''There is someone trying to attract your attention. A lady on a sedate cob.''

''Yes, I know,'' he replied, his voice tight with irritation. ''It is Miss Plantagenet—she has been there for some time watching your antics.''

''Oh, I see!'' exclaimed Emma, enlightened. ''You wish to speak to her, rather than ride after me. Let us by all means go over to her.''

''Miss Plantagenet is a model of decorum—I would have preferred you to make a good impression.''

Emma sniffed. ''She sounds extremely boring,'' she remarked bluntly.

''Behave, you dreadful girl,'' ordered her guardian, before assuming a polite expression as they joined the waiting lady and her groom.

Miss Plantagenet proved to be a very genteel person, a few years older than Emma. Her riding habit, while fashionable, was so sober in style and color that Emma could quite see why Sir Julian had taken a dislike to her own dashing outfit.

''So this is your little ward,'' said Jane Plantagenet, extending a hand. "How much I have wanted to meet you, Miss Beringer—and to offer any help and advice in my power. I do quite understand how different London ton must be to the company of soldiers."

Emma stiffened slightly. "That is very kind of you—but I assure you that the society with whom I mixed were very little different from that to be found in London. Indeed, I suspect that some may even be brothers or husbands of females quite like yourself! Lady Beauvale has good care of me and will tell me how to go on."

"How sensible—Sir Julian, what a little treasure you have here." She fell in alongside Emma as they rode back to the entrance. Leaning sideways, she said confidentially. "One little word, dear Miss Beringer. You are not acquainted with our ways, but to gallop so wildly is not the thing. Forgive my plain speaking, but Sir Julian and I have an arrangement." She paused delicately before going on, "So you must think of me as almost one of the family."

"One of the family, indeed!" snorted Elvira a little later, when Emma repeated the conversation to her. "Jane Plantagenet is so high flown that there is no tolerating her."

"Is she really . . . ?"

"Engaged? Not yet, but I'm afraid that she soon will be," said Elvira gloomily. "I think Ju likes her because his wealth means nothing to her—she is so full of her own importance. She claims to be descended from William the Conquerer and thinks that she is more royal than King George or the Prince Regent."

Emma had lost interest in Miss Plantagenet. "Was it very wrong of me to gallop in the park?" she asked.

"It's not usually done," conceded Elvira. "Ju is not usually so stiff, but I daresay that you gave him a fright, and he was annoyed that his *amour* was there and could disapprove. He has no liking for being put in the wrong."

"To own the truth, I do not care for these niceties of

polite behavior," observed Emma with feeling. "Life was much easier in the Peninsula—I do so miss the easy society there."

"Don't be too downcast. The invitations to our dinner-dance are sent out! Aunt Diana and Mrs. Melvin have arranged the picnic to Richmond for a week tomorrow. Now, all we have to wish for is good weather."

The skies were anxiously watched and many weather profits consulted; Hetty's ancient uncle declaring that the weather was set fair for a month, and Mrs. Frobisher, who went by the state of her corns, was sure that rain was on the way. At last the day dawned bright and cloudless to the participants' relief. Mrs. Melvin was to accompany the young people, and Emma and Elvira were already in the hall when Clarissa and her mother drew up in a chaise with the hood let down.

Happy greetings were exchanged and the girls handed into their own carriage by Freddie and his friend, who were accompanying the party on horseback.

"Is not this delightful?" called Clarissa as the little cavalcade set off, and, seated in the open landau, wearing a new lawn gown and a chip straw hat that she knew was becoming, Emma smiled happily and agreed with her.

The leading chaise paused at the approach to the bridge crossing the Thames, and a waiting horseman rode up and was greeted by Mrs. Melvin and her daughter.

"Oh, dear," murmured Elvira as the landau drew level. "I do believe that is—"

"Lord Devern," supplied Emma, a certain satisfaction in her voice.

"My dears," called Mrs. Melvin. "Pray let me present my cousin to you. Vivian—Miss Beringer and Miss Leyton."

Lord Devern bowed from the saddle. "Ladies," he said, sweeping his hat from his head with a gallant gesture. "Your servant."

His eyes lingered on Emma, and she felt constrained to ask, "Do you intend to accompany us, sir?"

His eyes dancing, he bowed again. "Nothing would stop me . . . *now*," he said softly.

# Chapter Six

' '*O*h, dear," repeated Elvira unhappily as the party set off once more, clattering over the bridge. "What *will* Julian say?"

"We cannot ignore the man," put in Emma, "so it will be best if we behave as if he was any new acquaintance." Privately she felt a degree of excitement at the occurrence, a shiver of anticipation sliding deliciously down her spine as she watched Lord Devern riding attentively beside his cousin and her daughter. Emma had wondered if he would ride alongside the landau, but as Freddie and Henry appeared reluctant to give up their places on either side, he smiled and seemed content to escort Mrs. Melvin and Clarissa.

By the time the party arrived at Richmond the young folk had developed hearty appetites, and luncheon was voted to be served at once. Both ladies' cooks appeared to have vied with each other in a contest to see who could provide the best and most. Cold pies, chickens, salads, and fruit tarts in profusion were produced from the hampers and lemonade and elderflower champagne put to cool in the nearby stream.

After the repast, Mrs. Melvin declared herself wishful of sitting peacefully on the bank to drink in the beauty of her surroundings while the young people had her permission to explore a little. At first they walked in a group, but gradually Emma found herself ahead of the others with only Freddie and Vivian Devern for company.

"Freddie," Lord Devern said suddenly, looking back. "I believe your mama is signaling to you."

"What can she want?" wondered the younger man, screwing up his eyes and squinting at the distant figure, who was indeed waving her arm in an unusually energetic manner.

"You'd better go and find out," suggested his kinsman.

Freddie looked from Emma to Lord Devern, reluctance plainly written on his face. "I believe it is you. . . ." he suggested tentatively. "I daresay she has suddenly remembered some family news and wishes to tell you."

"No," said the other firmly. "I heard her call your name. Have no fear, I shall look after Miss Beringer."

Freddie shuffled and kicked a stone, blushing as he pondered upon the effect of making an issue out of the affair. A glance at his cousin's stony face decided him upon the disadvantages of such a procedure, and, bowing awkwardly to Emma, he reluctantly set off back the way they had come.

"I daresay cousin Lizzie is feeling lonely," commented Vivian Devern blandly, with a sideways glance at Emma as he tucked her hand into his elbow. "Am I right, Miss Beringer," he went on as they walked on, "in thinking that we have met before?"

Emma admired the distant landscape before replying lightly, "I doubt it sir, for I have never been in London until recently."

"Perhaps we merely . . . *passed* somewhere. Portsmouth, maybe?"

Emma refused to be drawn. "As I am a soldier's daughter, I have often been in Portsmouth, so possibly you are right," she answered coolly, with an air of indifference.

Lord Devern stopped and turned toward her. "Do I detect a certain coolness toward me, Miss Beringer?" he asked, sounding amused.

"You must know that I am aware of old stories, Lord Devern," she replied, returning his bluntness. "I am only surprised that you sought this outing, knowing that Elvira and I would be present.''

"My dear Miss Beringer, that is unworthy of you," he chided gently. "If I had wished to renew my acquaintance with Miss Leyton, who was in the schoolroom when my unfortunate disagreement with Julian Leyton took place, I could have made the attempt any one of a thousand times. You are intelligent enough to realize that it is yourself whom I wish to know.''

Startled by such plain speaking, Emma raised her eyes to his face and found herself being studied by a pair of gray eyes. For a second their gazes held, while she tried to read his enigmatic expression, then suddenly, he visibly relaxed and smiled down at her.

"Have I shocked you?" he asked.

"I must own to some surprise," she replied candidly. "I had not supposed you to believe this rumor of the Beringer Heiress!''

Vivian Devern laughed. "So you have claws!" he said, reminding her of a similar remark made by Sir Julian. "No, my dear, I am not after your fortune. You are not in the usual run of insipid Society misses, I fancy, and I'll admit that I would like to know you better. . . . To be honest, I rather care for the idea of Julian being hoist with the guardianship of a wayward young lady who can ride like the wind—yes, I did see you in the park—and who is not afraid to speak her mind, beside having the looks of an angel for good measure.''

Not expecting flattery, Emma blushed furiously and feigned a sudden interest in the button of her kid glove which had come undone. The tiny pearl button proved difficult, and suddenly her wrist was taken by a masculine hand and the task performed competently. Before releasing her, Lord Devern carried her hand to his lips and lightly kissed the back of her fingers.

"Will you acknowledge me when next we meet?" he asked insistently.

Raising her eyes to study the face above her, Miss Beringer finally nodded.

"Julian will not like it," he pointed out, not hiding his satisfaction. "To upset his equilibrium would please me, but how do you feel, Miss Beringer? Julian can be . . . forceful."

Reminded of the many times when he had, indeed, been overbearing, Emma's resolve hardened. "My guardianship is purely a formality. I am sure that my father had no real intention of putting me into Sir Julian's care. I am far too old to be a ward and shall attain my majority in a few months. Of course I cannot invite you to the house," she added hastily, foreseeing possible difficulties, "but I shall be very happy to be friends."

"I am honored." Lord Devern smiled, setting her heart fluttering, as he bowed over her hand, holding it for longer than was strictly necessary.

"I—think that we should rejoin the others."

For a moment he looked into her eyes. "By all means," he said, releasing her hand at last and escorting her back to the party, handing her over to Freddie's care as soon as that youth approached along the path. "You see," he said, "Miss Beringer is none the worse for my presence," and went to pay attention to Clarissa who, having had only her mother for company, was feeling decidedly peevish.

Henry and Elvira had wandered a little along the riverbank in the opposite direction, and Freddie suggested that he and Emma should join them.

"Not too far, children," said Mrs. Melvin as they passed the picnic site. "We must start back to town soon."

As soon as they were out of earshot Freddie spoke. "I say, Miss Beringer," he began heatedly before falling silent, appearing to be at a loss for words.

Emma smiled encouragingly. "What *do* you say, Mr. Melvin?" she wondered gently.

Freddie thrust a finger into the folds of his neckcloth as if that garment were about to strangle him. "I say," he began again, "I wouldn't have you suppose that I knew—embarrassing and all that. Common knowledge that the Leytons don't acknowledge him. Nothing against Vivian myself, of course, and the fellow is kin—but not the thing to force the meeting on you. Give you my word that I'd no idea Vivian had invited himself along. Can't think why—a picnic's not usually to his taste."

"I don't feel that the coolness between the families has anything to do with me," Emma hastened to reassure her companion. "I have no intention of cutting Lord Devern, and so I shall tell Sir Julian if the point arises. I intend to choose my own friends."

She spoke bravely but did not feel nearly so bold when her guardian sent for her the next day. The sight of a tearful Elvira precipitously leaving the room did nothing to reassure her, and she answered the curt order to enter with a trepidation which she did her best to conceal.

Sir Julian was standing in front of the empty fireplace, one arm stretched along the mantelpiece. The look he turned on Emma was far from kind, his black brows almost meeting in obvious displeasure.

"Well, Miss Beringer?" he demanded in a tone which made her lift her chin. "What have you to say for yourself—and I want no such nonsense as I have had from Elvira."

Refusing to stand like an errant schoolgirl for what was clearly to be a scolding, Emma calmly seated herself and turned an inquiring face to her companion, determined not to be intimidated.

"As I have no idea what has put you in such a temper, it is only fair to tell you that I have very little to say," she answered coolly, folding her hands in her lap with the air of one prepared to give her attention to a fractious child.

Sir Julian's expression darkened. "You know very well to what I refer," he said. "Play no games with me, miss."

Remembering her father's advice that attack was the best defense, she sat up straight and met the angry black gaze directed at her. "Has no one ever pointed out what a bully you are?" she asked, almost conversationally. "Elvira passed me on the stairs in tears, and now I find you obviously intending to reduce me to the same state! Let me tell you, sir, that I am made of sterner stuff. *I* was not brought up by an overbearing brother, too full of his own consequence to care about others. I assure you, Sir Julian, that behaving like a bear with a sore head cuts no ice with me. *I* am not afraid of you!"

For a moment Julian Leyton looked astonished, obviously surprised by her attack before, schooling his features, he went on, "From what Elvira has said, it is perfectly clear that you are aware that Lord Devern is persona non grata."

"With you, Sir Julian—not with me," Emma interposed calmly, for all her heart was beating quickly at her own daring. "I understand that Mrs. Melvin is Lord Devern's cousin, and so it was perfectly proper for him to be invited to the outing. Elvira and I can hardly dictate upon the matter."

For his great height Sir Julian looked down at her, his expression harsh. "While in my house, Miss Beringer, you will obey my rules," he said.

Emma shook her head. "You can try to impose your will on me, I suppose, but I really cannot see how you can force it," she said candidly. "And you must know that I have no intention of obeying what seems to me to be a totally unreasonable dictum."

"While in my house—"

"Of course I would not expect Lord Devern to be invited here—but outside is quite another matter. Having been introduced in the proper manner, how could I cut him, without causing gossip and speculation in the matter? I am persuaded that you have no desire to attract attention."

Curbing his temper, Julian Leyton considered. "Very well," he conceded grudgingly. "But remember that Vivian Devern is a dangerous man."

Emma smiled angelically. "How exciting," she said.

Sir Julian's eyebrows lowered. "Have a care," he warned. "And remember that your friendship with Devern ends at my door."

Emma studied him, her head on one side. "How very autocratic," she observed.

Sir Julian's head came up, and once more she was the object of a cold stare, which made a tingle of anticipation slide down her spine.

"Have a care, ward," he advised. "I could very easily remove you to the country. I stand in place of a parent, remember."

Smiling, Emma stood up. "And what a grumpy one," she said sweetly, refusing to be provoked into losing her temper. "Really, Sir Julian, has no one ever told you that more battles are won by kindness and understanding than by bad temper and autocratic ways?"

Abruptly abandoning the contest, Sir Julian went to hold the door for her, merely remarking dryly that he had not supposed General Wellesley to be a mild-mannered man.

"No," Emma agreed cordially, "but he is fair to his troops who respect him in consequence."

Julian Leyton's expression grew thoughtful, and over the next few days he seemed to take care to court his sister's company. Elvira, who had become reserved with him, relaxed and even allowed herself to be teased and chaffed him in return. Indeed so pleasant became the atmosphere at Cumberland Square, that both girls allowed themselves to be a little disappointed when Sir Julian announced that business took him away and departed for Hampshire, promising to be back in time for the dinner-dance.

"A sirloin of beef, with fowl and fish—whatever Cook thinks suitable," said Lady Beauvale, making lists at her desk, "and supper refreshments for the twenty couples invited to the dance. We'll open up the ballroom and engage some musicians. . . . Flowers from the garden and glasshouse should suffice." Pausing, she looked up, her expression unhappy, "I must own to a wish that the Melvins . . . Unfortunately the invitations have gone out, so there is nothing to be done. I almost feel that I would not welcome them. . . . I can only be charitable and suppose that Lizzie Melvin did not know of the affair with her kinsman, or she would not have included him in the outing to Richmond. However, having been introduced and having received my apparent endorsement of the acquaintance, I do not see how you can end the friendship, but I must ask you both to reduce it as much as possible."

"They are the only young people we see," complained Elvira later. "Why should old quarrels affect us?"

"Your aunt was not definite—she did not *precisely* say that we had to cut them," Emma pointed out slowly.

"N—o." Her friend was doubtful. "Ju read me the most famous scold the other day. . . ."

"I know—at least I guessed as much. He seemed surprised when I told him he was a bully."

"You're very brave," Elvira told her in awe.

"Well, I'm not his sister," said Emma practically, "and was not brought up to admire and obey him. It's really not good for boys to be treated so—it gives them quite the wrong idea of their own consequence." She paused thoughtfully. "Though to own the truth, he can be charming when he sets his mind to it," she added honestly, thinking of the last few days.

The household, from Maria to Lady Beauvale, was thrown into a frenzy of activity, making ready for the dinner-dance, leaving Emma in no doubt as to the reason for Sir Julian's convenient absence.

The day arrived, heralded by the arrival of the hired musicians with their instruments, and for the rest of the morning their rehearsals added to the pandimonium. Elvira and Emma had been given the task of arranging the flowers, which the gardener had cut reluctantly and brought in grudgingly that morning. Dressed in their oldest clothes and enveloped in large aprons, the work was relaxing and much to their liking. Around them servants scurried about their work, as excited as the girls at the prospect of entertaining. Only Mrs. Frobisher showed signs of overwrought nerves, and her husband was heard declaring the fervent hope that she would not give way to the vapors until after dinner.

At last all was in readiness and the house in relative quiet as its occupants seized the opportunity to recover their energy before the coming event.

Emma obediently lay on her bed with the curtains drawn against the bright afternoon sun, but, even in the dimness, her new gown shimmered where it lay over a chair, filling her with excitement. At last she could bear inactivity no longer and, sliding off the high bed, crossed to the window to draw back the curtains.

The sun streamed in touching her with warm, golden fingers, and, sighing with satisfaction, she leaned her elbows on the hot windowsill. Resting her chin on her hands, Emma watched the scene below with interest; a few children under the watchful eyes of their governess played a desultory game with a ball, two nursemaids were flirting with a group of soldiers, resplendent in their regimentals, and a lady occupied one seat, oblivious to all that was going on around her as she read a book. For a while Emma occupied herself with imagining what she was reading so avidly and had just decided that it must be the latest offering from the pen of Miss Austen, when a clatter of hooves made her turn her head to see Sir Julian and his groom entering the square.

Mindful of her state of undress, she drew back a little but could not resist watching the arrival of her guardian. Instead of dismounting at the front steps and leaving his groom to take the horses to the mews, he continued round the corner of the house. A movement at her window made him glance up, and Emma found herself the object of his disconcerting black gaze. A decidedly unguardianlike grin crossed his face as she blushed furiously and hastily backed away into the darkness of the room behind.

Mortified, she sat down in front of her dressing table and was still pink and uncomfortable when Elvira entered a few minutes later.

"It *is* hot, isn't it?" she remarked innocently, noticing her friend's condition. "Have you decided upon how you are dressing your hair? Aunt Diana is lending Mrs. Hill to us." Seeing her friend's doubtful expression, she hurried to reassure her. "She is really very good, you know. Aunt Diana pays her a hundred pounds a year, just to be sure of keeping her."

When the elderly maid came to take out the curl rags with which her head had been decorated all day and arranged her hair in a becoming style quickly and easily, Emma found that Elvira had spoken the truth.

Maria watched closely and with obvious admiration as the older woman worked, following the other's deft handiwork with attention. Aware of her interest, Mrs. Hill, with a grudging air, explained some of her techniques, but Emma noticed that her austere manner had softened slightly.

"I'll leave Miss in your care," she said, having surveyed her work with satisfaction. "Lady Beauvale will be needing me." Looking down from her angular height she nodded at the diminutive form of Maria. "You show promise, I'll say that for you—but don't you so much as touch a hair of Miss Emma's head!"

Maria poked her tongue out at the closed door once Mrs. Hill was safely beyond it. "Old misery!" she commented.

"She is a bit grim," agreed Emma, dabbing perfume in various places about her person. Fastening her pearls around her neck, she found herself yearning for some more elaborate item of jewelry to enhance her gown. Ashamed of her avarice, she reminded herself how much the pearls meant to her and, remembering the loss of her father, had to blink back tears. Luckily a footman handed in two bouquets at that moment, distracting her thoughts as she examined the flowers.

One was an eminently suitable posy of cream roses, tied with ribbons that matched her dress.

"How clever!" she exclaimed, holding it against herself. "Who can it be from?"

"Sir Julian," Maria informed her with satisfaction. "He asked me what you'd be wearing."

"Oh!" was all Emma could think of to say before turning to the other gift. Unlike the first this bore a card, nestling among the arrangement of flamboyant cream and orange lilies. "From an admirer," she read and looked at the bouquet thoughtfully.

"Do you know who sent them, miss?" asked Maria curiously. "Aren't they lovely."

"I've a good idea, only one person would send anything so . . . unusual," Emma returned. "What a pity they don't go with my gown. Put them in water for me—I'll carry the roses."

But almost at once her decision was affected by the arrival of another offering, this time in the form of a single cream rose, with a spray of forget-me-nots trailing from it.

"Forget-me-nots!" snorted Maria, not hiding her disgust. "Everyone grows them. Why, we even had them in the yard of the George."

"I think it's very original," observed Emma, having ascertained that they were from Freddie. For a moment she hesitated, knowing that Sir Julian's gift was the more suitable and suddenly made up her mind. "Here, help me," she commanded, reseating herself in front of the mirror. "Pin them into my hair, just at the back."

"Mrs. Hill won't like it," Maria warned, doing as she was bid and pinning the flowers into the knot high on Emma's head without disturbing the arrangement of her fair curls too much.

Pleased with her tact, Emma went along to Elvira's room, and a little later both girls went downstairs together to join Lady Beauvale and Sir Julian in the drawing room.

"My dears, you look beautiful!" Lady Beauvale smiled.

"Without a doubt they'll be the toasts of the town," said Sir Julian with a gallant bow. "I had not realized that my little sister had grown into such a beauty—though I had an idea that my ward was something out of the ordinary."

"Thank you for the flowers," said Emma. "As you see they compliment my gown perfectly."

"An inspired guess," her guardian said blandly.

"And doubly clever to guess rightly a second time," she said dryly with raised eyebrows, indicating Elvira's pink satin and matching roses.

Sir Julian laughed. "I see I am found out—I confess to a well-organized spy service. Does that make my efforts less worthy?"

"Not at all," she told him amiably. "Though I own to a little disappointment that you did not use a crystal ball or a charm to read my mind."

"Alas, I am no wizard, kitten," he assured her quietly, smiling down into her eyes.

Emma found his expression disconcerting, and her own eyes wavered under his gaze. For a few seconds the other occupants of the room became so insignificant that they might have been alone. Her mouth softened, and as her hand crept up to play with her necklace, Julian Leyton's expression altered, and he drew back, turning aside to say something teasingly to his sister.

By the time the first guests arrived, Emma had recovered her composure and was able to join in the greeting with all the niceties of social behavior expected of her.

Miss Plantagenet arrived on the arm of her father, Tudor Plantagenet, a small man, whose lack of stature was more than made up for by his air of consequence and calm condescension. The other dinner guests consisted of family friends whom Lady Beauvale judged would advance the girls in their first Season.

As course followed course, Emma grew more nervous about the coming dance and almost wished herself anywhere but seated at the long table making polite conversation, while her mind was busy with the dread that no one would ask her to dance, and she would have to spend the evening trying to look happy and animated, while hoping for a partner.

At last the interminable meal came to a close, the gentlemen foregoing more than one glass of port, while the ladies retired to effect hasty repairs to their toilet, as the dance guests were expected any minute.

Emma found no need to repair her appearance and was about to leave her room, when the door burst open without warning and a pink-cheeked, bright-eyed Elvira appeared, waving a crumpled square of paper.

"Oh, joy!" she cried. "My dearest Bevis is here in London and begs me to meet him at the library in Bond Street tomorrow! This dinner-dance will be a great bore. . . . I can hardly contain my impatience at the prospect of dancing with old beaus in the hopes that their wives will invite us to *their* next rout!"

"Oh, Elvira! A moment ago you were excited at the thought."

"*That* was before I received Bevis's note," Elvira pointed out. "*Now* I can think of nothing else and only wish that this evening were over."

However, when the girls joined Sir Julian and his aunt to welcome their new guests a pleasant surprise awaited them; Emma had shaken so many hands and been introduced to so many strangers, that her head had started to spin when a familiar face appeared in front of her eyes.

"Johnnie!" she cried in pleased surprise and had her fingers taken in a strong grip as a young officer in the well-known green uniform bowed over her hand.

"I see you know Captain Gray," observed her guardian dryly. "Glad to see you, Gray. I am pleased that you could join us."

To her amusement, Emma saw Elvira brighten visibly as she was introduced to the soldier. When they could join their guests in the ballroom, it was not long before the rifleman approached, claiming a waltz from each to Freddie's ill-disguised annoyance.

"I say—are we going to waltz?" he asked. "I'd have put my name down if I'd known."

"Lady Beauvale is allowing just two—the rest are to be country and round dances."

"Then, may I put my name against the other?" Freddie asked quickly, reaching for Emma's card only to have it removed from his grasp.

"I see it is already spoken for," said Sir Julian, scribbling his initials and blandly ignoring the younger man's irritation. "A guardian's privilege," he explained, handing the card back to Emma.

"Well, dash it all!" Freddie was moved to exclaim as Sir Julian moved on. "If that isn't a dirty trick."

Both girls' cards filled up with gratifying speed, and Emma happily forgot her dread of being a wallflower. Waltzing was still considered a little fast, but she knew that Johnnie Gray was an accomplished dancer and under his guidance acquitted herself well. She approached the dance with Sir Julian with more trepidation. Feeling unusually nervous, she reached up to lay her hand on his shoulder, accepting his hand on her waist with outward calm but inwardly very aware of his nearness.

She was oddly pleased to find that he was a very good dancer, swinging easily to the lilting quick rhythm.

"Relax, Miss Beringer," he said into her ear. "I promise not to eat you."

Emma missed a step and apologized, careful not to meet her partner's eyes, wondering why her feet should suddenly fit so easily to his steps and why she should be sorry when the music came to an end.

# Chapter Seven

"*W*as not that the most delightful evening?" wondered Elvira late the next morning, sipping her chocolate, while curled up at the foot of Emma's bed.

"You sound like Clarissa," Emma pointed out teasingly.

"Oh Lord, so I do! But you must agree—it *was* enjoyable. Even Ju was charming. I will say that he makes a very good host. Everyone was so attentive. . . ." She broke off reflectively and gazed dreamily at a point above her friend's head.

"Johnnie Gray cuts a dashing figure, does he not?" put in Emma invitingly and was gratified when the other girl responded at once, confirming her suspicions.

"He is very handsome, certainly. That precise shade of red hair goes so well with his green uniform. I felt that I had known him for years—"

"Johnnie is an accomplished flirt but very attractive with it, and I am persuaded that there is not a scrap of unkindness or mischief in his soul. I always regarded him as an especial friend in the Peninsula."

Elvira looked disappointed. "Did you?" she asked, rather tonelessly.

Emma laughed. "*Friend*, I said. I have no other claim on him, I assure you. As far as I know he is heart free, so feel able to flirt with him as much as you like!"

Raising a shocked face, Elvira shook her head reprovingly. "Have you forgot Bevis?" she demanded. "Remember that I consider myself engaged to him."

Privately Emma had begun to grow tired of the absent poet. "Does that mean that you intend to refuse all invitations?" she inquired, a wicked twinkle in her eyes.

"Indeed, no. For that would excite suspicion," she was assured. "I shall just *regard* myself as affianced to him."

"Of course—and you are meeting him this afternoon."

"Oh, Emma, you will come with me, won't you?"

"I've no liking for the part of a gooseberry," Emma objected.

"Say you'll come—Aunt Di will never let me visit Bond Street alone."

Elvira looked distinctly panic-stricken, and Emma relented quickly. "I was only teasing—of course I'll wish to change my library books this afternoon." She looked at her friend a little doubtfully. "Perhaps," she suggested, "if you asked Lady Beauvale, Bevis would be allowed to call upon you, and then there would be no need for deception."

"Ju would never agree," was Elvira's positive response. "He made it quite plain that he would do his best to prevent Bevis and I meeting." She looked closely at Emma. "You are not crying off, are you?" she demanded.

"I—just thought that it would be better if your relationship was known."

"What nonsense! Ju may be showing his pleasant side at the moment, but underneath he is just as arrogant and objectionable as ever," stated his sister positively.

It was in a state of high excitement that Elvira entered the library that afternoon. The obliging Hetty was sent on a reconnaissance and returned, beaming, to report that Mr. Bevis was to be found in the far corner, which happened to be suitably private. Emma promised to keep watch, and Elvira vanished into the depths of the book-lined room.

Hovering near the door, Emma took down a copy of *Mansfield Park* and divided her attention between Fanny's adventures and the library entrance. However, she became engrossed in the story, forgetting her duty until her arm was lightly touched and a well-moderated voice spoke.

"Miss Beringer—how pleasant to find you here. I trust you are not feeling tired after the exertions of last night?"

Recognizing the voice, she managed to hide her dismay before she turned and greeted Jane Plantagenet as affably as possible.

"H-how delightful to meet you, Miss Plantagenet. Are you a devotee of Miss Austen?" She held out the book. "I think she is very clever and amusing. . . . Do not you think her a wicked tease?"

Miss Plantagenet looked disapproving. "I prefer more sober authors," she said, a gently chiding note in her voice. "An improving book is to my taste. My papa has taken great pains with ordering my mind. I daresay that you have not been lucky enough to have an educated man guide you in your reading matter. I believe that I still have the reading list my father set out for me when first I came out of the schoolroom."

"H-how interesting," Emma felt called upon to say and was at once rewarded by Miss Plantagenet kindly offering to lend her the list.

"No thank you," she said firmly. "*My* papa, who was a man of extreme good sense, taught me not only to be discriminating in my choice, but also that one should *enjoy* a book!"

Jane Plantagenet looked down her aristocratic nose. "I daresay, my dear Miss Beringer, that he was alluding to the reading matter for a young, unformed female. If you will just consider—"

Having grown tired of the subject, Emma firmly changed the conversation. "Did you enjoy the evening—I noticed that you and Mr. Plantagenet left early?" she asked, maneuvering so that she could keep her eyes upon the discreet corner into which Elvira had vanished.

"We believe that early hours are good for a healthy mind."

"Dear me, that must make your social life a little diffi-cult!" exclaimed Emma involuntarily.

"Not at all," she was told comfortably. "Our *friends* are all aware of the restrictions we place upon late hours."

Emma smiled sweetly. "That would explain why I have not seen you in Cumberland Square," she could not resist saying.

"Sir Julian is well aware of our feelings and has com-mented upon the wisdom of them. He gives us the civility of leaving our house before ten o'clock and understands that it was only because of our . . . *particular* circumstances that we stayed until thirty minutes past eleven last night."

"I'm sure he was very honored." A movement at the back of the room attracted Emma's gaze, and for one moment she encountered Elvira's horrified stare as her friend rounded a tall bookcase before, realizing her danger, she popped out of sight again.

"Is there someone you know?" inquired Miss Plantage-net, turning to follow Emma's eyes and peering at the back of the library. "Surely you are not here alone?"

"Yes—no . . . I mean . . ." Emma stammered, but Jane Plantagenet was not listening.

"Oh, I see Hetty at the back," she exclaimed, starting forward, "so dear Elvira must be there, also. Of course she should be the one to come to me, but I was never one to stand on ceremony."

While speaking, she crossed the room, Emma following unhappily in her wake.

"Elvira is looking for a particular book," she announced loudly, hoping to warn her friend of their imminent arrival and was relieved when Elvira stepped out from behind the bookshelves.

"Why, Miss Plantagenet, how nice to see you," she en-thused, unaware that the bright spots of color in her cheeks and the sparkle in her eyes hardly coincided with the mun-dane task of changing her reading matter.

"Elvira, my dear," Miss Plantagenet stopped and viewed the other's flushed face with some alarm. "Are you not well?" she asked. Alerted by the girl's guilty expression, she looked behind Elvira and for the first time became aware of a male figure hovering in the space between the lines of books. "Who is this?" she demanded. "Was he annoying you—I shall call the proprietor."

Emma stood steadfast, refusing to step out of her way. "This is Mr. Bevis Browne—an old friend," she said, hoping that the older woman would accept the explanation and that that would be the end of the affair.

Miss Plantagenet quivered. "Browne—is not that the name of the person whom Sir Julian has forbidden you to see? Elvira, I am shocked! To meet him here, alone and against your brother's express wishes."

"Elvira is not alone, I am here and so is her maid," Emma pointed out, while Elvira looked about to burst into tears. Emma looked up, expecting Bevis to join them, but that gentleman had taken the opportunity to slip away, and, turning her head, she saw him leaving the library and hurrying across the street, heedless of the traffic.

"I will take it upon myself to escort you home," Miss Plantagenet declared with self-righteous piety. "My papa is collecting me any minute in the barouche—we will take you up. I am sure he will understand the need and that it is what Sir Julian would wish. After all I almost consider myself as a sister."

"There really is no need," said Emma, as Elvira appeared incapable of speech. "Lady Beauvale knows we are here, and you really should not trouble yourself with our affairs, for we are quite able to walk home."

"I would be lacking in my duty if I did not see you safe into Lady Beauvale's care," she was assured, and Miss Plantagenet, who saw her duty only too clearly, hurried officiously to the door, searching for her father's carriage among the lines of approaching vehicles.

"Quick!" urged Emma, nudging her friend who seemed in a state of shock. "Out through this door before she comes back."

Pushing a stunned Elvira and followed by an excited maid, she opened a door in the back of the library, and they almost fell into a large room, piled high with books. An old man on a high stool glanced up from the ledger in which he was writing as they passed and nodded, not at all put out by their presence. Scurrying across the room, the girls headed toward another door and, upon opening it, found themselves in a small alley. Traffic rumbled to their left, and as they started toward the sound, Emma caught Elvira's arm.

"What shall we do? The wretched woman will see us if we go that way," she cried.

"I knows a back way, miss," offered Hetty, and the two girls gratefully followed her stolid figure through the narrow streets, returning eventually to Cumberland Square by a back route. Even so, a familiar black barouche was just driving away as they arrived.

"Oh dear," cried Elvira, looking ready to faint. "What shall I do? Julian is so fierce in a rage, and she is bound to have told all—"

"And made the worst of it," added Emma grimly. "Hetty—go in the basement way, and ask Mr. Frobisher to open the door for us. That way we need not ring the bell."

"I feel quite ill. . . ." murmured Elvira faintly and, putting one hand to her head, began to sway. "Julian will be waiting—"

"You can't swoon here," said her friend firmly. "Only think of the fuss that would cause, the very last thing we want."

Her bracing attitude revived Elvira enough to enable them to hurry up the steps when the butler obligingly opened the front door. Flashing a smile of thanks, Emma urged Elvira up the stairs, and the two girls almost fell into Elvira's bedroom.

"I shall die—I shall die," moaned Elvira, falling headlong onto the bed. "I know I shall."

"Nonsense," rallied her friend robustly. "No one ever died of mortification."

Bursting into hard sobs, Elvira seemed to lose interest in the situation. With tears running down her cheeks and her bonnet hanging down her back by its ribbons, she seemed like a travesty of the girl who had left the house in such high spirits a short while before.

"I sh-shall n-never see Bevis ag-gain." She sobbed, shredding her dainty lawn handkerchief.

"That would be no great loss," said Emma. "He sneaked off like a ninny!"

"How can you say so? Anyway Bevis is easily upset. A poet feels more th-than others," defended Elvira.

Deep in thought, Emma tossed her bonnet onto the bed and paced about the room. "Papa always believed in attack," she said. "We should confront Sir Julian—"

"Oh, no—I could not!" Elvira shook her head vehemently. "Indeed, I think I am about to be extremely unwell."

Hetty, who had been hovering, produced a bowl just in time and nodded knowledgeably to Emma. "Always takes miss in this way. A nervous disposition, milady calls it—the poor lamb'll be in bed for days now."

Thinking it was a convenient way of avoiding life's troubles, Emma regarded her friend doubtfully. The pale face and shadowed eyes convinced her that Elvira was not strong enough to cope with adversity, and, steeling herself, she decided to use her own strength on her friend's behalf.

Adjourning Hetty to stay with her mistress, Emma left the room, and, hurrying downstairs before her courage should fail, she knocked on the library door where she knew she would find Sir Julian.

The voice that bade her enter told her nothing of its owner's state of mind, and Julian Leyton appeared immersed in his correspondence when she opened the door.

Clasping her hands behind her back and leaning her shoulders against the door panels, she broke into speech.

"I know that Miss Plantagenet has felt called upon to tell tales," she began, "but I feel that you should listen to Elvira's side before making up your mind."

Sir Julian looked up. "And what makes you think that I would not?" he inquired.

For a moment Emma was taken aback by the unexpected reply. "The fact that she is upstairs sick with fright," she said. "Do you know that your sister is afraid of you?"

It was Sir Julian's turn to be surprised, but he recovered quickly. "If my sister has, indeed, been sneaking off to clandestine meetings with a man with whom I have expressly forbade her to associate, then she has every reason to be afraid." He paused, looking at Emma closely. "However, if it was totally by chance that she met Mr. Browne, then, of course, a different complexion is put upon the case."

Obligingly, he waited for her reply while Emma felt her cheeks burn with mortification.

"I see," he went on, noting her flushed face. "It was an arranged assignation. No doubt with your connivance, Miss Beringer, and Hetty as messenger. Very romantic to be sure. I had thought better of you, Emma!"

The unexpected use of her first name and the note of sorrow in his voice conveyed more to Emma than any angry words would have done, and, startled, she looked up to meet an accusing black gaze.

"Oh, no!" she cried. "It was not like that—well, not *quite* . . . but, really, you are treating Elvira in quite the wrong way." One black eyebrow rose disdainfully, but her guardian did not speak, and she hurried on, "To refuse to permit her to meet Bevis—Mr. Browne—is only to make him appear more romantic. At the moment he is unobtainable, ill treated . . . and to be desired. Only allow her a little more leeway, and she will soon lose interest—already she has seen a side to him that she cannot like. Instead of staying to defend her like a hero against Miss Plantagenet's accusations, he neatly took himself off, leaving her to cope with the unhappy situation. I have only to remind her of his lack of bottom, and she will gradually fall out of love, I do assure you.''

A grim smile flitted briefly across Sir Julian's frosty countenance. ''You seem well versed in such matters.''

''Yes—well, many of the junior officers applied to me for help in their affairs of the heart,'' Emma confessed. ''Besides, one has only to listen to Elvira to soon realize that her poet is a complete ninny hammer!''

Sir Julian bit back a laugh. ''Do I take it that you have no admiration for Mr. Browne?'' he inquired.

''To be honest, I've only met him once—and that was this afternoon, which could hardly be termed a salubrious meeting. Elvira needs a strong man, with vitality and spirit, not some dreamy, mooning youth, more interested in his poetry than her.''

''Do you have someone in mind?''

The question was asked in an amused drawl, and Emma relaxed imperceptibly, aware that she had gained her objective. Flashing Sir Julian a wicked grin, she nodded, ''Johnnie Gray would be just the thing and entirely suitable from your point of view. . . . But whatever happens, do not mention him or put him forward. To do so would only antagonize Elvira and ensure that she regarded him with dislike.''

''I beg of you to take care—Captain Gray may already have other plans.''

''I happen to know that Johnnie is looking for a wife. . . . I've known him since I was at school. He is the best and dearest of friends—and no fortune hunter.''

''Indeed? I'll bear him in mind when I am looking to settle Elvira's future—which reminds me—I have received a command to present you to Mrs. Hodge within the week.''

Emma was intrigued. ''A *command*?''

"No less." He picked up a letter and began to read from it. "Mrs. Hodge's compliments, and she will receive Miss Beringer on either next Wednesday or Thursday."

"That's all?" Emma asked as Sir Julian looked up.

"Apart from the letter heading," was the dry answer.

"How strange . . ."

"Rich people can afford to be eccentric—"

Wide-eyed, she looked artlessly up at him, until he responded with a gleam of amusement at the back of his dark gaze.

"Behave, Miss Beringer," he admonished gently. "Be ready to set out on Monday—and tell Elvira that I wish to see her."

Emma turned at the door. "I do not think her well enough. She was being put to bed when I—"

"Decided to beard the lion in his den," her guardian finished as she hesitated, making her blush with the truth of his words. "Very well, I will come up and put her mind at rest."

Which he did to such good effect that Elvira was able to leave her bed the next day and take luncheon with Emma in the small room allotted to them for their own use.

"I shall be eternally grateful," she announced, helping herself to cold chicken. "I cannot imagine precisely what you said to Ju, but he was very understanding and even seemed to hint that Miss Plantagenet had taken too much upon herself in running to Aunt Diana with tales. He seemed rather shaken by her taking a sisterly role upon herself."

"Good! Maybe he'll think twice before inflicting her on his family. Miss Prunes and Prisms would have us all dance to her tune," observed Emma darkly.

Elvira cocked her head. "What a suitable nickname, though it would be best not to let Ju hear it. She is certainly prism, and that cold, dissecting eye makes one feel like an insect being examined under a magnifying glass. Oh, Emma, I truly do *not* wish for her as a sister-in-law. She will make us all extremely uncomfortable."

"Yes," agreed her companion thoughtfully. "I can quite see that. . . . Do you think that Sir Julian is truly enamored?"

"Pooh!" ejaculated the other girl. "He is just tired of being the object of every matchmaking mama. . . . Besides, even Aunt Di says it's time he had an heir."

"Good Lord! Can you imagine a nursery full of little Plantagenets?"

"Do you know that it is rumored that she has a crown encircling a branch of broom embroidered on her underwear? The crest of the Plantagenet kings, you know."

Emma blinked. "How ostentatious!"

Elvira was doubtful. "Well, it doesn't show," she pointed out. "And Ju does have a coronet on his handkerchiefs."

"That is not the same at all," cried Emma, surprising herself and hastily changing the subject by telling her friend of her proposed visit to Hampshire.

"It's like having a fairy godmother," murmured Elvira dreamily. "I daresay that she will be dainty, still retaining a hint of her past beauty and will have a head of silver curls. Did she suffer unrequited love in her youth?"

Stiffling a giggle at her friend's overromantic yearnings, Emma answered roundly, "No such thing—she married a rich merchant and was disowned by her family, save my mama."

"Oh." Elvira digested this information, saying at last with a hint of regret, "While a merchant cannot be considered in the best *romantic* light, to have given up her all for love is still very touching." Sighing deeply and pushing aside the last morsel on her plate, she took up a tragic pose. "I—understand her feelings, you know."

"Are you still forbidden to see the beautiful Bevis? I quite thought from your manner that Sir Julian had more or less withdrawn his objections."

Relinquishing her role of tragic muse, Elvira helped herself to vanilla pudding. "He did—but I view his change of mood with suspicion. I cannot allow myself to feel entirely safe.''

"I should take what is offered and send for your beloved at once in order that he may call and charm Lady Beauvale with a hasty sonnet or two." She looked up as her friend was silent and saw from her expression that Elvira was not happy.

"I have," she said dolefully. "Hetty took a note this morning. A maid took it in and then returned to say there was no answer. It's very odd."

"Perhaps he thinks that you meant to scold him for running away," suggested Emma.

"I am persuaded that he retired for my sake. After all, to have confronted Jane Plantagenet would only have made matters worse, would it not?"

Emma reflected that she preferred someone who gave support in moments of difficulty but kindly murmured an affirmative.

"How long will you be away?" asked Elvira. "Our dance has already had effect and several invitations have arrived."

"Only a few days, I imagine. Sir Julian said that if the weather holds, we will travel in his phaeton, and I *do* so hope that my new traveling outfit arrives in time—" Becoming aware that Elvira was regarding her in wide-eyed, open-mouthed astonishment, she broke off to ask what was the matter.

"Taking you in his phaeton! You must be mistaken. Ju takes *no one* in his precious phaeton. Why, he only took me round the square once—and that grudgingly—and set me down as soon as I remarked upon the height making me dizzy. He was probably teasing you and intends to take the chaise."

But to her immense gratification when, a few days later Miss Beringer descended the front steps becomingly attired in her new forget-me-not blue merino wool traveling dress and matching pelisse, she was confronted by an elegant carriage, its double seats perched high over enormous, delicate wheels.

"Ooh, miss, we aren't never going in that!" cried Maria who, until that moment, had been eager and excited at the thought of accompanying her mistress into the country.

"Of course we are," said Emma bracingly. "Sir Julian and his groom are waiting—put on a brave face, do. We don't want to be taken for a pair of nervous females, do we? The wretches are hard put to hide a grin at our expense already."

Hiding her own fears, she stepped forward and allowed herself to be helped into the high perch seat. The vehicle swayed and dipped in an alarming manner, but with great control she managed to refrain from clutching the sides in fright. Behind her she heard the little maid give a faint squeak as she arrived on the seat, and then Sir Julian stepped up easily beside her, gathered the reins into capable hands, and flicked the two matched horses into motion. Leaving their heads, the groom ran back to scramble into the seat beside Maria and Emma who just had time to wave to Elvira and Lady Beauvale, who were watching somewhat disapprovingly from a window as the equipage started off.

For a while Emma was occupied with controlling her nerves as they bowled through the London traffic. The ground was nearly five feet away, allowing her to look down on other road users, which she found slightly disconcerting. At first the motion of the well-sprung vehicle was unusual, but gradually she relaxed and at last began to enjoy herself, nodding with panache to passing acquaintances as she looked about with interest.

"Well done, Miss Beringer," her guardian murmured, tooling his horses neatly into a narrow space between a poste-chaise and a loaded wagon.

Emma flashed him a brilliant smile, happily conscious of the picture she must present and feeling a lady of the first fashion in her new outfit with a matching bonnet, dashingly decorated by two cream ostrich feathers.

"I like it above anything!" she declared, flushed with enthusiasm and excitement. "*Thank* you, Sir Julian—if I were very wealthy, I would travel only in a phaeton!"

"You'd find it cold in winter," was the dampening reply, and she fell silent until noticing the occupants of a closed landau which was held up in a stream of traffic going in the other direction.

"Only observe, Sir Julian," she said, touching his arm, a hint of wickedness in her voice. "Is that not the Plantagenets? Would it be proper to wave, do you think? Perhaps that would be too forward, and we should merely nod genteelly?"

"A bow and a smile will suffice," she was told and was gratified to observe a flicker of mortification cross Jane Plantagenet's face as she caught sight of the dashing equipage and its occupants bowling past.

The journey progressed more speedily than Emma had thought possible; first the royal house at Kew, then Hampton Court, affording a quick glimpse of the red brick palace, were quickly passed, and luncheon was taken at Esher. Late in the afternoon they arrived at Farnham, where they were to stop for the night. A weary Maria had to be helped into the inn, but Emma, who had enjoyed every moment and blessed the fortitude acquired during the years spent with the army in the Peninsula, stepped down from her high seat, still fresh and alert.

# Chapter Eight

*H*aving inspected the private room provided, Emma followed the landlady upstairs to her bedroom, where Maria had already taken the luggage.

"Dinner's ready when you are, miss," she was assured. "There's a ham and salad, roast beef, or one of my pies."

There was a note of pride in the landlady's voice as she put a particular emphasis upon the word "pie," and, rightly interpreting this, Emma announced her wish to sample a slice, which met with beaming approval.

"Though I says it myself, miss, you can't do better. Bessie Long's pies are famous for miles around—even as far as London, I daresay."

Urged on by the hope in the proud cook's voice, Emma agreed that the name *did* seem familiar and was rewarded by the promise of a special pie to take home with her. Smiling and bobbing, Mrs. Long left to go about her business, and only after they were alone did Emma realize that Maria was uncharacteristically quiet.

Looking at her more closely, she saw that the girl was very pale and going about her duties without her usual verve and chatter.

"What is wrong? Maria, are you ill?" she asked, concerned.

"Oh, miss, that journey didn't half make me feel bad— I've a head that's fit to burst, what with all that bumping and swaying and rushing along like a whirlwind! It's not natural!"

"I didn't know—I thought that you were enjoying it as much as I was," cried Emma. "Though, now I think of it, you hardly ate at lunch. How unkind of me—I should have realized that it was not to your liking."

"I'll be better soon, now that my feet are back on the ground. What I'd have done without Jem Bowls's arm to hold me in, I don't know."

"Oh, Maria, what a bad mistress I am," Emma said, chagrined at her own negligence. "You should have said." A speaking glance from the younger girl made her realize the foolishness of the statement, and she felt even more uncomfortable as she realized the dependence of servants upon the whim of their employers. "That was unrealistic of me, of course you could hardly complain—I should have had more thought for you. I apologize, Maria, and promise never to be so high-handed again."

Maria, who had been staring in astonishment, burst into tears. "I'm ever so sorry, miss, I really am. If only I could have a cup of tea, I'd be as right as ninepence. I know all my duties. Mrs. Hill didn't half drum them into me, when she knew as I was coming with you. I'm to unpack your clothes, set out your dinner dress and night things, arrange hot water for your bath—"

Despite her brave effort, her voice wobbled, and she sniffed into a handkerchief, obviously feeling very unwell.

"Nonsense," said Emma robustly, tugging at the bell pull. "You shall have a cup of tea and then go to bed—no arguments. I shall look after myself while you recover."

Opening her mouth, Maria wailed loudly. "If I ain't of use, 'm, you'll turn me off. I know all my duties—I do!"

"I'm sure you do and can perform them admirably," soothed her mistress, "but not tonight."

A little maid appeared in answer to the summons and quickly returned with a tea tray. Turning maid herself, Emma helped Maria into the bed in the small room off her own and, leaving her ensconced against the pillows with a steaming cup of comforting beverage, set about repairing the ravages of travel and dressing herself for dinner.

Knowing that they would be dining in an inn, she had hesitated over the choice of a gown and had finally chosen a pale yellow crepe, which she felt would not be too formal. Surveying herself in the mirror, she was pleased with her choice and twined a matching ribbon through her curls as her only adornment.

Sir Julian was waiting for her at the foot of the stairs and came forward to offer her his hand. He had changed out of his riding clothes into a gray jacket and tight paler gray pantaloons, his crisp cravat was tied into a perfect waterfall knot, while his carelessly brushed black curls would have been the envy of less fortunate straight-haired people.

"Simple, yet elegant," he approved. "Your taste, Miss Beringer, is delightful."

Emma paused and opened her eyes wide. "Compliments, Sir Julian?" she marveled. "You'll spoil me!"

"I am persuaded that you have a very sensible head upon your shoulders," he said, leading her into their private room. "And it would take more than a few pretty words to turn it."

"Perhaps . . . to own the truth, I am feeling very mortified with myself."

Sir Julian looked at her closely. "How so?"

"It's Maria—the journey has made her quite unwell. I, who should have noticed, was so wrapped up in my own enjoyment that I did not see her discomfort. The poor girl was doing her best to carry out her duties, despite feeling sick and ill, and all the while afraid to say anything in case she was turned off!" She turned speaking eyes to her guardian. "I feel such a thoughtless wretch," she admitted candidly. "And how are we to get her back to Cumberland Square?"

"I see no difficulty. She shall go by poste-chaise or

coach," he answered promptly. "As to your suitability as mistress—the fact that you are upset shows your kind heart."

"I am not used to having a maid—"

"No more than Maria is to being one. You must learn together. I am sure that you both will prove apt pupils."

He helped her to soup from the tureen already presiding in the middle of the table, and for a while they both enjoyed slaking hearty appetites. While they waited for the soup plates to be taken away, Emma urged Sir Julian to partake of the landlady's prestigious pie.

"Very wise," he agreed. "To put oneself on the right side of one's landlady can only be sensible."

Once the main meal had been served and they were alone again, Emma could control her curiosity no longer and felt impelled to ask: "What manner of lady is Mrs. Hodge? Pray tell me—will we be welcome?"

She could not hide a faint tremble in her voice, and Sir Julian smiled at her vain attempt to hide her agitation.

"Mrs. Hodge is—unique. Quite unlike any other," he told her. "And as to being welcome, Jem Bowls is this moment riding there to inform her of our arrival in the area."

"You have not answered my question, sir. Is she . . . formidable? The stuff of fairy stories? Or—a kindly, gentle aunt?"

Julian Leyton considered. "Mrs. Hodge is a law unto herself, and she would answer to none of your descriptions," was all he would say, his black eyes twinkling with amusement.

Reflecting that he would not tease if Mrs. Hodge was, indeed, an ogre, Emma remarked in a composed manner, that in that case she supposed it just as well that she had provided herself with a piece of silver.

"To ward off witches?" asked Sir Julian, catching her meaning. "You need have no fear in that direction. Mrs. Hodge is more in the mode of a fairy godmother, I'd say."

With that Emma had to be content, for he refused to enlarge upon his interesting statement, shaking his head and assuring her that he had given his word to present her to her great aunt with her mind free from preconceived notions.

The next morning a note from Sir Julian informed Emma that Jem Bowls had returned bearing an invitation to luncheon, and, consequently, they would be setting out soon after breakfast. Maria, who was feeling herself again, helped her to dress in an almond pink, muslin morning gown. After hesitating between a long silk shawl and the cream jacket which had been one of her first purchases in London, Emma chose the spencer and allowed Maria to set the chip straw milkmaid hat on her fair curls and tied the long pink ribbons under her chin in an elegant bow.

"Well, miss, I hope as you won't mind if I say as how you look bang up to the nines in that outfit," the maid remarked with satisfaction. "Sir Julian should feel proper proud with you on his arm."

"What nonsense, Maria—he won't even notice!" Emma murmured, smoothing her eyebrows.

"I don't know about that, miss," was the knowing reply, "but I've seen his eyes on you—"

Emma turned a surprised gaze on her companion. "Sir Julian is my guardian," she pointed out, a little breathlessly.

"Not for long, miss. You've said so yourself."

Realizing the impropriety of the conversation, Emma crisply told her maid that such speculation was not to be tolerated and pulled on her gloves, bright spots of agitation in her cheeks. Unhappily aware of the thought put into her mind, her manner was constrained when she joined Julian Leyton a little later, and, bending his head, he peered under the wide brim of her hat and inquired upon her state of health.

"Perfectly well, I assure you," she told him and, seeking an excuse for her manner, added truthfully that she was feeling somewhat nervous.

"Hodge Hall is a delightful house," Sir Julian began, setting the horses in motion. "In parts medieval, I believe—the windows and fireplaces may not be entirely to our modern tastes, but the surrounding gardens make up for any inconvenience.''

Emma had heard only part of this attempt to set her at ease and, turning her head, inquired, ''*Hodge* Hall? Surely you are mistaken.''

''No. I inquired most particularly, and Hodge Hall it is. I believe the late Mr. Hodge renamed it so upon acquiring the property . . . rather in the manner of cocking a snoot at the local gentry, who were none too pleased at a merchant joining their select circle and had obviously made their feelings clear.''

Emma chuckled. ''He sounds a man to be reckoned with.''

''Until then it had been called 'Wherlam House,' '' supplied her guardian, negotiating the bend at the end of Farnham High Street, preparatory to beginning the road toward the hamlet of Wrecclesham.

''I'm beginning to wish that I had met my uncle,'' remarked Emma appreciatively as they drove alongside the river.

Turning left just before arriving at the little town of Alton, they drove along a leafy road before leaving it and taking a smaller lane cut deep into the earth, like a green cave between the fields of ripening crops. Hodge Hall was set in a sunlit clearing, its flint walls and silky, gray beams so old that the building appeared to have grown there. The offset mullioned windows and huge oak door stood open, as if inviting the travelers into the cool, dim interior, and as Sir Julian stopped the phaeton in the shingled courtyard, Emma could only sit entranced as she drank in the ancient tranquility of the old house.

''It's . . . *beautiful*,'' she breathed, before accepting his arm to aid her descent.

A small boy ran to catch the reins, and a woman in the black dress and lacy apron of a housekeeper appeared in the open doorway.

"Miss Beringer to see Mrs. Hodge," Sir Julian informed her, and the woman curtsied gravely.

"If you will step into the library, sir, Mrs. Hodge will see the young lady in the garden," she said.

With a reassuring smile, Julian Leyton followed a small maid into the depths of the house, and as he vanished from sight, the housekeeper stepped out onto the front step.

"If you will take that way, miss," she said, indicating a path that led under an arch of greenery and into a colorful walk, bounded by high herbacious borders. "Mrs. Hodge is waiting."

Obediently following her pointing arm, Emma set off and, having passed under the arch, was astonished to find herself in the midst of a riot of color even more brilliant than had appeared from the doorstep. Never had she thought that so many flowers could be coaxed to bloom together in such harmony. The air was filled with their scent and the humming of bees and insects. Enchanted, she wandered along, half forgetting her errand in the pleasure of exploring the marvelous garden.

"Well, miss, what do you think of it?" asked a voice, and Emma, who had thought herself alone, noticed a shabbily dressed woman enveloped in a sacking apron, looking up at her from where she knelt among a tangle of plants.

A large straw hat shadowed her face, but Emma could see a pair of sharp eyes regarding her with interest.

"It's the most beautiful place I've ever seen," she answered truthfully, and the woman relaxed her stare somewhat and returned to the weeds she had been attacking.

"Know anything about gardening?" she asked, abruptly plying her fork vigorously.

"I've never been lucky enough to have one," answered Emma. "Do you work here, Mrs. . . . ?"

The old woman sat back on her heels. "I own it, miss. I am Emma Hodge. You were named for me." Emma looked at her, unable to hide her surprise, and Mrs. Hodge gave a loud snort. "Took me for the gardener, did you?"

"I've never seen a lady on her knees with muddy hands," Emma admitted honestly.

"And I've never seen a female following the drum, as I know you and your mama did," retorted the other. "I imagine that you weren't ladylike at times."

"No indeed," Emma agreed readily. "The niceties of social behavior were ignored most times in the Peninsula."

She spoke with an unconsciously wistful note in her voice, and her aunt turned a sharp gaze in her direction.

"Miss it, do you?" she asked abruptly.

"Oh, yes!" Emma sighed. "I do find many of the rules of Society irksome."

"And Sir Julian, how do you like him? I hear that he can be autocratic and keeps his sister on short reins. Does he do the same to you?"

Emma smiled. "He tries," she answered enigmatically.

"Good for you. I don't hold with this superiority men feel they have. My Ned and I had a partnership, we were as good as each other—that's how it should be. Though, I've a suspicion that Sir Julian holds different views. I daresay he believes that females need looking after." She paused thoughtfully before giving what could have passed for a cackle. "Come to think of it, I would have enjoyed showing him differently forty years ago!" She turned shrewd eyes on her great niece. "How do you feel?"

"I—" began Emma, only to break off as the fiery color flooded to her cheeks. "I don't care for being told what to do," she answered stiffly, while Mrs. Hodge watched her confusion with interest.

"Heavy-handed, is he?" she asked, amused. "I've heard that he's as good as engaged," she remarked provocatively.

"Miss Plantagenet should suit perfectly. She is a paragon of virtue and knows all the nuances of behavior upon which she kindly instructs us all."

Again Mrs. Hodge emitted the sound like a cackle. "High-blown, you mean? A proud sort of woman?"

"Exactly," was the dry answer as Emma's color returned to normal. The emotion she had felt at her aunt's question had surprised her, and, puzzled by her own response, she decided to ignore the event until she was alone and could give the strange occurrence her undivided attention.

Mrs. Hodge rose stiffly to her feet and dusted earth off her apron. Shaking out her skirts, she trod out of her muddy patterns which had protected her shoes and stepped onto the gravel path.

"Luncheon," she announced. "I'm famished, and I hope you are, too. I can't put up with females who think it's genteel to eat like a bird."

"I enjoy my food," Emma told her, and, at ease with each other, they walked toward the house side by side.

Vegetable soup, a succulent ham, and new potatoes and peas, followed by an apple pie and thick cream, were satisfactorily disposed off, Mrs. Hodge setting to without feeling the need for polite conversation.

"My compliments to your cook," said Sir Julian, accepting another helping of pie. "And to the person who grew the provisions." He raised his glass to his hostess who, to Emma's surprise, became quite pink and flustered.

"We'll take our tea in the garden," she announced, fanning herself. "It's too hot by far in here."

The tray was carried out to an arbor, where a stone seat and overhanging roses provided shade and coolness. Mrs. Hodge dispensed china tea from a rotund silver pot, and for a while they contentedly sipped the aromatic liquid and nibbled ratafia biscuits. When their cups were empty their hostess sat up straight and fixed Sir Julian with a compelling eye.

"Sir Julian," she said, "I am convinced that you will find the watering system, which my gardener has arranged, of the utmost interest. Men are always interested in things mechanical, I know. Just follow the path to the green shed—"

Obediently Julian Leyton rose, bowed, and sauntered away. Watching his tall figure, Emma marveled upon the ease with which her aunt had dismissed him.

"Now, niece," began Mrs. Hodge, turning to her. "As you know, I had intended to leave my wealth to your mother. . . . So you became my heir. I daresay that I have been remiss in my treatment of you, and we should have met before now. I am a selfish old woman with my own interests, and only now, when I am faced with the prospect of my demise, have I felt the need to meet you."

For the first time, Emma studied her aunt closely and detected signs of fragile health beneath the sun-tanned, weathered face and involuntarily put out her hand toward the other's work-worn, wrinkled claw.

"No sympathy, miss," said the old woman. "Age comes to us all—I merely wish to be sure that you will care for Hodge Hall. I—do not want it to be neglected."

On the last word she looked round her domain, and, seeing the expression in her eyes, Emma understood how much the property meant to her aged relative.

As if reading her mind, her aunt said almost to herself, "I never had children and this . . . has become my child. Some folk would not agree, but I find that the earth and mother nature are more rewarding than people. They certainly have served me better."

Emma could find no comment to make, realizing how disillusioned her aunt must have been to retreat from the world in this way.

"I—will come and see you, if you will permit me," she said quietly at last.

Mrs. Hodge shook her head. "No need," she said decisively. "We have met, and I'm satisfied that you will have a care for Hodge Hall. Count yourself my heir, niece, but don't let it go to your head. Take my advice and look out for fortune hunters. Look for a husband as rich as yourself. . . *He* won't be after your inheritance." She nodded her head in the direction Sir Julian had taken. "*He's* as good as any, I'd say."

"Sir Julian is my guardian," Emma pointed out, shocked.

The older woman cackled. "At the moment, but if I've done my sums aright, in a short while you'll be of age."

"Besides . . . he's as good as betrothed. . . ." murmured Emma, following her own line of thought.

"As good as, isn't final. Take my advice, niece, and put in a bid. I don't think the man himself would be exactly averse."

Emma was very quiet on the drive back to Farnham, disturbed, not only by her aunt's unusual character, but by the advice which she had given. Sensing her wish to be quiet, Sir Julian drove without speaking, allowing her time to assimilate the experience.

At last she sighed and relaxed, peering round the deep brim of her bonnet to say: "It is really rather sad, don't you think? Mrs. Hodge appears to have no wish for relationships with people. Her garden is her all."

"Did you hope to find an affectionate aunt, kitten?" Julian Leyton tooled the phaeton round a bend and let the reins out again before going on: "*She* seemed perfectly happy to me—"

"Oh, no!" was Emma's shocked exclamation. "Everyone needs someone to love! The garden was beautiful—but it isn't *human*. It merely blooms in response to her care and the seasons. No one loves my p-poor aunt and . . . I find it very sad."

Sir Julian stole a look down at her abstracted face. "As her heiress, you must. . . ." he suggested tentatively.

"Of course I don't," Emma objected, indignant at the idea. "How could I, when I've never met her before? One does not love to order, Sir Julian."

"Some would be more than willing to try, for a fortune," her guardian pointed out dryly, causing her to shoot him a sharp look.

"H-how very cynical," was her comment. "What a poor set of people you must know—"

"My friends are limited—by choice, I'm afraid. *You* are just setting out on the career of heiress. I, my dear Miss Beringer, have been wealthy this sixteen years or more. I can spot a scrounger from the other side of the street and a match-making mama from across a ballroom with unfailing ability. Card-sharps have tried any means to inveigle me into a game, and wastrels have courted my acquaintance since I was a beardless youth. Believe me, ward, I am well aware of humanity's foibles."

Emma glanced at his unusually severe face. "Dear me!" she said softly. "Is it that bad, in truth?"

"Worse," she was told briefly. "Money brings out the very worst in people, as you will undoubtedly find."

"Then I shall give it all up," she answered promptly, causing her companion to raise a quizzical eyebrow. "I prefer to be as I am . . . with friends who like me for myself. I shall return to the idea of becoming a governess."

"Huh!" Her guardian snorted. "A fine governess you'd make, hardly out of the nursery yourself!"

"If that is so, I must be the oldest baby in Christendom!" retorted Emma. "You must be aware that in only a few weeks I shall attain my majority."

"And then what, miss? Let me remind you that you have only expectations until your aunt dies."

"I sh-shall think of something," cried Emma. Until that moment, she had not thought beyond the present, content to stay in London and enjoy the Leytons' friendship. Suddenly she was confronted by a bleak future and one for which she did not care. The prospect of leaving Cumberland Square filled her with dismay, the strength of emotion surprising her as she contemplated the dreary possibility.

Sir Julian touched her hand briefly. "Don't look so worried. We shall be happy to have you as long as you wish."

"Thank you, but no. I am grateful for your kindness, but

I intend to earn my own living,'' she said bravely, wondering where her independent spirit had gone and why the thought of doing something which she had always known she would have to should suddenly fill her with sadness.

''What nonsense! Why seek another post, when Elvira needs you? Stay with us until you have a home of your own.''

Emma shook her head, while longing to agree, and said firmly, ''I cannot *scrounge*.''

Sir Julian's mouth tightened, and, sensing his emotion, the horses jibbed a little. ''You know I did not mean *you*,'' he said, when he had calmed them.

Emma was contrite. ''I had not supposed. . . . I did not mean that—I used the word, because it had been brought to mind. But you must know that the same applies, no matter which word is used. I will not take charity.''

''Charity?'' He sounded savage. ''From *friends*?''

Emma turned to him impulsively, her expression earnest. ''You all have been so kind,'' she said, ''and I am eternally grateful, but I must be allowed some independence. You, Sir Julian, of anyone must surely see that.''

He smiled a little grimly down at her, but she was relieved to see that his expression had softened somewhat. ''Are you accusing me of pride, Miss Beringer?'' he asked.

She shook her head. ''Only in having pride in your achievements. I cannot be a 'hanger-on.' ''

''No one would expect you to be,'' he told her. ''We will leave the matter for the time being; perhaps the situation will resolve itself. However, I would like your word that you will do nothing rash without first consulting me.''

Having considered, Emma gave her promise willingly, and they fell into general conversation for the last few miles to Farnham. Their former talk, however, gave her cause for thought and occupied her mind for the rest of the day. Noticing her preoccupation, Sir Julian eyed her speculatively once or twice during dinner but said nothing when she announced her wish to retire, beyond reminding her of their early start the next morning.

A place on the stagecoach had been procured for Maria, and, conscious of her recent neglect, Emma insisted that the groom, Jem, should accompany her. Beyond remarking that he thought such care a little excessive, Sir Julian made no comment and to his obvious chagrin, for he regarded the phaeton and horses as his charge, Jem was dispatched to London in the cumbersome public vehicle, while his master and Miss Beringer set off in the elegant, light-wheeled carriage.

"Our relationship will never be the same," murmured Julian Leyton. "Jem is convinced that without him behind me, I shall wear out the animals, have an accident . . . or at the very best, fall foul of highwaymen."

Laughing at his lugubrious tone, Emma asked, "Will he be very upset?"

"I daresay that upon arriving in Cumberland Square I shall discover the need for a new groom."

Emma raised her eyebrows. "I quite thought that he had a *tendre* for Maria."

"You surprise me. . . . I believed Jem impervious to female attractions."

"Maria was grateful for his strong arm which held her in her seat on the way down, so she said, and while no one would willingly let another fall out of a carriage, it *did* seem to me that his arm lingered a little as he helped her into the inn."

"You surprise me! Can Jem's cold heart have melted at last?" questioned her companion. "I thought him as inviolate as myself!"

Emma turned to look at him, studying the handsome profile beneath the glossy hat, noting the lazy eyelids above the black eyes and the firm mouth before, shaking herself out of her reverie, she repeated, "Inviolate?" in an interrogatory note. "I had assumed that Miss Plantagenet had won your heart,'' she finished lightly, careful to hide the fact that her own heart had chosen that moment to race madly.

For a moment Sir Julian looked savage as various expressions fleeted across his face. Blank surprise was quickly superceded by what seemed to be dismay, followed by anger, and then his features were schooled into a calm lack of emotion, and he turned a bland countenance to his passenger. ''You are somewhat premature, Miss Beringer,'' she was told coldly.

''I—thought that your engagement was imminent.''

''My dear girl, even if it were, nothing so common as 'love' would enter into it. You may be sure that my heart is entirely free,'' Sir Julian answered briefly.

Emma's heart surprised her by giving an unexpected leap at the news. Even though Sir Julian appeared to be indicating that love and marriage were not coupled together in his estimation, she greeted the idea that he had not yet offered for Jane Plantagenet with relief, telling herself that they would not have suited, while Elvira had need of a lighter-hearted sister-in-law. She decided that it would be better for all if the engagement never came about and spent several pleasant hours reviewing a campaign to thwart Miss Plantagenet's plans.

High summer was drifting into early autumn, the heavily leafed trees were showing the merest touch of brown, while the ripe fields were full of people intent upon bringing in the harvest. Watching from her high perch, she found the journey home even more enjoyable than the outward drive, even when one of Sir Julian's matched grays lost a shoe and they had to trail slowly into Esher and wait while a smith replaced it, she retained her good humor, wandering down to look in the shops of the busy town until the work was done.

''We shall be later than I intended,'' commented her guardian as they set off once more.

He appeared not to have noticed the dark storm clouds gathering behind them. For a moment Emma contemplated pointing them out but, realizing that Sir Julian would almost certainly decide to put up overnight rather than risk a soaking, while she was enjoying the drive and preferred to go on, she said nothing.

Not until they turned right at Hampton Court did Sir Julian become aware of the dark sky. Realizing that dusk was falling quickly and earlier than usual, he glanced over his shoulder and, smothering a curse, slowed the horses to a walk.

"If that decides to break, you'll be soaked," he said, looking down at his companion.

Eyes dancing with excitement, Emma smiled at him. "I'm no sugar baby," she declared. "And have survived worse in the Peninsula. Let's make a run for it—there can't be far to go."

For a moment he considered, eyeing her animated face as a rising wind swept free tendrils of blond hair and played with the feathers in her bonnet.

"Oh, *do!*" she pleaded. "It's an age since I felt the elements . . . I've always liked the wind and rain, and I've been cooped up in London for months. I don't really care for the calm, secluded life of a Society miss, you know. I miss the natural life. A little rain never hurt anyone."

Sir Julian showed his teeth in a grin. "Very well, but I'll not be responsible if your best bonnet is ruined and my aunt reads you a scold for unladylike behavior."

With the words, he flicked the reins, and the high-spirited beasts, who had been chaffing at the bit, sprang into action, tipping Emma back in her seat and making her clutch at her bonnet. The exhilarating speed and rushing wind brought bright color to her cheeks and made her eyes sparkle with excitement as she gripped the edge of her seat. The horses settled into a steady trot, which ate up the miles, making the body of the phaeton swing and rock on its springs.

Sir Julian was an exceptional driver, but even he could not foresee the disaster which struck; one of the enormous, delicate wheels struck a stone in the road, the blow shattering several of the slender spokes, and, without warning, the vehicle fell sideways, pitching out its passengers. The empty carriage was dragged on by the terrified horses before finally coming to a halt, slewed across the road.

In the few seconds available to him, Sir Julian had the presence of mind to wrap his arms around his ward, protecting her with his body as they flew through the air and taking most of the force as they landed. For a moment Emma lay still, the air knocked from her lungs before, gathering her scattered wits, she realized that Sir Julian lay across her, alarmingly still and strangely heavy.

# Chapter Nine

Shaken by fear, Emma called Sir Julian's name and when her urgent voice elicited no response, pushed and heaved against his unconscious body until, with a final effort, she could wriggle free.

Kneeling beside her guardian she hastily felt for broken bones but found no sign of injury until she moved his lolling head and felt her fingers grow warm and sticky with blood. An involuntary exclamation broke from her, and at that moment, the scene was lit by a garish flash of lightning, which highlighted his pale face and the black trickle of blood dripping down his forehead.

"Oh Lord!" she moaned, wishing desperately that she was in the middle of a nightmare and that she would wake up. A violent flurry of rain convinced her that she was not dreaming, and her old training from the Peninsula, when everyone had to be able to survive on their own wits, came to her rescue. Looking round, a convenient lightning flash showed her a low building of some kind a short way from the road, and, glancing over her shoulder at the remains of the phaeton which lay across the road, she saw that the horses had regained their feet and appeared unharmed but were obviously nervous and frightened.

Tossing their heads and neighing shrilly, they gave every sign of being about to take off, and she knew that the next crack of thunder would send them hurtling along the road to their doom and danger of others.

Turning Sir Julian on his side, she felt in his pocket for the penknife which she knew he always carried and, leaving him for the moment, went to the horses' heads, murmuring soothingly. It was the work of a minute to cut their traces, and, hoping that they would not sense her own nervousness, she took a hold of each bridle and coaxed them toward the building she had seen.

Nearer to the building, she discovered that it was a low shed with one open wall. Luckily there was a wooden railing separating it into two, and she tied the horses to this before going back to her guardian. The remains of the phaeton proved too heavy for her to move, and, praying that no one would ride into it, she returned her attention to the unconscious man, lying where she had left him.

Under her fingers, Sir Julian's pulse seemed light and erratic, and he showed no signs of regaining consciousness. Staunching the blood with his cravat, Emma wondered what to do for the best, deciding that the increasing rain would definitely bring on a chill, while she hoped that he would suffer no further injury from being moved. Luckily he was wearing a riding coat, and, gathering the edges of one of its capes, she pulled the material over his head and began to drag him toward the shelter of the cartshed.

Although slim, Sir Julian was tall and broad shouldered, and Emma was exhausted by the time she reached the shelter and only had strength to pull him onto the straw piled in the part away from the horses before collapsing beside his limp form. Lifting his heavy head onto her lap, she wrapped her arms around him in an effort to keep him warm.

"Don't die," she whispered as the desperation of her situation hit her, and two scalding tears slid down her cheeks. "Wake up, Ju—I don't like it here," she whimpered, but only the horses snickered behind her. Chiding herself for her lack of spirit, she drew some comfort from their presence and kept watch until in the early hours sleep finally overcame her.

Waking just as dawn drew a few faint gray fingers in the eastern sky, she stared around, puzzled by her strange surroundings before, remembering the circumstances, she gazed anxiously down at the man cradled on her lap. Sir Julian looked strangely young and vulnerable, his long black lashes curved against his pale cheeks. A lock of hair had fallen over his forehead, and she brushed it gently aside.

During the night the bleeding had stopped, but now she could see the deep gash and discolored bruise a little below his hairline. Bending nearer, she called his name and thought she detected a flicker of the shadowed eyelids, but at that moment the sound of a swiftly approaching vehicle came to her ears.

Quickly disentangling herself, she lay Sir Julian against the straw and ran onto the road, almost into the path of a small tilbury which was being driven at breakneck speed. Seeing her, the driver slowed his equipage and managed to stop, narrowly avoiding the wreckage of the phaeton. Staring down at her disheveled figure, a look of blank surprise crossed his face before he schooled his features into the calm, blank expression fashion decreed and bowed blandly.

"By Jove, Miss Beringer, fancy meeting you," drawled Lord Devern. "Can I be of assistance?"

"Of course you can!" returned Emma, nettled by his unconcern. "I should have thought that anyone could see that! Surely you can see Sir Julian in the building—?"

"I thought it more polite to pretend that I hadn't noticed."

Emma was not impressed by this sign of delicacy. "Oh, do not, I beg you, be such an idiot! Apart from the fact that he is my guardian, would we be likely to choose an open shed for an assignation and leave a broken-down vehicle on the road to point the finger?"

Lord Devern smiled. "That does seem a little unlikely on Ju's part, he is usually *much* more discreet."

Drawing his carriage into the side, he climbed down, tying the reins to a branch of a tree, while Emma, seeing that he was about to offer aid, hurried ahead to the reclining figure in the shed.

When Vivian Devern joined her, she was kneeling in the straw, anxiously surveying Sir Julian. Crouching on his heels, the newcomer examined the other man critically.

"Pale, ain't he?" he observed, earning a furious glance from Emma.

"If you can make no more useful remark than that, then I suggest that the best thing you can do is to go for help," she said scathingly.

"Do you know," he agreed, conversationally, "I was just about to make the same suggestion."

Miss Beringer was surprised to find a sob rising in her throat at this unsympathetic attitude; she had spent a cold and worrying night alone with an unconscious man and now was in need of a little support herself.

Lord Devern regarded the tears hanging on the edge of her lashes with interest. "Don't mind me," he counseled more kindly. "Ju and I are old enemies; he'd feel the same about me."

"Let me tell you, sir, you are h-horrid!" cried Emma, losing any wish to cry.

"That's better," his lordship observed cheerfully. "Now, let's see what's wrong with the fellow." He bent over Julian Leyton and felt along his limbs as Emma had done.

"I don't think anything is broken," she said, "but he's been unconscious since late last night."

"Said anything!"

She shook her head. "Just muttered—"

"Well, that's a good sign." He looked more closely at the unconscious man. "I'd say he's asleep—" He looked up, meeting her anxious gaze, and smiled suddenly. "It really would be best if I go for help, you know. There's not room in my tilbury for him. I'll ask at the nearest farm or inn for a wagon to be sent out."

Unexpectedly, he took off his greatcoat and wrapped it

round her shoulders. "Bear up, Miss Beringer," he said. "I give you my word not to be long."

Touched by the kindness, Emma looked up and smiled briefly before, with a gesture half-wave, half-salute, Vivian Devern straightened and walked briskly to his tilbury.

Once alone again, Emma was overcome by a sense of helplessness and touched the unconscious man's face.

"Oh, Ju—do wake up," she begged and was both startled and relieved to find herself being regarded by a pair of hazy, black eyes.

"H-allo, kitten," Sir Julian said weakly, and tried to sit up, only to sink back with a groan. "I've the devil of a headache," he complained. "Did you hit me with something?"

"Indeed, I did not!" Emma exclaimed. "We had an accident—the wheel hit a stone, and we overturned."

"Did we, by God!" The haze had cleared from his eyes, and he sent her an inquiring glance. "Are you all right? And the horses—?"

Again he made to rise, but she pressed him firmly back into the straw.

"Lie still," she commanded. "The horses are well—if you'll look behind me, you will see them both, with only their prides hurt. The carriage, I'm afraid to say, appears beyond repair—Lord Devern has pulled it away from the road, but it resembles nothing so much as firewood."

Apparently not interested in the fate of his vehicle, Julian Leyton frowned. "Devern! What the deuce is *he* doing here?"

"I have no idea, but he was passing a short while ago and offered to go for help."

"Very civil of him."

"He *could* have driven by," Emma pointed out, watching anxiously as her guardian again attempted to sit up.

This time he managed to pull himself up enough to lean against a hay bale, lying there alarmingly pale and quiet.

All this while she had been straining her ears for an approaching vehicle and at last heard the welcome rumble of wheels and, looking down the road in the direction taken by Lord Devern, saw a low farm wagon, pulled by a large, gray shire, advancing steadily with his lordship riding beside it.

"Here they are," she announced thankfully.

"There is an inn, of sorts, down the road," said Lord Devern, dismounting. "I've bespoke a bed and sent a man to bring the nearest doctor." Looking down, he noticed that Julian Leyton had returned to consciousness. "I see you're awake—how do you feel?"

"Well enough—apart from a tendency to see two of everything."

Vivian Devern laughed. "Pleasant enough when Miss Beringer is the view, but I am well aware that *one* of me is more than you care for!"

"At the moment even that is very welcome," admitted Sir Julian, allowing himself to be helped to his feet.

As he swayed alarmingly, Emma hurried to his free side, offering herself for a prop.

"Kitten—I'd crush you," her guardian whispered weakly, closing his eyes.

"I am stronger than I look," she assured him, taking his arm across her shoulders, and together she and Lord Devern supported him to the wagon, while the wagoner watched the proceedings with interest.

" 'Urt bad is 'ee?" he inquired, not moving from his perch. "Best get the poor gentleman on board as quick as you can, like."

"We would be a lot quicker if you helped," Emma pointed out with asperity.

"Now there my dear, you are mistaken," murmured Lord Devern. "The fellow is, I assure you, totally devoid of wits—"

"Very well, missy, I'll just take old Dobbin here to that

121

there tree—'' said the driver obligingly, and shook the reins along the broad back of his patient animal.

"No—no!" shouted Lord Devern as the vehicle began to move.

"Can't leave the 'orses' 'ead, master—can't be done, no 'ow. 'E'd take off, see. And if the young leddy wants me to 'elp the poor gennleman—''

"Stay where you are," commanded his lordship, while a sound suspiciously like a smothered chuckle escaped the injured man.

"No need to shout at I," said the aggrieved wagoner in injured tones. "I be doing my best, like. It's the 'orse, see—just can't be left. Tisn't my fault—''

"Yes, yes," broke in Lord Devern as the man appeared prepared to continue. "We quite see how it is—if you will just contrive to hold the 'orse—horse, we will manage very well."

Again Sir Julian's shoulders shook, and Emma looked up suspiciously, only to catch a grimace of pain cross his pale features.

"Bear up, sir," she encouraged, patting him comfortingly. "In just a little while we shall have you safe in bed."

"I am d-doing my best," he answered, his voice shaking slightly and, with surprising strength and dexterity, Lord Devern ignored his protests and lifted him, almost bodily, into the cart.

Emma was swung up to join him, landing in a flurry of skirts and indignation in the straw at his side. Meeting her outraged eyes as he threw in the luggage which had been rescued from the wreck of the phaeton, Lord Devern grinned and touched the brim of his hat in an ironical gesture.

"Allow me to take a little pleasure in my work," he murmured, smiling into her stormy gaze, and, blushing, she found her rage abruptly subsiding.

"Pray . . . let us hurry," she said, avoiding his gaze. "Sir Julian should be got to shelter as soon as possible."

With a skill that surprised her, the wagoner turned his horse and set off back the way he had come. Looking over her shoulder, Emma saw Lord Devern collect the carriage horses from the shed and, leading them by their long reins, fall in behind the wagon.

She had taken little notice of Vivian Devern's description of an "inn of sorts" and was dismayed to see a run-down, decrepit building of almost a ruinous appearance. However, there was no alternative in sight, and, against her better judgment, she reluctantly allowed Sir Julian to be carried inside.

A thin, melancholy man, in complete contrast to the usual style expected of a landlord, met them and escorted them glumly upstairs to a room overlooking the road. Emma, who had been expecting the worst, was agreeably surprised by its clean state. The floor had recently been swept, and the bed linen appeared newly laundered. A glowing fire warmed the room, obviously lit some time ago. Mildly surprised, Emma wondered briefly upon the extravagance of keeping a fire lit upon the chance arrival of a guest, something which even the most popular inns did not do. Lord Devern arriving at that moment with the intention of divesting the invalid of his clothes, she retired and, mindful that they had not eaten since the previous day, determined to find something suitable for Sir Julian to eat.

Sometime later, she returned to the bedroom carrying a tray laden with a jug of weak ale, four boiled eggs, and a plate of bread and butter.

"The kitchens are disgusting," she announced, "however I've read the cook a homily, and she has promised to mend her ways. I think really she was quite glad to find someone interested. . . . The poor woman is troubled with swollen ankles. I told her to drink barley water and put her feet up when possible."

While she was speaking, she had poured out a beaker of ale and now offered it to Sir Julian, who was lying in bed, looking pale but more alert than he had done.

"I had not thought of you in the role of ministering angel, Miss Beringer," remarked Vivian Devern, sounding amused.

"Well, I cannot say that I had thought of you as a rescuer," she returned conversationally. "And I am sure that Sir Julian had never viewed you as a possible valet, so we are all as surprised as one another."

Refusing to be fed, Sir Julian firmly took the spoon out of her hand and attacked his own egg. "Eat your breakfast," he advised. "Devern is desirous of starting for town as soon as possible."

Emma began upon her breakfast, offering kindly to share it with the impatient man by the window. "An excellent idea, my lord," she said. "Allow me a moment, and I will make a list of things which Sir Julian's valet should bring with him."

"No need," put in her guardian. "You can tell him yourself."

Miss Beringer looked up. "If you suppose for one moment, Sir Julian, that I am prepared to leave you here in the hands of a slovenly wretch and a sluttish cook, then I must tell you that you are quite mistaken." With those words she returned composedly to her breakfast and continued eating as if the matter were settled.

Lord Devern gave an appreciative chuckle. "There's a facer for you, Ju," he remarked. "Your little companion is showing her mettle."

Sir Julian sent him a quelling look. "Miss Beringer," he began in a reasonable tone, "it is not practical that you stay here. . . . Such a thing will not do, as you are well aware."

Emma studied him with a practiced eye. "If you mean that folk will gossip, then I'd say that you were nearer falling asleep than attempting to seduce me," she said bluntly. "And, if you think that *your* honor might be in danger from me—" A sharp glance from his black eyes made her cut off what she had been about to say, and, changing tactics, she suggested sweetly that she should send a note to Miss Plantagenet. "For then, you know," she went on brightly, "she could come and nurse you—or would that not be quite proper, as you are not *officially* engaged?"

Sir Julian ground his teeth, and Vivian Devern stepped in quickly. "There is no need for any such arrangement, I assure you. The valet and a maid can be here by this evening with a carriage to carry you both to London tomorrow."

"Then, all is settled," said Emma promptly, jumping to her feet to urge him on his way before her guardian could argue further.

"Devern." A voice stopped him at the door. "Not a word, mind."

"It's too good a story to hide," was the soft answer, and before anyone could say anything more, his lordship closed the door quietly behind his departing figure.

Going to the window, Emma looked down into the road and saw him come out of the inn, deep in conversation with the loutish landlord. After a moment, something changed hands, then Lord Devern climbed into his tilbury and, with a flourish of his whip, drove away.

"Do you think he will spread it abroad?" she wondered aloud and, receiving no reply, glanced over her shoulder to find Sir Julian asleep, the spoon still in his hand and the tray perched precariously upon his chest.

Removing the tray, she tucked the covers around his shoulders, unable to resist smoothing aside an errant lock of dark hair that had fallen over his brows. She studied his face, finding it both interesting and different without the amused arrogance with which he usually viewed the world. Much later that morning the doctor arrived, showing himself upstairs and into the bedroom.

"Dr. Bartholomew," he announced, "at your service, dear lady." Bowing as deeply as his rotund figure would allow, he crossed to the bed and peered at his patient who had just awoken. A plump hand was placed on Sir Julian's brow, the physician shook his head, and murmured "tsk

tsk," before taking the injured man's pulse to confirm the worrying diagnosis. "How many fingers, dear sir?" he inquired, waving his forefinger and going on to examine the wound, without waiting for a reply.

With a mournful shake of his head, he joined Emma, who had been watching this performance from the window. "A sad business, dear lady," he began, "but with great care we shall pull him through."

Emma opened her eyes. "Pull him through!" she repeated in a sharp, disbelieving whisper. "Good God—it's only a slight concussion, isn't it?"

The doctor regarded her carefully. "Have you had experience of such matters, may I inquire?" he asked, losing some of his bland manner.

"Indeed, I have," she said smartly. "I was with the army in the Peninsula."

The complacent smile faded. "Then . . . with your aid, the patient will do very well, I have no doubt of that," she was assured smoothly.

Dr. Bartholomew opened his bag and delved inside, bringing forth a knife and kidney-shaped bowl, a proceeding which Emma viewed with deep suspicion.

"I hope you have no intention of bleeding Sir Julian!" she cried. "For that is something I will not allow."

"Dear lady, if the sight of blood is too much for your delicate sensibilities, you have only to step outside—"

"I do not turn faint at the sight of blood, sir." Taking up a defensive position between the bed and the hovering doctor, she looked the physician firmly in the eye. "He has no fever, so there is no need for such an old-fashioned remedy."

"Indeed? What a knowledgeable young lady you are, to be sure. My advice would be to let blood, but if you are so averse to the old and tried method, then we will use leeches— if a fever should result, I shall absolve myself of all blame."

Again his hand reached into his bag, but Emma's curt voice made him stay his search.

"No leeches," she said firmly.

Dr. Bartholomew withdrew his hand and surveyed the resolute, diminutive figure confronting him with steady resolve. "May one inquire, madam, why you sent for me?"

"To tell the truth, I did not, but I suppose that the person who did thought that you would be of some use. However, I see that he was quite mistaken; I even doubt very much whether you are really a doctor—your methods are more those of a quack! You can do nothing here, so I will bid you good day."

The doctor stared at her with total disbelief, while a sound fast becoming familiar issued from the bed.

"The lady is right," Sir Julian agreed. "I do not need a doctor. Give the man a guinea for his troubles, kitten. Let us detain you no longer, Dr. Bartholomew."

"What a *quack*!" exclaimed Emma when the disgruntled physician had closed the door behind his indignant back.

"What a fierce defender I have in you," commented Sir Julian, making her blush.

"I only hope I was right," she said anxiously. "But the army doctor never bled without cause, saying an ill person needed his blood to get better."

"I prefer to keep mine," her guardian assured her with a smile. Cautiously sitting up, he looked round, moving his head experimentally. "The giddiness has gone," he announced. "I shall get up."

With difficulty Emma persuaded him to relinquish this idea, pointing out the foolhardiness of such a proposal. "Only stay abed until the morning," she suggested.

With every sign of reluctance, Julian Leyton, who had been unpleasantly surprised by how weak he felt even lying against the pillows, allowed himself to be persuaded. In better accord with each other than either would have thought possible only a few weeks previously, the day passed pleasantly; Emma making her patient laugh with her colorful accounts of her adventures with the army, and Sir Julian contributing pithy tales of his youth.

A dinner of roast beef was served, which the diners had just finished when the sound of hooves and rumbling wheels brought Emma hastily to the window. Looking down into the road below, she saw the angular figure of Mrs. Hill alighting from a chaise, aided by the slim form of the baronet's valet.

Recognizing the despondent droop of her shoulders, Sir Julian spoke sympathetically from the bed. "Back to the everyday round of things, Miss Beringer."

Surprised that her feelings were understood, Emma turned to study him. "Do you get tired of the Social round?" she asked.

Julian Leyton grinned. "I have an escape, as you may have noticed—the estate business often calls me out of town."

Emma looked hopeful. "I find that I, too, much prefer the country," she remarked artlessly.

Sir Julian did not pretend not to understand but shook his head. "It would not do," he said. "You are my ward, and we must take care to obey the rules and not cause gossip. As it is, we must hope that Devern does not find amusement in spreading a colorful account of our adventure."

# Chapter Ten

"*Oh*, how exciting—just like a romance from the library!" declared Elvira enviously the next day, when Emma was recounting the tale over an informal dinner shared by the ladies of Cumberland Square.

"I daresay you are disappointed at there being no haunted ruins nearby," teased Emma. "Thunder and lightning are the best I can offer in the way of Gothic effects. The inn was rather ghastly, but only because it was drab and dirty, not because of any mystery surrounding it."

"I *wish* I had been with you—a *real* adventure. How I envy you, Emma."

"You would not have cared for it," stated her friend positively. "Only think how my new traveling gown and pelisse are quite ruined, and you know you are afraid of the dark."

"Emma did very well," put in Lady Beauvale quietly. "I am only glad that you had experience of such things and knew what to do. I am sure that I would have had no idea of the best action—Julian speaks very highly of you, Emma dear."

"Really?" Emma blushed with pleasure. "I am only happy that I was there—though, that is a silly thing to say, for if Sir Julian had not taken me to visit my aunt, *he* would not have been on that road in the first place! I feel quite guilty!"

"What nonsense." Lady Beauvale laughed. "Such an accident could have happened anywhere, and, with the miles

Julian drives, it is pure luck that he has not had an upset before. He much prefers the country and, I daresay that as soon as he is well enough, will be off to Hampshire.''

Her words proved true; Sir Julian had no sooner lost his interesting pallor than he took himself away on estate business, leaving the house in Cumberland Square quiet and dull without his masculine presence. Emma, who had thought that they were on good terms and had been surprised to find that she was looking forward to his company, found herself cast down in dull spirits, viewing the rest of the Season with disfavor and lack of interest.

"Why we cannot go to Brighton or Bath, I do not know," complained Elvira, who appeared to share her feelings. "Aunt Diana is quite happy to stay in town all the year round, and Ju is the most selfish wretch, taking himself off like that without a word. Even the country would be *different*! If only Jo—" She broke off and sent a guilty glance at her friend.

"Jo—?" Emma repeated innocently. "Now who can you mean?" Eyes dancing impishly, she pretended to wrack her brain, sighing elaborately at last and appearing to give up, only to ask suddenly, "Have you seen Johnnie Gray recently?"

Her ploy worked, and Elvira jerked upright, her eyes wide, vivid color burning in her cheeks. "I vow that you are a wicked girl, Emma Beringer," she cried. "To even think that I—"

"Johnnie Gray is so charming that I own I would have been surprised if you did *not* like him."

Elvira managed to look both relieved and downcast at the same time. "Of course he is gallant to all. . . ."

"He is nice—a dear, kind man," said her friend. "But I must confess that he seemed particularly interested in you from the first moment he saw you."

Elvira looked gratified. "What nonsense," she said loftily, but could not restrain a little wriggle of pleasure. "I hardly regarded him."

"Did you not? Well, he obviously regarded you," observed Emma. "I am afraid that all the other females paled into insignificance. Even so old a friend as I found myself being viewed as a means of introduction!"

"He is certainly very handsome."

"Do you think so?" queried Emma teasingly. "That precise shade of ginger hair . . ."

"Ginger! Why, it is the most beautiful auburn!"

Emma laughed. "I thought that you had hardly regarded him," she reminded her friend.

"Indeed—but hair such as his can hardly be ignored."

"And that dashing green uniform—together they make a striking effect. There is something romantic about a soldier, is there not?"

Lifting her chin, Elvira looked at the other girl. "So I believe most females feel," she answered steadily. "To me, however, a poet is by far the most romantic of callings."

"Oh, *Elvira!*" cried Emma. "I had thought that you had discovered a *tendre* for Johnnie Gray."

Tears rose in Elvira's dark eyes. "How could you suppose me so disloyal, so changeable in my feelings?" she asked. "I know that you think him lacking—that he should have faced Miss Plantagenet. . . ."

"Indeed he should. I did not care for the way he made off, but I daresay he was afraid that his benefactor would hear of his liaison with you and turn him off."

"Precisely. He has written to explain that he must retain his position at all costs. His suit will never be acceptable until he has made his way in the world. Our—relationship must be kept even more secret. . . . You *do* understand, Emma? *No one* must know of our . . . attachment. Bevis says it would be fatal to all our hopes if it were to become known."

Muffling a snort of disgust, Emma allowed her silence to be taken for agreement. "Your loyalty does you credit, Elvira. I hope that your poet deserves it. But are you sure that you are not making a mistake? Johnnie Gray—''

Elvira stopped her with a gesture. ''Is all that any female could wish for,'' she finished, an unconsciously wishful note in her voice. ''But Bevis and I exchanged vows, Emma. I could not break an oath. We exchanged tokens. . . .''

Her interest caught, not having been aware of this, Emma raised an inquisitive eyebrow, and Elvira, after an initial hesitation, produced a tiny ring on a chain round her neck. Inspecting it, Emma privately thought it bought in some fairground but did not say so.

''It was his mother's,'' explained Elvira sentimentally, dropping the trinket back down the neck of her gown. ''I gave him Papa's pocket watch in return—you must promise me never to mention this, for Ju would be mad with rage if he knew. He wanted it, you see, but Aunt Diana said that I should have it. Being so young at the time, it was the only thing of Papa's which I could remember.''

''Oh, Elvira!'' Emma sighed. ''You seem to positively *look* for trouble. Could you not have used something else to plight your troth?''

Elvira shook her black curls. ''No—it had to be of immense value, you know. If Bevis loved me enough to give me his mother's sapphire, then I had to prove my own devotion by giving him something of equal value.''

Her voice was unhappy, and Emma could see that she was regretting her action. The younger girl was caught in a situation from which she could not extricate herself without admitting that her love for the would-be poet had waned, and neither her loyalty nor pride would allow her to do so. Understanding her difficulty, Emma sighed sympathetically, privately deciding that Bevis had forgone all right to Elvira's heart, and that she would take a personal hand in the matter.

She was rather pleased to have this task to occupy her mind; she had thought that she and Sir Julian were in accord and had looked forward to confirming their friendship once he was better. However, far from seeking her company, her guardian appeared to be avoiding her and, since his recovery, had taken himself out of the house as much as possible, spending most of his evenings at White's, the gaming club, and at the moment was absent on a visit to a friend, who lived on the other side of London.

More hurt than she cared to admit, even to herself, Emma was also puzzled by his actions. Upon the rare occasions when they happened to meet, Julian Leyton had behaved with punctilious correctness which froze her into a matching remote manner. For some time she pondered upon the cause of his coldness, and then one day, an overheard scrap of Lady Beauvale's conversation provided the answer.

Emma and Elvira had just returned from changing their library books and were crossing the hall as a maid was taking a tray of tea into Lady Beauvale's sitting room.

". . . gossip," she was saying, "is the bane of any man in Society. One word that he has impinged on a female's honor in any way, and the poor fellow is obliged to offer for her. Many an unwanted marriage has been caused by rumor or speculation. And, of course, gossip can only too easily be arranged by a malicious person—"

The door closed, cutting off the rest of Lady Beauvale's words, leaving Emma shaken and dismayed as she realized that the scrap of conversation could all too easily refer to herself and her guardian.

"Emma, dearest—whatever is the matter?" asked Elvira with concern. "You look as if you'd seen a ghost. Are you unwell?"

"What? No—no, I am quite well, I assure you," was the distracted answer as Emma looked blankly round the hall, without seeing her surroundings. Putting a hand on the banister, she began to climb the stair, her movements so slow and labored that her friend grew alarmed.

"Let me call Aunt Diana," she cried, turning to run across the hall.

"No!"

The word was so definite that Elvira stopped abruptly, turning to look at her friend in surprise.

"I—would rather that you did not," said Emma, softening her curt command. "I am quite well, I give you my word. I have just realized something. . . . And it was an unpleasant shock."

"Oh, Emma, whatever do you mean? Surely no one here has upset you? I know that I have not, Aunt Diana is the kindest of females, and we have hardly seen Ju since his accident, so it cannot be him—"

Emma tried to smile. "You are right, I am just being foolish, pray take no heed—it was just silliness on my part. Nothing at all to bother about. Let us both forget the incident and think of other things."

Determined to take her own advice, she began to discuss the new fashions in the magazine they had just bought and succeeded in diverting Elvira's attention. However, her own thoughts were less easy to distract, her anger growing that Sir Julian could have supposed her capable of attempting to inveigle him into a proposal. Once Elvira caught her grinding her teeth with suppressed rage, and it was only with difficulty that she managed to convince the other girl that it was merely a manifestation of her disgust for the extremes of fashion as portrayed in the periodical.

When, later that afternoon, Freddie Melvin was announced, Emma was so grateful for the distraction that she greeted him with a pleasure that made that young man blink.

"Freddie! How delightful to see you. We were in need of company." Struck suddenly by his ill-at-ease, nervous manner, she studied him more closely, finally flinging herself down on a chair and commanding him to make a clean breast of it.

His eyes flickered from one to the other, while he ran a finger around the edge of his stock, which had obviously become suddenly uncomfortably tight. "You won't like it," he said unhappily. "Dash it all—I mean to say—a fellow don't want to tittle-tattle. I ain't one for blabbermouths. . . ."

"Go on, Freddie," encouraged Emma, as he fell unhappily silent.

"Don't care for cards much," he suddenly announced, "but there was a game set up on the other side of Hampstead Heath last night. Went there for something to do, you know. Never play deep—" With a significant glance at Elvira, who looked puzzled, he added meaningly, "Not like *some*."

"Oh, go on, *do*," cried Emma, exasperated as he again became silent. "Who is in trouble . . . surely not *Julian*?"

Freddie choked at the thought but shook his head. "The fellow's as rich as Croesus, ain't he? No, not *him*—"

"Who, then?" demanded the girls in unison.

"Several cronies there," Freddie went on, determined to tell the tale in his own way. "Saw Vivian Devern, wandered over to say 'How do'—surprised to see that he was playing with that poet fellow you're so fond of, Miss Leyton."

"You're not supposed to know," began Elvira involuntarily, before realizing what had been said. "You saw Bevis in some gambling den, playing cards with Lord Devern?"

"Not a gambling den, a private house. In pretty deep, though."

"Are you sure? He h-hasn't any money, so how could he be gambling?"

Freddie looked at her, and with a thrill of anticipation Emma realized that he had come to the crux of his story. "He wasn't playing for money. . . . A gold and enamel pocket watch lay on the baize, and it was *that* he'd used as a stake."

Elvira looked shocked and turned quite pale. "What was it like?" she asked faintly.

"Prussian blue enamel-patterned case with a circle of diamonds around the edge, white face, and a gold filigree cover to the works," was the prompt reply. "I noticed especially because I like watches—quite a collection, myself. However, not the point. Thing is, the poet had just lost it to Devern.''

Elvira gave a faint moan, and Emma hurried to her side. "It can't be yours," she said, taking both her hands. "Surely Bevis would not pledge your gift in such a way?''

Elvira's hands were icy cold and trembled in hers. "There cannot be two,'' she whispered. "It was made especially for my papa. Oh, Emma, I am betrayed! What shall I do? Ju will never forgive me . . . to have lost Papa's watch in such a way and to Lord Devern, too.''

Two large tears trickled down her cheeks, splashing onto the bodice of her dress. She looked so devastated that her friend was moved to wrath.

"The wretch!'' she cried, though whether she meant Lord Devern, Bevis, or Sir Julian himself was hard to tell. "I'd like to call him out—''

"Can't be done, you know—you're female,'' Freddie pointed out, adding reasonably, "Wouldn't do anyway, the whole thing needs to be hushed up. Happen to know that Vivian Devern is staying there until tonight, friends of his, y'see.''

"So he hasn't come back to town, you mean?''

"Not yet—but he's invited to dine with us tonight and hasn't cried off, as far as I know.''

"So there's a chance that he still has the watch?''

Freddie looked uncomfortable. "Every chance. More than likely, I'd say. Don't like to rat on a kinsman, but don't care for this kind of thing. Thing is, I'd say that he intended to use it against Sir Julian. My guess is that's why he made a play for it. Devious fellow, Vivian. It would amuse him to produce it one day and watch his face.''

"Despicable!'' exploded Emma, while Elvira sat down abruptly as if her legs would no longer support her. Moaning faintly, she clutched Emma's hand and stared at her pleadingly.

"Don't worry. I have a plan,'' Emma whispered, and,

having a shrewd idea that Freddie Melvin might not approve and would prove difficult if he knew of her intentions, she thanked that young man for his news and used her considerable charm to persuade him that, having done his duty, all would now be well.

One last item of information was needed, and she casually elicited the fact that the Melvins habitually dined at nine o'clock before the flattered but dazed Freddie took his leave.

"Now," she said, turning to the other girl the minute they were alone, "I am feeling a headache coming on, and you, my love, are in the best of spirits! I shall take to my bed, while you dine with Lady Beauvale, concealing your true feelings and convincing her that all is normal. It is imperative that she suspects nothing."

"I cannot—I cannot! Do not ask it of me."

"Only do as I ask, and I give you my word that the watch will be returned to you, with Julian and Lady Beauvale none the wiser."

Stifling a succession of sobs, Elvira sat up and stared at her, wide-eyed. "What do you mean to do?" she asked, half-fearfully.

Emma shook her head. "It's better that you don't know," she told her firmly. "Just keep your aunt busy this evening. I'm going to my room now. . . . If you would send for Maria, and make sure that the servants all know that I have retired with an incapacitating headache . . . ?"

Much depended upon Maria, and Emma awaited her arrival with some trepidation, looking at her intently as the maid entered her bedroom. "How well do you know Jem Bowls?" she asked, without preamble.

"Well enough, miss," she was answered in surprised tones, while a lively color flooded into Maria's cheeks.

"If I gave you this evening off, would you be able to persuade him to take you for a walk?"

"He lives above the stables, so once he's done his work, his time's his own. . . . We walked to the river last week."

Emma was faintly surprised at this evidence of her maid living a life of which she was unaware but merely inquired, "So it would not be difficult?"

Maria grinned. "No, miss. I could manage it."

"Very well. Here's a shilling for you and the evening off, provided that Jem is away from the stables at dusk."

"Whatever are you up to, miss? Not running away, are you? Course, if you was, I'd come with you, much as I like it here."

"No, nothing like that," Emma assured her, touched by the concern for her own welfare.

"What, then? It wouldn't be right, you wandering round a town alone, like. You're no more than a babe in arms, where some folk are concerned."

"Maria, I've dealt with bandits before now—besides, I'll take my pistol with me, so you need have no fear on my account."

Her maid remained uncertain, and her mouth assumed a mutinous appearance.

"Trust me, Maria. I give you my word to take care." Maria still looked unconvinced, and her mistress began to wish that she had no need of her help. Realizing that she must take her into fuller confidence, she said, "Lord Devern has something belonging to Miss Leyton. If Sir Julian finds out, she will be in great trouble. I intend to make him return it."

The maid seemed somewhat reassured at this expurgated version, accepting, as Emma had hoped she would, that her mistress intended only riding to his lordship's London lodgings.

"He's not a man to trifle with," she pointed out dubiously.

"I will be careful," Emma assured her. "So—now you know my intentions, will you undertake to keep Jem away from the stables? I've an idea that he would make difficulties about my taking out a horse."

"Wouldn't he and all," agreed Maria, a faint hint of pride

in her voice. "No idea of his station, has Jem. Why, he thinks himself as good as the master, and, by what I hear, Sir Julian allows him his head in a great many things."

"Yes . . . well, I'm sure Jem is a very sensible young man, but will you do as I ask?"

The maid nodded her head. "But you're to take care, mind. Wouldn't it be best to let the master deal with it?" she suggested invitingly.

"As he is not here, that would be rather difficult. I have a plan. . . ." she said, proceeding to repeat the expurgated version of her intentions.

Satisfied with the explanation, the maid drew the curtains, and Emma retired to bed in the darkened room, assuming the frail air of an invalid when Lady Beauvale appeared to inquire after her well-being. Feeling a little guilty, Emma accepted the offer of a vinaigrette and allowed her brow to be cooled by the application of lavender water. Having satisfied herself that it was nothing serious, Lady Beauvale advised sleep and retired to dress for dinner, leaving the patient to the tedium of whiling away several hours with nothing to do.

At last dusk began to fall, and Emma climbed out of bed and dressed herself in her riding habit. Mindful of her errand, she took a black velvet "loo" mask from a drawer and slipped it and her pistol in her pocket before cautiously opening the door and listening intently. Distant sounds of muted conversation and laughter told her that Elvira was keeping her promise to distract her aunt, and the chink of cutlery and crockery spoke of the servants' intent upon the business of serving dinner.

Clutching her shako, Emma crept downstairs, pausing on the first floor landing as Frobisher and the footman crossed the hall with an assortment of entrée dishes and trays. As soon as they had gone into the dining room, she ran down the last flight of stairs, across the checkered floor and into the long drawing room, which ran the length of the house.

As she had hoped, the full-length window at the back was open, and she had only to step over the sill to be in the garden.

Taking to her heels, she ran down the path, trusting to luck that no one would see her flying figure and let herself out of the gate at the bottom, which gave onto the stable yard beyond. Refusing the temptation to take her guardian's powerful animal, she went to the mare she had ridden before and, murmuring soothingly, set about saddling her. Old skills returned quickly, and she soon had her ready for the road. Leading her out of the stall, she was met by one of the stable lads who had come to see who was in the stable at such an unusual hour.

"Hallo," she said in a friendly, informal voice. "You're just the person I needed to open the gate for me."

Giving him no time for argument, she indicated that he should help her to mount and then, with as confident an air as she could manage, waited while he opened the gate onto the road. With a salute of her whip, she trotted by his hesitating form before he could pluck up the courage to query her actions and quickly turned into the square and out of his sight.

During her stay in London she had become familiar with its maze of streets and, avoiding the main roads, made her way by the back streets, peopled by respectable tradesmen's families, toward the north of the city. Assuming an air of self-confidence, she affected ignorance of the curious stares her lone figure was attracting and, skirting Hyde Park, headed toward the Great North Road. Soon she was on unfamiliar territory and with gathering dusk began to wonder about the wisdom of her venture.

Chiding herself for a cowardly lack of backbone, she had only to reflect briefly upon her friend's predicament to strengthen her resolve. When she reached a suitably deserted stretch of the road, she unbuckled her riding skirt and removed it with some difficulty to reveal a pair of tight army breeches. Thankful that her father had had the forethought to insist that the masculine garments should form part of her riding habit, she rolled the heavy skirt into a manageable bundle and fastened it with some difficulty to the pommel of her saddle before riding on, confident in her masculine disguise.

Soon the road became more deserted and empty of any sign of human habitation, the lights of London behind her serving only to highlight the loneliness of the heath. As she looked about, Emma felt a growing tinge of unease and could well understand how such a place had become notorious for the felons who inhabited it, playing upon the travelers who were unwise or foolhardy enough to use the old highway.

Choosing a convenient clump of trees to shield her from view, she settled down to await the arrival of Lord Devern and before long heard the rumble of wheels as a carriage approached. Remembering her mask just in time, she kicked the mare into motion and plunged down the incline to the road.

"Stand and deliver!" she shouted in the manner culled from the news sheets, flourishing her pistol and wishing it had been bigger and more impressive.

The carriage was brought to a halt, and she realized with dismay that it was too big and cumbersome to carry her quarry, whom she suspected would be driving his tilbury.

"Well, damn me, if the army hasn't taken to High-Tobying! What would the general say?" exclaimed a voice, and she found herself the object of a furious glare from an elderly man in a bob wig. "Here's my purse, damn you for a dog—drive on coachman!" he cried, hurling something to the ground between the feet of her mount.

The mare took exception to such behavior, and by the time Emma had regained control the coach was trundling hastily toward the safety of the city. Struck for the first time by the effect of the military uniform she was wearing, Emma reflected upon the trouble it might cause the regiment but, as there was nothing to be done about it, could only hope that with growing darkness it would become less easily recognized.

The evening wore on, becoming darker and colder, a hooting owl added to the ghostly atmosphere, and, when it began to rain, Emma wished devoutly that she had never set out upon the enterprise. At last, after what seemed like hours, she heard the approach of another traveler and squeezed her mount with her heels. Tired of inactivity, the mare plunged eagerly onto the road, nearly unseating her rider, who had been in the act of pulling down her mask. Regaining her seat, she flourished her pistol and again demanded that whoever was approaching should stand and deliver.

To her mortification the light carriage showed no sign of abating its pace, the driver even appearing to urge on his animals. Too nonplussed to move from the middle of the road, Emma watched helplessly as her intended victim galloped toward her. As the moon broke through the clouds and bathed her in a shaft of brightness, the bells in the city behind began to toll nine o'clock, and she had the time to think fatalistically that she must have missed her quarry, anyway, as he would be sitting down to dine at that very moment.

Abruptly the approaching carriage, which she now identified as a phaeton, swerved aside from a collision course, swinging wide as the horses were slowed, finally stopping almost opposite her. For a moment rider and driver stared at each other, mirrored amazement on both their faces.

"Good God—Emma!" exclaimed Sir Julian, penetrating her disguise without difficulty.

"W—what are *you* doing here?" she demanded furiously and spun her mount round in a tight circle, preparatory to flight.

"Stay where you are, ward," ordered her guardian in a voice which brooked no argument. Seeing that he was being obeyed, he went on in a steely voice. "Dismount, if you

please, Miss Beringer. Tie your mare to the back of the phaeton and then sit up here beside me.''

Reluctantly Emma did as she was bidden, while Julian
Leyton sat tight-lipped and still. Reaching down, he seized
her wrist and with an almost contemptuous gesture, flicked
her into the high seat beside him. Acutely conscious of her
attire and the tight overall breeches which revealed the length
of her legs, Emma stared ahead as her guardian started toward the lights of the distant town.

''I'm waiting for an explanation,'' he said at last. ''I am
sure you must have a perfectly valid reason for masquerading
as a soldier and making a very bad attempt to hold up the
users of the highway, but I find such outrageous behavior
somewhat surprising—even for you.'' He paused while his
passenger stared uncomfortably ahead, seeking desperately
and without success for some explanation which would sat-
isfy him and yet not involve Elvira. ''I am waiting, Miss
Beringer,'' he went on inexorably, making his ward wish that
she was anywhere but where she was.

When the silence had lengthened, Sir Julian put his hand
into his pocket and dropped a small object onto Emma's lap.

''Could that have anything to do with this escapade?'' he
asked quietly.

Looking down, Emma could not stop herself giving a gasp
of amazement; there on her knees was a gold and enamel
watch, the ring of diamonds decorating its edge, sparkling
coldly in the light from the moon.

# Chapter Eleven

ℰnjoying the moment, Sir Julian glanced down at her, grim amusement at her consternation showing plainly on his face.

Emma sighed bitterly. "You knew all along—and let poor Elvira make herself ill with worry," she accused, thrusting the offending timepiece toward him.

Pocketing the watch, Sir Julian drove on. "I had no idea that my sister was even aware of its loss. I only knew because, by good fortune, Captain Gray was in the party and had the sense to acquaint me of the matter."

"Johnnie Gray! I had no idea—"

"May I inquire as to the identity of your informant?"

"Freddie Melvin. He came at once to tell Elvira."

"He would have done better to come to me," said her guardian, adding as he eyed his ward in no kindly manner, "And so would you, my girl."

Feeling that he was probably right but refusing to admit as much, Emma shrugged eloquently. "You forget, Sir Julian, that you were from home when the matter arose. In fact you seem to have been much from home of late—and that being the case, pray tell me, how we were supposed to apply to you for help?"

Sir Julian glared at his companion only too aware of the truth of her words. "Be honest, Miss Beringer, and admit that this harebrained scheme was your idea of adventure—something to enliven your life and annoy me!"

Emma looked interested. "Why should I wish to annoy you?" she inquired.

"I am well aware, ward, that that is your prime desire."

"Oh, pooh!" she exclaimed. "You forget the times when we have been f-friends. Why, I even thought—" realizing the impropriety of what she was about to say, Emma abruptly bit off her words and finished lamely, "that you would be pleased if I restored the watch."

Sir Julian was not entirely deceived. "Now that, Miss Beringer, is quite untrue. If you thought at all, which I doubt, it was that you would have scored over me."

"Why would I want to do that?" Emma wondered again and was rewarded by a tightening of Julian Leyton's fingers on the reins.

"Because you are the most infuriating girl I know," she was told grimly, and was jerked back in her seat as the horses responded to the mood of the driver and bounded forward.

The journey through London was achieved in silence, Emma admiring the knowledge which enabled her guardian to avoid all the main roads, save for a brief crossing of Oxford Street.

"I find this most interesting," she told him brightly, refusing to be put down by his manner. "I used the back streets as much as I could, but even so had to skirt the park—you have managed to avoid all the thoroughfares."

"If we should be met and recognized, your reputation would be in rags," he pointed out curtly.

"How kind and thoughtful you are," Emma murmured ironically.

"Don't try me too far," she was warned. "So far you have come off unscathed—due to the fact that I am prepared to believe that you were acting, however misguidedly, in what you thought were Elvira's best interests. However, I am no fool, Miss Beringer, and am well aware that you were spoiling for an adventure. . . . And that this henbrained scheme of yours was put into operation without care or thought."

"Now, that is untrue," said Emma in a small voice. "I thought of it a great deal and could come up with no better solution. Would you have me let those wretches, between them, ruin Elvira's life?"

"No," admitted her guardian after a pause. "I'll accept that your motive was of the best and, for that reason alone, have not read you the lecture you deserve. Good God, ward, have you no idea of the danger in which you ran? You were playing at highwayman, but the real thing is to be found on Hampstead Heath—and a tobyman does not care to find a rival on his ground. Many an amateur highway robber has been found with a bullet in his body."

Emma shuddered and hung her head. "I—did not think—"

"I daresay—and what if you *had* stopped Devern? Have you not considered that he would very likely defend himself?"

Beginning to feel that she had, indeed, been foolish, Emma was saved from having to admit as much by the fact that they arrived at the gate of the stables at that moment. Sir Julian climbed down, taking the reins with him, and unlocked the gate, just as a sleepy groom appeared to take the carriage and horses into his care.

With an uncomfortably tight grip on her elbow, Sir Julian led her through the garden, letting himself in the back door and, without bothering to light a candle, urged her past the kitchen, from behind the door of which came sounds of laughter and loud conversation, up a flight of dark stairs to the hall. Here, he allowed her the luxury of a light, retaining his own grip on the candlestick as she reached out to take it.

"Who besides ourselves knows of this escapade?" he asked quietly.

"Elvira—and my maid."

He nodded grimly. "Keep it so," he advised, dropping the watch into her hand, "and make sure that my sister does the same." Releasing his hold on the candlestick, Sir Julian bowed ironically and stepped back. "Good night, Miss Beringer."

Glad to have escaped retribution, Emma ran quickly up the stairs, glancing down from the landing to see her guardian standing where she had left him, watching her retreating figure. The sweet sound of Elvira playing the piano and singing carried from the room behind. For a second they exchanged gazes before, with a curious gesture, half-salute half-dismissive flick of the fingers, he turned away, and she continued up to her bedroom to await the arrival of an expectant Elvira.

"And that was *all*?" As soon as she was able, Elvira had made her escape from the withdrawing room and hurried to her friend's bedroom. "He didn't rage and threaten to beat you?" she asked incredulously.

"Of course not," replied Emma stoutly, not willing to admit that physical violence had been her first fear in the moment when she had recognized her victim. "In fact Sir Julian was surprisingly forebearing." Even to herself she sounded a little puzzled and added lightly, "I begin to suspect, Elvira, that he is not *entirely* the ogre you would have me believe."

"Is he not?" wondered the other darkly. "Then, all I can say is that something has caused a change of character—that bump on the head, perhaps. I've heard of such things."

Relief and excitement had caused her voice to rise, and Emma put a finger to her lips in warning.

"What I don't understand," she went on more quietly," is Ju's behavior. He came in as if nothing untoward had happened. Why, he even kissed me and asked most kindly after your welfare the instant Aunt Diana acquainted him with your indisposition. It makes me feel quite uneasy."

"Mmm," agreed her listener thoughtfully, "but what I'd *really* like to know is—*where* was Lord Devern? I swear he did not cross the heath, and yet Freddie said he was due to dine with the Melvins."

Elvira stared at her, wide-eyed with sudden supposition. "You don't think that they . . . duelled again?" She gasped.

Emma considered and then shook her head. "I expect Sir Julian made him see the error of his ways in that cutting way of his," she said.

Elvira looked at her. "Don't you like him?" she asked. "At one time I quite thought . . . that is, I hoped—well, to be honest, I began to think of you as one of the family."

Suddenly Emma found her hands of immense interest, studying each pink fingernail with care before replying lightly, "What nonsense, Elvira. You know that we took an instant dislike—nothing has happened to change that. Indeed, I find myself quite set in my ways."

"You just said that you did not believe him the ogre—"

"That was a figure of speech," Emma interrupted quickly. "Sir Julian is—just a normal man. A trifle more arrogant and indifferent to other's wishes to be sure, but still the embodiment of the fashionable male."

The other girl could not hide her disappointment. "I thought that when you said he had been so—understanding and when he had asked so pleasantly after you, that you had made up your differences." Aware that her friend was regarding her frowningly, she faltered to a stop, her lip trembling.

"Sir Julian and I do not have *differences*," Emma announced grandly. "We have insurmountable *divergencies*! Besides," she went on in a determinedly bright tone, "we are forgetting Miss Plantagenet."

"How I wish we could!" exclaimed Elvira feelingly. "I *dread* her marrying Ju. She will make life quite dreadful with her interest in her elevated ancestry and her single-minded determination to make everyone conform to her own idea of social behavior. I daresay she will expect me to curtsy to her whenever we meet! I've a good mind to mention the family legend," she finished darkly.

Emma was interested. "What legend?" she asked. "Do tell."

"Well, it's only a story I heard from my old nurse years ago—it's nothing, really, and I daresay totally untrue. . . ." Seeing her friend's growing impatience, she went on. "The tale is that it was one of our ancestors who actually unseated Richard the Third and Henry Tudor knighted him for it—"

Emma sighed with bliss. "And our dear Jane has no idea of this?"

"She can't have, can she?" Elvira answered ingenuously. "I do not think that she would care for it at all, do you?"

"I am very sure that she would not," agreed the other girl and fell thoughtfully silent, certain that the information could be used to advantage.

Any qualms she may have had about putting a halt to any hopes of a betrothal between Sir Julian and Miss Plantagenet were dissolved when Lady Beauvale, a woman who rarely saw bad in anyone, remarked after a visit from the paragon that she really was a most tiresome girl.

"As you know, Emma dear, I would not for the world have it go further, but I do find Miss Plantagenet a little difficult. To expect Mrs. Beaufort, who is rising eighty, apart from being a cadet branch of the Lovat family, to bow first, is quite unacceptable. She really does place herself too high! To think of her and my dearest Ju—I fear that she will *not* make him happy."

Diana Beauvale looked so worried that Emma hastened to reassure her. "They have not made the announcement, yet. There is time for the affair to come to nothing."

"How I hope so," Lady Beauvale sighed before, conscious of indiscretion, she again counseled Emma to silence. "Let us talk of other things," she said. "Your birthday is almost upon us. We must consider how to celebrate, though to be sure, I hope that the fact of your majority will make no difference to how we go on. Now, would you like a dance, perhaps?"

"You are too kind and have done so much for me already," protested Emma.

"Nonsense, my dear, I've enjoyed every moment. I insist upon this little gesture. . . . Surely you would not disappoint Elvira, who has been waiting upon this event?"

"I should like above all things a visit to the theater," replied Emma, giving in gracefully, as a half-formed plan slipped into her mind. "A family party, if you please."

"Made up of your young friends, you mean?" asked Lady Beauvale doubtfully.

"Not entirely," replied Emma. "You and Elvira and Sir Julian—"

"That would mean that Miss Plantagenet must have an invite, too," warned the older woman.

"If it must be so, I shall make her very welcome," Emma agreed soulfully.

Any one of her Peninsula friends would have suspected her of duplicity, but Lady Beauvale did not know her well enough to recognize the danger in the voice of innocence and merely inquired kindly, "What is there at the theater that you so want to see?"

"Edmund Kean is playing at Drury Lane; I saw a broad sheet the other day."

Lady Beauvale looked even more doubtful. "It sounds rather intellectual, my dear. I had supposed that you would prefer something lighter . . . Garibaldi, perhaps."

Emma shook her head. "I have never seen Mr. Kean and have heard so much of him. Do, *please* say that I may have a theater party, dear Lady Beauvale."

"Very well, Emma, if that is what you want, though, I believe Elvira will be sadly disappointed."

And so she proved to be, gazing at her friend in undisguised horror. "The theater?" she cried, as if threatened with a torture chamber. "And Shakespeare—not even a burlesque! *Shakespeare!*" she repeated bitterly. "A modern play would have been a little better. How could you choose Shakespeare? Why, he is old-fashioned and *full* of history and deadly boring to be sure.''

"You'll enjoy it, you'll see—''

"I won't—I hate blood, and Shakespeare is forever putting out people's eyes and cutting heads off! I vow that you are a ghoul, Emma Beringer,'' she told her spiritedly, "and do not deserve a birthday treat, if you waste it so!''

"You will enjoy it when you get there,'' Emma told her firmly and would not allow herself to be talked into changing her mind.

"Well, it's the strangest thing I have ever heard of,'' pouted Elvira, admitting defeat. "And to wish to invite Jane Plantagenet is above all astounding!''

Emma would only say that if the lady in question was to become a member of the family, then it was time the effort was made to cultivate her acquaintance.

The younger girl could only look at her askance. "Pooh!'' she retorted, suddenly looking enlightened, "what nonsense. Only Ju could want to cultivate Miss Plantagenet— you, wicked girl that you are, are planning some mischief, I do declare.''

Emma merely looked the picture of shocked innocence and firmly denied any such intention, retiring to the library in order to make herself acquainted with the play, the better to enjoy it, so she informed her friend. However, a few days later when Miss Plantagenet, arriving to pay a morning call on Lady Beauvale, met them in the hall on their way to walk in the park and insisted upon accompanying them, her goodwill was sadly tried. At first all was well as they exchanged idle pleasantries and then, making sure that their maids were out of hearing, Jane Plantagenet turned to both girls and assured them in superior tones that they both had her heartfelt sympathy and understanding.

"What for?'' Emma demanded, while Elvira turned a guilty shade of pink and murmured confused apologies.

"As nearly a sister, I feel able to give my advice and

support, you know,'' began Miss Plantagenet, with a gentle smile.

"Forgive me, Miss Plantagenet,'' Emma said, a dangerous note in her voice which most people would have heeded, "but, in the interests of fact, I must point out that you and I are not in any way related nor likely to be.''

"Not in the usual sense,'' agreed the other kindly, "but in the near future—'' She paused delicately before going on with an arch smile. "You shall be my . . . ward-by-marriage—if all goes well, of course.''

"If Sir Julian comes up to scratch, you mean,'' put in Emma baldly, tired of the other's delicate mind.

Miss Plantagenet's smile vanished. "My dear Miss Beringer, it pains me to hear such a vulgar expression!''

Emma went on relentlessly. "*If* Sir Julian comes up to scratch as you hope, we shall still not be kin, I am happy to say. In a week's time I shall be of age!''

Surprise and quickly concealed dismay crossed Jane Plantagenet's face before haughty disdain superceded them as she looked down her nose at Emma. "Good manners make me refrain from comment, Miss Beringer, apart from saying that no doubt Sir Julian will be as relieved as I at the news.''

"It is not news; Sir Julian knew when was my birthday all the time—though, believe me, he will be no happier than me at ending it!'' Emma was goaded into saying. "This year my birthday is even more welcome than usual. To be out of leading reins and irksome control will be a joy.''

Miss Plantagenet gave her a withering gray stare before she turned away, pointedly engaging an unhappy Elvira in a light conversation that totally left out her companion.

Irritated, Emma dropped back, and when a few minutes later, a pleasant baritone spoke her name, she greeted Lord Devern guardedly but allowed him to walk beside her.

"I am relieved, Miss Beringer,'' he told her, bowing. "I had thought that I might be in danger of being given a setdown.''

Emma raised her eyebrows. "What a foolish female I would be to draw attention in such a way," she murmured. "Besides, I cannot believe that any action of mine would seriously discompose you, my lord."

Vivian Devern laughed. A sound which caused several heads to turn in their direction, including that of Miss Plantagenet, who, seeing who was Emma's companion, was obviously caught in a quandary of both wishing to ignore Emma and yet feeling the need to save her from the attentions of Lord Devern.

"The paragon is about to descend on us," he murmured, an amused smile on his lips as he looked down into Emma's face. "Do you wish to be rescued?"

"Not at the moment," she assured him.

"Then, let us turn down this side path."

Walking quickly, they were soon lost among the twists of the hedge-lined path, alone apart from the distant sounds of voices, and suddenly Emma was aware of the indiscretion of her action.

Sensing her unease, Lord Devern turned to her, barring her path as if by accident. "Dear Miss Beringer, do not, I pray, fail me now," he said softly. "I thought that I had found that unusual female—one who cared little for comment. . . . Do not disillusion me by turning into a nervous, spinsterish paragon."

Emma eyed him, his rueful expression making her smile. "I am no missish old maid," she said, "but neither am I prepared to risk my reputation, which I would be foolish not to care about. Let us turn back, if you please."

He folded her fingers into the crook of his elbow and held them there in a firm grip. "If we continue this way we shall rejoin the main thoroughfare shortly—and in the meantime we will have the opportunity of a private conversation."

An exploratory tug telling her that her hand was tightly held, Emma could not but fall in with the suggestion and walked calmly beside her companion.

"Very well," she said composedly, "we shall talk of inconsequences. . . . The weather is very good for the time of year, do you not think? I believe that the harvest has been exceptional, though fashionable Society is sadly depleted at this time of year."

"Naughty!" her companion admonished, nipping her fingers, "when I stayed in town merely to be sure of a moment of your company."

"Pooh—let me tell you, my lord, that I am not henbrained enough to believe such blatant flattery. I know very well that you have not left for the country for some good reason which has nothing to do with me."

Vivian Devern raised a mocking eyebrow. "What a knowing minx you are."

Not liking the familiarity of this address, Emma lifted her chin and inquired sweetly as to the time.

Lord Devern lost his smile, and for a moment his gray eyes narrowed into slits before a rueful expression twisted his lips. "That damned knuckleheaded cousin of mine, I'll be bound," he exclaimed.

Emma saw no reason why Freddie should bear the blame alone. "And Sir Julian," she supplied quietly.

They had come up to a seat set back in the hedge, and here he obliged her to sit. "How much do you know, Miss Beringer?" he asked.

Emma considered. "Most of it, I'd say," she answered coolly. "Save precisely how Sir Julian obtained the return of the watch."

Lord Devern appeared amused. "I suppose that you and Miss Leyton imagine a dramatic duel, no less."

His companion nodded. "As neither of you bore signs of fisticuffs, as far as we could see," she said lightly.

Apparently having regained his good humor, Lord Devern laughed. "My dear, Ju merely asked!" he told her surprisingly, going on to explain as she raised her eyebrows in polite disbelief. "Once he knew I had the bauble, there was no point in continuing the affair."

Emma regarded him thoughtfully. "Why do you dislike Sir Julian so much?" she asked.

"Old business, my dear." Seating himself beside her, half-turning to shield her from view with his shoulder, he returned her gaze for a few seconds before remarking, "I have an idea that you do not exactly love him yourself."

"Love!" she was startled into repeating. "Indeed it would be very improper for me to love my guardian." Realizing from his interested expression that she was being too vehement, Emma took a breath to allow time for her brain to clear and then went on more calmly. "While it would be true to say that Sir Julian and I have not always seen eye to eye, that circumstance is about to change. I attain my majority very shortly."

For a moment she found herself the recipient of a shrewd, assessing stare, which discomforted her, before Lord Devern relaxed his gaze and offered her his felicitations. "May I be the first to wish you a happy birthday?" he asked, taking her hand to convey it to his lips in a gallant gesture.

It was at that inauspicious moment that Miss Plantagenet came upon them. Having spent a quarter of an hour searching for the errant Emma, she was clearly satisfied to have her suspicions well-founded.

"Miss Beringer, there you are," she cried in well-bred accents, bustling forward and acknowledging Lord Devern's bow with cool civility. "How we came to miss you, I do not know, but now we must make haste—"

"Lord Devern has taken good care of me," said Emma coolly, standing up and shaking out her skirts. "You need have had no worry on my behalf, I do assure you."

Miss Plantagenet was forced to acknowledge Vivian Devern's presence more than she cared. "My thanks, for your care," she said, inclining her head graciously.

"Not at all, Miss Plantagenet. I was happy to be of some service, and now I shall be delighted to escort you all home."

Shooting a quick glance at his bland countenance, Emma thought she detected a hidden amusement, but his bow to Miss Plantagenet as he proffered his arm was a model of polite manners, and the conversation he offered as they walked toward the gate could not be faulted.

"Well, that *was* clever," admired Elvira as she and Emma dutifully followed, "for now the snide cat cannot tell tales on us."

In that surmise they were mistaken, as Emma found out the next morning. She was up early as usual, intending to take her habitual ride in the park, however, instead of Jem Bowls, she found Sir Julian waiting to accompany her. One glance at his set face showed that this was intended to be no pleasant outing, but, choosing to ignore his glowering countenance, she remarked brightly upon the pleasure of his unexpected company and rode beside him with unconcern as they trotted through the quiet streets.

"I shall gallop," she announced once through the gates and without giving her guardian the chance to comment, clapped her heels into the sides of her mount and dashed away across the grass at a reckless pace. The mare had settled into a steady, exhilarating gallop which seemed to leave her worries behind, when she was chagrined to notice an equine nose appear alongside her elbow. Out of the corner of her eye, Emma was aware of being overtaken as the head steadily advanced and drew slowly ahead. Although she knew that it was useless, she urged her own animal to greater effort. The mare responded willingly with a surge of power, but the gain was only momentary, and Sir Julian passed her, riding on to win the race easily.

Turning at the far end of the open space, he waited for her, resting easily in the saddle as she approached.

"Well?" she demanded, halting the mare a few paces in front of Sir Julian's horse.

Her guardian raised his eyebrows and regarded her coldly.

"Pray say what you have to," Emma said. "By your expression it is clear that you did not choose to ride with me for reasons of enjoyment, therefore you must wish to say something which you prefer me to hear privately. I take it that Miss Plantagenet has let drop a little insidious poison in your ear."

Sir Julian looked a little surprised at this attack but countered quickly, "I wonder, Miss Beringer, how you dare, not only to place yourself in a position of some question, but force Miss Plantagenet into the invidious position of having to accept Lord Devern's company?"

"I thought that she would come running to you!" commented Emma in a satisfied voice. "In the nicest way, of course, and only because she felt it her duty!"

"She—Miss Plantagenet did no such thing. She was very diffident about acquainting me with the matter, and only her thought for you persuaded her to mention your behavior."

"Indeed? Well, you really must be a ninnyhammer to believe such fudge. She told you to bolster her own self-esteem and importance."

"Unfair, Miss Beringer. To have sneaked away to an assignation with Lord Devern and to have been found in intimate circumstances with him in a trysting place is behavior no one could condone."

The heat of Emma's rage abruptly departed, leaving her cold and icy. "Is that what you believe—that I would behave so?" She stared at him, eyes like chips of blue glass. "Then, sir, I have nothing to say. I shall leave your house immediately."

About to ride away, she recalled her plan and, for Elvira's future happiness, swallowed her pride and, with shoulders drooping in clear despair, bravely smothered an audible sob.

"Emma!" cried her guardian, stricken.

With bent head and dejection expressed in every line of her body, she put her horse to a slow walk, conscious of the picture she presented as she headed toward the park gate. Almost, she whistled a funeral march, but managed to refrain.

"Miss Beringer—Emma, stay. If I was too harsh, I apologize."

"So I should hope," she said, lifting her head to meet Sir Julian's gaze.

Staring at the tears still sparkling on her eyelashes, he took a steadying breath and shook his head admonishingly. "Don't bamboozle me, kitten," he said, the harsh note gone from his voice.

Flicking the teardrops away with a finger, Emma accepted his offer of a handkerchief and blew her nose. "You really should listen to both sides of a tale," she remarked.

"Miss Plantagenet was doing only what she saw as her duty," he repeated, sounding defensive.

Lifting her head, she gave him a steady gaze. "Yes? Well, then I must accept it as being so, but to me it seems that the lady is prone to see the worst in things. I know that she often upsets Elvira, whom you know is very sensitive. Of course Miss Plantagenet may mean well, but Elvira is easily hurt. I will give Miss Plantagenet the benefit of doubt, but, even so, Sir Julian, I am not in need of a nursemaid. Miss Plantagenet may be as she puts it 'a nearly sister' to Elvira, but she is no such thing to me, and, to be honest, I resent her interference. I make no excuses and feel no need for explanation, except to say that I have no need to be ashamed of my behavior."

Sir Julian, who had listened gravely, searched her face and nodded thoughtfully. "Then nothing more will be said," he told her. "Let us not quarrel—"

"Indeed no, for I have only a few more days in your wardship, and to end our relationship in acrimony would be of all things foolish," she said ingenuously.

Her guardian agreed, an expression she could not read in his black eyes, despite which, Emma chattered brightly as they rode home. Sir Julian appeared thoughtful and unusually quiet during the journey. Leaving her at the entrance to the mews, he took her hand and conveyed it to his lips before riding off without a word.

Watching his tall, straight back, Emma slowly rubbed the back of her hand, a faint smile curving her mouth, before she rode under the gate and into the stable yard.

# Chapter Twelve

*A*n ordered calm prevailed in Cumberland Square for the next few days, even extending as far as Mrs. Melvin, who presented her card with some qualms and was gratified when, for the first time in weeks, she found that Lady Beauvale was at home.

"I do not believe in bearing grudges, my dears," remarked her ladyship comfortably. "Of course, I would not extend my friendship as far as Vivian Devern, but Lizzie Melvin is one of those poor creatures more put on than putting upon."

And so the girls were forced to endure the regulation twenty minutes of light gossip with as much fortitude as they could raise. The only item which caused them to prick up their ears was Mrs. Melvin's announcement that Lord Devern had been called away yet again on urgent business.

"Now, what can that be?" wondered Emma as soon as they had retreated to their own room.

"Personally I believe he is a smuggler," supplied Elvira. "He is always out of town on some business or other—look how you met him when Ju had the accident."

Having given the matter her attention, Emma shook her head. "I cannot see him as the mysterious leader of a gang," she remarked. "More a spy, perhaps . . . someone alone and answerable to himself."

"Oh, yes," breathed her friend. "He'd make a very good

sinister spy. Have you noticed how he always appears quietly *just* when you don't expect him?''

Emma laughed. "Like J—your brother! Who is forever popping up to discommode me.''

"I assure you that Ju is no spy,'' said Elvira huffily.

"No—and I daresay that Lord Devern is not either,'' agreed the other. "We are just looking for excitement because we are bored.''

"How I *wish* I was a man!'' mourned Elvira. "They are forever going to prize fights and shooting clubs and other places *we* cannot.''

"I don't think I would precisely care to attend a fight— but to go where and when one wished, *alone* and without bother would be above all marvelous!''

"Oh, *yes*—imagine just ordering a horse and setting out wherever one pleased without having to ask permission and make arrangements to be accompanied—''

"And all too often one is told that it is not considered suitable for young ladies.''

"Do you think Miss Plantagenet will cry off from your birthday party?'' asked Elvira, having followed the train of thought caused by the subject of their conversation.

"I hope not!'' cried Emma involuntarily, causing Elvira to open her eyes in surprise. "I mean—I wouldn't want to spoil Sir Julian's enjoyment, and, after all, they are *nearly* engaged!''

As Elvira looked disbelievingly at her, she hurried on, eager to change the subject. "What do you intend to wear?'' she asked, knowing that the inquiry was one sure to distract the other girl, and, to her relief, the conversation turned to Elvira's new gown, the precise hang of which was proving difficult even for the nimble fingers of the dressmaker.

The evening of Emma's birthday was wet, but the rain did not dampen her spirits, particularly as she had a new dark green evening cloak as yet unworn and, by good fortune, had chosen to wear a silver gauze dress with an emerald green underskirt.

Lady Beauvale had given her a pair of emerald earrings, and with these in her ears, she sat in front of her mirror and drew on the new pair of kid gloves, which had been Elvira's present, and smiled back at her reflection, well-pleased with her appearance.

"Oh, miss, you do look lovely!" Maria sighed, putting the finishing touches to her mistress's hair. "Like a fairy—all green and sparkly!"

Sir Julian was waiting at the foot of the stairs as she descended. For one moment the expression she read in his dark eyes made her catch her breath, before he veiled his thoughts and assumed a bland smile as he came forward to offer his hand.

"Happy birthday, Miss Beringer," he said formally, dropping a long, slender parcel into her hands.

The tissue paper parted to reveal the carved ivory sticks of a fan, and, flicking it out with a practiced gesture, Emma gazed in delight at a delicate painting on sea green silk. "It's beautiful," she breathed, "and just the right color."

"I had some help there," Sir Julian confessed. "Little sisters have their uses!"

"My dear, you look beautiful," exclaimed Lady Beauvale, hurrying forward. "Julian, does she not do us credit?"

Emma held her breath while dark eyes swept over her. Not hiding his admiration this time, Sir Julian made her a gallant bow.

"Miss Beringer, you will put all other females in the shade." Without looking round, he was aware that Elvira had pouted comically behind his back and went on blandly, "Except for the ladies of my family, who, without exception, have the good fortune to be born with outstanding good looks."

Elvira dimpled happily, and all three woman swept elaborate curtsies in unison.

"You have no idea how much searching of pattern books and how many visits to Bond Street it took, Ju," Elvira told her brother.

"Oh, I have little sister, I have," he murmured dryly. "And Aunt Di, may I say how fine you are looking—indeed, I am sure that there will be no finer looking set of ladies in the whole of London."

Lady Beauvale inclined her head graciously, pleased with the compliment and conscious that she was looking very well in a cream satin dress with a royal blue overgown.

"We must be going, children," she advised. "To be late is fashionable—to miss the first act altogether would make the rest of the play unintelligible. And we have yet to collect Miss Plantagenet, you know."

The landau was already waiting at the door, and the ladies set about disposing themselves and their finery on the leather seats. Lady Beauvale, sitting beside her nephew, eyed the two girls opposite with a worried expression.

"Julian dear," she said. "I think we should have used two carriages—there is very little room to spare, and you know how particular Miss Plantagenet is. She will not like being cramped."

"Nonsense, Aunt," replied Sir Julian robustly. "Elvira and Emma are both as slim as reeds, and Miss Plantagenet is no prize fighter. To take two carriages would merely have added to the traffic congestion outside the theater. We are much better as we are."

The travel arrangements did not entirely please their guest, who did not hide her lack of enthusiasm as Sir Julian handed her into the vehicle.

"Oh—I see we are all here," she murmured. "I had expected two carriages. I am to sit with the girls, to be sure—no, Lady Beauvale, do not move. I can manage quite well, I promise you."

Diana Beauvale, who had made no move, looked quite startled at the newcomer's suggestion.

"Pray be still, Lady Beauvale," put in Sir Julian quietly. "Miss Plantagenet would not dream of accepting your place, were you to offer it. She has too much sense of what is due to a lady of your age and rank."

Elvira nudged Emma with a sharp elbow while, after an initial pause, Jane Plantagenet made a show of high-minded agreement and settled herself beside the younger women. For the rest of the journey, which Emma would have preferred to spend gazing at the passing traffic and crowded, brightly lit streets and houses, she made polite conversation, somehow conveying that her good breeding prevented her from being "put out."

All the occupants of the landau were glad when their destination was reached and the carriage stopped outside the bright entrance to the Theater Royal. Here all was hustle and bustle, people were ascending the steps, while carriages arrived in a queue at the entrance. Sir Julian managed things with his usual aplomb, and his party was whisked up the winding, red-painted staircase and quickly found themselves in a box.

Emma had almost forgotten the heady smell of the theater and sniffed ecstatically at the scent of burning candles, greasepaint, and wet clothing.

"Phaw, what a fug!" exclaimed Elvira, forgetting to be ladylike in her distaste.

"One must forget one's sensibilities, dear Miss Leyton, in the cause of intellectual achievement," observed Miss Plantagenet soulfully.

Both girls gazed at her silently, unable to think of a suitable reply, and it was left to Julian Leyton to step into the breech and arrange the seating.

"Of course, Miss Beringer must have the best seat," agreed the paragon, as if giving up her position. "In a *family* I believe that a birthday counts above rank, do not you, Sir Julian?"

She spoke playfully, but the others in the party did not

smile, even Sir Julian appeared somewhat irritated by his intended's self-consequence.

"What a wretch," Elvira whispered in Emma's ear, "and what possessed her to choose such a color?"

Indeed the brilliant shade of mustard yellow, while fashionable, did little for Jane Plantagenet's sallow skin and nothing at all for her sandy hair. However, she gave every sign of being well-pleased with her appearance, nodding graciously to acquaintances, fanning herself languidly, and smiling in a restrained, genteel manner at Sir Julian's conversation.

The ladies had been too taken up with the excitement of their arrival to notice the play-board, and it was not until the auditorium lights had been snuffed out and the curtain up for several minutes that the precise nature of the play dawned upon Miss Plantagenet. Emma heard a stifled exclamation as Edmund Kean declared that now was the winter of his discontent and was aware of the yellow-covered shoulders stiffening into a rigid attitude. Studiously ignoring her companions, she gazed as if entranced at the stage, allowing nothing to draw away her attention, while Lady Beauvale and Elvira exchanged rapid whispers behind the cover of their fans.

Emma found the great actor as enthralling and his stage presence even more exciting than she had expected. Rapidly, she found herself engrossed in the play, her whole attention fixed on the stage and the magnetic personality of Edmund Kean as he portrayed the hunch-backed King Richard in so evil a manner that he was heartily hissed by the audience.

The curtains fell on the first act, and, as the candles were relit, Emma blinked and shook herself, as if awakening from a dream.

"Oh . . . was not that marvelous?" she cried ecstatically. "Surely you enjoyed it, Elvira."

"W-ell," murmured her friend doubtfully. "I may have— but the paragon most decidedly did not!"

Emma had almost forgotten her ploy and glanced at the other girl in some surprise before recalling her intentions, the very moment Jane Plantagenet declared her wish to go home.

"Oh, surely not!" Emma exclaimed. "I chose the play especially, Miss Plantagenet, knowing both how you enjoy culture and that the subject would interest you—you have told us all so many times of your ancestry. And after all, it cannot be often that two old antagonists meet in their descendants!"

Miss Plantagenet had risen, prior to leaving, but Emma's words caught her attention, and, frowning, she turned to the younger girl.

"Antagonists," she repeated. "What do you mean?"

"Why—that your and Sir Julian's ancestors met on Bosworth Field. Surely you know the story?"

Jane Plantagenet's eyes widened, and her nostrils flared, giving her the appearance of a startled horse. "What story?" she snapped.

"It's an old tale . . . so long ago that it hardly matters, except to people like you, Miss Plantagenet," Emma told her mendaciously, conscious of the listening silence of the other occupants of the box. "After all, it happened more than three hundred years ago, so what can it—"

"Miss Beringer, I insist that you make clear to what you are alluding," cried Miss Plantagenet, remembering her grammar even in her extremity.

Sir Julian had returned from his errand to retrieve his amour's cloak in time to hear the last exchange and now stepped forward. "I imagine she is referring to the legend that my ancestor was the means of unseating King Richard," he said as Jane Plantagenet gazed at him in undisguised horror.

Tottering back, she fell into her recently vacated chair, moaning faintly, with every sign of one who had received a fatal blow.

"To think . . . to hear such news," she cried in distraught

tones. "To allow me to hear in such a fashion—Sir Julian, how *could* you?"

Julian Leyton looked down at her. "I thought it no such great thing," he said, and sealed his fate with one sentence.

Miss Plantagenet struck a pose, one hand to her forehead, shielding her closed eyes. "No great thing?" she repeated in an anguished voice. "Sir Julian—how can you be so lacking in sensibility? When we have spent so many hours talking about my lineage? Discussing the convolutions of my pedigree?"

"You are mistaken, Miss Plantagenet, *you* talked and discussed. Doubtless you will remember that I was given very little opportunity of doing either."

Behind her, Emma felt rather than heard Lady Beauvale catch her breath.

"I believe that the first Sir Thomas Leyton was knighted by Henry Tudor," she said, adding this promising tinder to the conversation.

Miss Plantagenet drew herself up to her full height, angry red patches flaming in her cheeks. "Is this true?" she demanded in awful tones.

Sir Julian eyed her inscrutably. "That Harry Tudor dubbed Sir Tom?" he asked, with a lift of one eyebrow. "Yes—on the field of battle, for services rendered. I've always been rather proud of it."

"Sir Julian, I am *shocked*," proclaimed Jane Plantagenet. "I find that I have been sadly mistaken in your character. Far from being the superior man I thought, you are a *Philistine*." She gazed at Sir Julian with loathing before, turning to her hostess, she announced that she had a headache and wished to be escorted home.

Julian Leyton bowed and assured her of his service, settling her cloak about her thin shoulders with all the gallantry of a courtier.

"I hope they don't make up on the way," observed Elvira,

not bothering to hide her satisfaction as the box door closed behind them.

" 'Pon my word, I do not call that nice behavior," declared Lady Beauvale's mild tones. "If I believed for one minute, Emma, that you managed the whole affair, I would be seriously displeased. . . . However, I will admit that I think it is for the best. Jane Plantagenet and my dearest Julian would not have done. Someone more interested in the modern world would be more suitable for him. Oh dear!" she exclaimed, struck by a sudden thought. "Now he is a free man once more, he will be the object of all the matchmaking mamas again, and *that* will not please him. Life can be so difficult. I daresay he will take himself off to the country, and I do so like having a man around."

However, the next morning a note from a country solicitor arrived which threw the household into confusion, pushing the affair of Miss Plantagenet to the back of everyone's mind and relieving Emma from any lingering fear she had that Sir Julian intended seeking her out to read her a scold over her unfortunate choice of play.

Not long after breakfast, she was called to Lady Beauvale's sitting room and found the lady and her nephew awaiting her, looking very grave.

"My dear, pray sit down," began Diana Beauvale kindly. "I am afraid we have bad news for you. Your great aunt has died. This letter is from her man of business."

"Oh, poor Aunt Hodge!" exclaimed Emma, taking the chair Sir Julian held for her, unbidden tears springing to her eyes. "I hardly knew her—but she was my only k-kin."

"The lawyer says she was found in her bower and seemed just to have fallen asleep," put in Sir Julian, seeming to understand her wish that the old woman had not suffered. "Mrs. Hodge had just finished weeding a flower bed, and the housekeeper had taken out a tray of tea."

"I'm glad she was not ill. . . . But I wish I could have seen her again." Emma sounded unconsciously desolate, and Julian Leyton placed a comforting hand on her shoulder. "What happens now?" she asked. "Do I attend the funeral? Forgive me, but I do not know how to go on. I've never been an heiress before."

Sir Julian patted her shoulder. "I shall represent you. It would not do for a young lady to attend."

"You are quite right, Julian. I feel it would be most improper for Emma even to host the funeral meats. As her guardian, you can act in her place—"

"Dear Aunt Di, you forget that I am no longer in that happy position."

For a moment Lady Beauvale looked nonplussed, before furrowing her brow in thought. "You can be her representative," she announced triumphantly.

"If Miss Beringer so wishes," said Sir Julian gravely, a question showing clearly in the look he bestowed upon Emma.

"I would be grateful," she said frankly.

Lady Beauvale nodded approvingly. "Very sensible, my dear," she murmured.

"The only funerals which I have known have been military affairs, and, of course, those were very different from civilian ones, apart from being arranged by the army."

"Surely you did not attend?" exclaimed her ladyship, quite shocked by the idea.

"No—we females watched from behind the window shutters."

"So you would have me drive down to Hampshire? I daresay Mrs. Hodge's man of business will be there. There will be much to attend to and papers for you to sign."

"Of course I am sorry that your aunt is dead, Emma, but is it not exciting to be an heiress?" cried Elvira, when acquainted with the news.

"I hardly know," admitted her friend. "So far there has been little difference."

"You will be the object of fortune hunters," declared the

younger girl enthusiastically. "Every man with his pockets to let will immediately set about wooing you!"

And indeed, Mr. Frobisher was heard to declare on his way to answer the front door for the umpteenth time that if that dratted door knocker did not give over, then he would give notice, see if he did not. The drawing room mantle piece was decorated with condolence cards, and Emma found herself inundated with posies and nosegays from all manner of people.

"Who is Cecil Marmaduke?" she asked, examining the card attached to a somber arrangement of purple flowers and laurel leaves.

"The most awful old fogie," supplied Elvira. "He must be at least forty and lives with his mama, who spends her time cosseting his health between looking out for a meek wife, who will bring a goodly fortune, while taking second place to her mama-in-law."

"I think it rather ill mannered to send me flowers when we have never met," observed Emma, discarding the bouquet and going to look out across the garden.

Her simple black mourning dress flattered her fair coloring, making her hair appear more golden and her skin resemble the pale translucence of a pearl. Bathed in a shaft of sunlight, she was totally unaware of the effect created and stared at her friend in surprise when Elvira admitted to envy.

"What do you mean, Elvira?" she asked.

"It is not *fair*! Not only are you an heiress to an unspecified sum and your hair naturally golden—but black, which is usually the most fatal color to wear, actually suits you! It is *not* fair!" she repeated bitterly, making Emma laugh.

"Oh, Elvira, you are not exactly poor, and you are the prettiest girl I know," she told her.

"Yes," agreed the other, "but I look a positive fright in black!"

Emma laughed again but quickly became sober. "I— really do not know how to go on," she said unhappily. "It would have been so much easier if I had been an heiress from birth—or not one at all! I was quite used to the idea of being poor, indeed I hardly noticed it, and was resigned to becoming a governess. Now, all is changed and I feel . . . disturbed and cannot be easy.''

''As to that, you may be assured that Aunt Diana will have a care for you and tell you how to go about things. She is dependable and well-versed in such matters. For all Jane Plantagenet's show of knowledge, Aunt Diana, with her quiet manner, is far better able to set you right. She has no pretentions, you know.''

''I know. I am foolish to worry over trifles, but I have this feeling that life will never be as easy again.''

''You have no need to worry, we will all take care of you, Ju, Aunt Diana, and I,'' Elvira assured her robustly.

Smiling, Emma allowed herself to be comforted but privately still felt ill at ease. To her heightened imagination it seemed that the whole world knew of her changed circumstances and that she was the object of concern and gossip. Even a trip to the library was fraught with tension and supposed stares, and when, the day after Sir Julian arrived home from Hodge Hall, he escorted her to the London office of her aunt's lawyers, she felt almost ill with nerves.

''Bear up, kitten,'' he said as he handed her into the carriage, apparently aware of her turmoil of feelings.

''Everything is different,'' she told him miserably. ''All my life I've been on the move—first at various boarding schools, then with Papa. . . . I enjoyed following the drum. but since living here with you, I've discovered that stability and security can be enjoyable, too. And now I'm an heiress with responsibilities—everyone tells me to be on my guard against fortune hunters and false friends who will toady to me because of my wealth. I feel that no one will like me for myself anymore, only for what I possess!''

''You belittle yourself, my dear,'' Sir Julian told her. ''With your engaging personality you will always possess true friends. I am sorry if I have lectured you overly and put you too much on your guard. Wealth always attracts the wrong kind of folk, but there are others to whom your inheritance means nothing. Do you think it will make any difference to Johnnie Gray?''

Emma shook her head, smiling faintly. "Not in the slightest," she stated positively, but could not forebear pointing out the inordinate number of smiles and bows they were receiving.

"That is because I am such a popular member of Society!" said her companion with such a display of complacency that she burst out laughing and felt happier than she had done since hearing of her aunt's death.

The lawyer was a rotund man, dressed in dull black, which seemed to have acquired a patina of dust from the piles of deeds and documents which littered his room. Mr. Dunwoody had started life in Edinburgh and, after nearly forty years in London, still retained the precise accent of his youth.

"My dear lady," he said, having read the will to Emma, "*far* be it from me to do more than suggest, but my advice would be to sell the Hampshire property."

"Oh, no!" cried Emma, shocked. "I promised my aunt to look after it."

Horace Dunwoody sighed and cast his eyes to Heaven. "The legal profession is strewn with promises, Miss Beringer—none of them worth a pennyfarthing."

"I daresay," interrupted the heiress, "but I gave my word and intend to keep it."

Mr. Dunwoody looked to Sir Julian for help. "We cannot expect a worldly head upon young shoulders, can we, Sir Julian?" he remarked. "But in this case, dear lady, allow yourself to be swayed by older and wiser heads than yours."

Emma shook one of the heads mentioned. "No."

"Pray take my advice, Miss Beringer. An offer has been made—advantageous, in the extreme, I may say—for the property."

"Who by?" demanded Emma. "One of those old brutes who were so horrid to my aunt, I'll be bound!"

"The offer *was* made by Sir Joshua Twill, I see no reason why you should not know—he is very keen upon acquiring Hodge Hall. . . ."

"Indeed, and may I inquire, Mr. Dunwoody, what you advise me to do with the money from the sale?"

Thinking he had won, the lawyer settled back in his chair and, joining his short fingers together in an arch, contemplated them with satisfaction. "Invest, Miss Beringer, my advice would be to invest. I know of several firms which would be sound, paying good dividends."

Behind her, Emma heard Sir Julian move suddenly but spoke herself before he could interrupt. "I am sure you do, Mr. Dunwoody. And I am sure that they all pay a good commission," she drawled, making the lawyer look up quickly, suspecting for the first time that his client might not be an empty-headed, easily malleable female, after all. "As I have told you, I intend to keep the house. Also, I wish to transfer my business to the firm which deals with Sir Julian's estate. I am sure that you can take care of that for me. The firm is—?"

She turned to Julian Leyton, who supplied the name. "Snodgrass and Brown. Good day to you, Mr. Dunwoody."

With a brisk nod of her head, she turned and sailed out of the door which Sir Julian hastened to open for her, leaving behind a shaken and shocked man of business.

"Well done, Miss Beringer," murmured Julian Leyton, catching up with her on the front door steps. "I am glad you were so decisive."

"The fellow is a charlatan—anyone could see that."

"Indeed, I agree with your estimate but was afraid that he would take you in."

"Pooh! He reminded me of an army supplier my papa dealt with. I had *his* measure before I was in the Peninsula a sixmonth.'' She suddenly gave him a brilliant smile. ''I feel better,'' she announced brightly. ''Perhaps I shall like being an heiress after all.''

Sir Julian smiled encouragingly. ''If you deal with all your problems in a like manner, you will have no trouble,'' he commented.

Emma cocked her head to one side and looked up at him. ''You—did not interfere.''

''No. Did you want me to? I rather thought you had no need of my protection.''

''I am glad that you allowed me to settle my own affairs.''

''I had an idea that you would.''

On an impulse, she gave him her hand and was surprised when, instead of shaking it as she had intended, he carried it to his mouth and touched the back of it to his lips. Emma's heart fluttered pleasantly, and a delightful feeling of excitement coursed through her. Her gaze widened as Sir Julian smiled down into her eyes. For a moment they stood on the steps of the building oblivious to the interested stares of passersby, until suddenly recalled to their surroundings.

''L-let us walk,'' suggested Emma, and with a gesture Julian Leyton dismissed the waiting carriage.

Tucking her fingers into his elbow and holding them there, he escorted her along the busy thoroughfare. A little self-conscious of their promenade, Emma was somewhat surprised to discover herself inordinately happy. Even Sir Julian seemed content to saunter along, pausing equably to gaze into shop windows whenever his companion chose.

Suddenly a playbill stuck to a wall attracted her attention. The name Rourk sprang out as if printed in letters of flame. Emma was about to point it out to her companion but, recalling the circumstances of her last meeting with Sergeant Rourk and his company, decided not to bring the gaudily printed poster to Sir Julian's attention. Instead, she read it surreptitiously as they walked by, hoping that his gaze would not be attracted.

"A benefit performance, whatever is that?" asked Elvira when told the news.

"It means that the money will go to the Rourks. I believe it must signify that they are retiring and hope to make enough from the benefit to keep them for a while. They are performing the 'Sultan's Slave.' "

"The very play in which you took part!"

"Yes. Oh, Elvira, I must see them. The sergeant was always so kind, and in Portsmouth, you know, he did his best to help me. Nothing will stop me—I intend to visit them at Sadler's Wells Theater."

# *Chapter Thirteen*

*P*recisely two weeks after her visit to Mr. Dunwoody, Emma received a letter from Sir Julian's solicitors and found to her surprise that not only did she own Hodge Hall as expected but had also inherited a large amount of money, the estimated range of which quite took her breath away.

"My goodness—you *are* worth knowing!" commented Elvira, who had retrieved the sheet of paper after it fell from her friend's lifeless fingers and who had not scrupled to glance at the contents.

"I feel quite ill," murmured Emma faintly, tottering to a chair. "When I think of the economies my poor papa practiced to keep our heads above water—and now this! If only we had had a fraction of the amount, we'd have thought it riches indeed."

"You must admit that it is better than the dreary prospect of becoming a governess."

"Oh, *I* always intended to marry the handsome heir!" Emma assured her.

"They are hard to find. Ju is the only one I know of—" Elvira broke off to eye her friend with a considering gaze.

For a moment there was a taut silence before Emma went on, speaking quickly to hide her feelings. "How lucky he is, that you no longer have need of a governess. It would never do to have him in the claws of a grasping fortune hunter."

"N-o," Elvira agreed slowly, "but now he has escaped

the clutches of the paragon, he is free to choose where he will. . . ."

"Indeed," said Emma lightly. "Let us hope he makes a wise choice." Desiring to change the subject, she sat up abruptly with a show of a dawning thought. "I know—I have several guineas still left in my purse, which I was endeavoring to make last until I heard from the lawyers. Now that I have, there is no longer need to be frugal. There is a hat in Bond Street that I have been coveting. Shall we go shopping, you and I?"

Elvira agreed warmly as her friend had known she would, and shortly they set out, accompanied by Maria and Hetty. The hat was everything Emma had thought it to be: a beige concoction of silk and ostrich feathers, which sat on her head like a cloud of thistledown, sophisticated and flattering.

"It was made for you, madam," said the milliner, and Emma knew that she was right, buying it at once, only wishing that she could wear it and not have to wait until she was out of mourning.

Turning to the other girl, she urged her to choose something for herself. "A present," she said softly. "To show my affection, for you and Lady Beauvale have made me the happiest of girls."

Encouraged, Elvira chose a bonnet in her favorite pink, and together they decided upon a cap made of lace and silk flowers for Lady Beauvale. With that and scarves for Maria and Hetty, Emma's purchases were complete, and they set off slowly homeward, lingering along the street to gaze into the windows and admire the merchandise on display.

"Ladies—may I bid you good day?" said a voice, and, turning from their contemplation of the newest materials, they found themselves confronted by Lord Devern, bowing, hat in hand.

"My lord," they said, curtsying in unison.

"May I walk with you?" he asked punctiliously, but ruined the effect by taking their consent for granted and falling in beside them as they continued on their way. "My condolences, Miss Beringer," he continued. "I would have sent a card but felt that my contribution, even if acceptable, might well be lost beneath the amount you were bound to receive. There is no one so popular as an heiress."

"I am pleased to accept the sympathy of a friend," said Emma quietly.

Vivian Devern smiled down at her. "I am flattered," he said. "While I hoped you would think of me so, I know there are circumstances which must make friendship difficult between us."

A sharp cry from behind made them all turn in time to see Maria, who had received a hearty nudge from a laughing Hetty, stumble, catch her foot in her hem, and fall sideward into the path of a wagoner's dray. The heavy horse reared, neighing shrilly as the driver pulled on the reins in an endeavor to avoid the supine figure in the roadway. Lord Devern had presence of mind to plunge forward and seize the animal's bridle, bringing him down to earth and away from Maria, but even so the wheel of the cart passed over her leg with a sickening jolt.

Hetty's laughter turned to shrieks, and Elvira gave a faint scream as Emma ran forward and, heedless of the danger, caught hold of her maid's hands and dragged her from under the cart before the other wheel could follow the path of the first.

Kneeling beside Maria, Emma bent forward to sooth the girl, murmuring comfortingly as her hands felt along her leg. The strange angle told her that it was broken, and at once years of experience returned to her aid.

"Hetty!" she said sharply. "Stop that noise at once." The girl bit off a shriek in midflow and sobbed loudly, watching the kneeling Emma. "Good girl," Emma encouraged. "Go into that shop, and ask them for something long and firm—a broom handle would be ideal."

Elvira had crept nearer, regarding Maria with wide,

shocked eyes, and Emma at once put her to use. "The scarves we bought—can you see the packet?"

Elvira darted forward to retrieve it from the gutter and presented it to Emma, who smiled encouragingly as Lord Devern returned, having calmed the horse and assured the indignant driver that the accident had not been his fault.

Hetty appeared with a broom, complete with bristly head, which Vivian Devern knocked off before handing it to Emma. Using the scarves, she bound Maria's leg firmly to it, talking calmly and brightly all the while.

"What a brave girl you are, Maria dear. Just one moment and you will be a great deal more comfortable—yes, I know it hurts, and you are bearing up like a Trojan. There now, is that not better? My lord, if you could procure a carriage, we could makeshift to carry her home."

"I have engaged the dray already—it is empty, and its length would make it ideal as I imagine the girl should lie straight."

Emma smiled her thanks but kept her attention on her patient, who had begun to shiver.

"Would you be good enough to give me your coat?" she asked. "Maria needs to be kept warm, and we females have nothing of substance between us."

To his credit, Lord Devern hesitated only a moment before stripping off his blue superfine coat and wrapping it round Maria. His shirt sleeves and yellow waistcoat seemed very out of place in the middle of Bond Street, but as he supervised the invalid's removal to the dray he gave every sign of being unaware of the strange appearance he cut.

Emma climbed up beside the injured girl, cradling her in her arms against the worst of the shocks from the rutted road, while Lord Devern joined them, ready to support them both on the open-sided cart. Elvira scrambled up to sit with her legs dangling over the back, but Hetty swallowed her sobs long enough to declare that she would walk home as nothing would get her up on that contraption.

Several excited small boys ran behind, eager to see the last of the incident, and the shopkeeper, who had supplied the broom, marched alongside, carrying his broom head, intent upon retrieving his handle when it was no longer needed.

Lady Beauvale, who was just returning from shopping, met the ill-assorted procession on her doorstep and blanched visibly before, rising to the occasion, she pulled herself together and ordered the doctor to be sent for.

Taking matters literally into his own hands, Vivian Devern carried Maria indoors, Frobisher supporting her legs. Under Emma's guidance, they took her upstairs to the room she shared with the other maids and left her there in the care of Mrs. Hill, who surprised them all by showing a maternal side which no one had suspected.

Feeling that Maria was in good hands and knowing the difficulties that Lord Devern's entrance would cause, Emma left her there and followed him downstairs in time to hear him ask Frobisher if Lady Beauvale would see him.

"Come and be my advocate," he invited wryly as Emma descended the last few steps.

"Of course," she agreed readily, "but I doubt . . . ."

To her surprise the butler returned at that moment and, begging his lordship to follow, led the way to Lady Beauvale's sitting room.

"Ah, Emma," said Diana Beauvale calmly as they entered, "I am glad you felt able to leave the invalid." She looked at Lord Devern and raised her eyebrows, saying coolly, "My Lord," as he made a formal bow.

"My apologies, Lady Beauvale, for making such an unauthorized entry."

For the first time in their acquaintance Emma could see that Vivian Devern was less than confident and felt called upon to ease the difficult moment.

"Maria fell under a horse, Lady Beauvale, and Lord Devern was most brave and helpful," she said simply. "We could not have managed without him."

180

"I only did what anyone would—"

"Stopping a runaway is beyond the usual range of good manners."

He smiled at her but spoke to the other woman. "Miss Beringer does not mention her own place in all this. At one time I recall seeing her diving under the cart wheel to pull the injured girl free—without a care for her own safety, I would say. . . . However," he turned to his hostess, speaking with an obvious effort and no attempt to hide the discomfort he was feeling, "I am pleased to have this opportunity of renewing our acquaintance, Lady Beauvale. I know that I behaved badly some years ago and have very much regretted it ever since."

"That, Lord Devern, is understandable," her ladyship told him severely, but seemed prepared to listen to him.

"I was a callow youth at the time," he pointed out, almost diffidently. "And, while youth is no excuse in itself, I can only admit that I had not the upbringing a loving family would bestow. I snatched at what happiness I could."

Lady Beauvale's look softened, and she extended her hand, saying quietly, "The past cannot be forgotten, Vivian, but time does ease the anger and disappointment. We can never return to our former relationship, but it is time our enmity was at an end."

"And Ju?"

"Julian felt betrayed and is known to be singularly unforgiving. I speak only for myself, I am afraid."

"And—Eleanor?" Lord Devern spoke almost painfully and seemed suddenly intent upon a knot in the floorboards at his feet. "Is she happy?"

Diana Beauvale seemed to hesitate before replying. "I believe so—the . . . episode spoiled the first years, but now, with a growing nursery and the parish work, she and Charles have reached something like peace."

"You should have let us be," Vivian Devern said bitterly.

"You both would have been ostracized. *You*, my lord, may not have cared, but Eleanor could not have born it."

"What of her now? Shut away in some country parsonage."

"She is the respected wife of a loved vicar." Lady Beauvale spoke severely. "Love does not conquer all, Lord Devern, remember that. It is a very overrated commodity and very seldom lasts longer than a year or two. Kindness, liking, and respect are a better foundation, believe me."

He bowed and smiled. "I will bear it in mind," he promised, with a return to his usual manner.

Lady Beauvale nodded and smiled slightly in return. "I am glad we have had this little talk."

Accepting his dismissal, Vivian Devern stood up and bowed to both the ladies, acknowledging Emma's presence for the first time in several minutes. "Your servant, ladies," he said, and took his departure.

"Well, Emma dear," said the older woman when they were alone. "You had best hear the whole sorry tale, since you have heard so much."

"I have no wish to pry—"

Diana Beauvale seemed not to hear, her expression far away as she recalled events which had taken place almost a decade ago. "Julian, Vivian, my daughter, and Charles Lindsey all grew up together. Charles and Eleanor had an understanding since quite an early age. He was a quiet boy destined for the church, like his father, and I knew he would make a good husband. Vivian left on a tour of the Continent, and while he was away Charles and Eleanor were married, and I came to London to keep house for Julian. Upon his return, Vivian presented a glamorous, suave appearance, so different to poor Charles, who was now his father's curate. . . . My Eleanor took leave of her senses, caring nothing for her husband or position. She and Lord Devern were the talk of the county, and finally they ran away together. You may imagine my feelings—I prevailed upon Julian to go after them and bring Eleanor back. Which he did. Of course things were not the same—Eleanor had lost Charles's faith and her own happiness.''

''Oh, how sad,'' murmured Emma.

Lady Beauvale again appeared not to hear her, going on reflectively, ''The boys fought, of course. . . . It is always so much worse when friends discover feet of clay, and Vivian seems since to have gone out of his way to demonstrate his indifference to Julian's dislike.''

''Perhaps that was because he cared,'' suggested Emma thoughtfully.

Diana Beauvale looked at her. ''I've often wondered,'' she admitted. ''Maybe this accident is all for the best—though poor Maria will not think so. Things could never be comfortable between Eleanor and Charles and Lord Devern. . . . But it would be pleasant if I could acknowledge him in the street. He was such a charming little boy—I was very fond of him. . . .''

Vivian Devern obviously agreed with her sentiments, for the next day a posy arrived for the injured Maria, accompanied by a delicate corsage for Lady Beauvale. Both recipients were pleased with the offering, Maria insisting upon it being placed beside her bed, and, while Diana Beauvale did not wear the spray, she touched the soft grayish foliage with a finger and smiled softly.

''What is it? It looks like an herb,'' Emma asked curiously.

''It's rosemary—for rememberance, according to Shakespeare,'' she was told as the lady retired to her boudoir, sniffing gently at the herb, a reminiscent smile playing across her face.

''Well! Do you think he is about to be reinstated?'' wondered Elvira, when acquainted with this interesting happening.

''I rather think he hopes to be,'' said Emma, and, during the next days, her surmise proved correct.

Lord Devern presented his card, was admitted, and inquired kindly after the invalid, his conversation so unexceptional that it could disturb no one, and when after the regulation length of time he took his leave, Lady Beauvale could only comment upon the correctness of his manner.

A few days later, finding Captain Gray upon the front steps, he joined him, and both were admitted together. The rifleman had come expressly to make promised arrangements to take the girls to an exhibition of Greek art, and upon hearing this, Vivian Devern expressed so great an interest that he could not but be included in the outing.

"That was very well managed, to be sure," commented Emma dryly when she and Elvira were alone.

"Do you think it was contrived?" asked the other innocently. "He seemed very interested in the ancients. He spoke very knowledgeably about Homer and Socrates—and he knew all the gods by name."

"As would anyone with a classical education. I think he was bluffing!"

"But why? Oh!" Elvira's eyes widened in sudden understanding. "Do you think he is a fortune hunter?" She gasped. "You know more of his financial position than I—"

"Well, I've never heard of his part of the family in straightened circumstances—of course the Melvins are never more than able to manage." A slow smile spread over her face as she considered her friend thoughtfully. "Perhaps he has formed a *tendre* for you," she suggested teasingly.

"How exciting," said Emma. "I must own to a little disappointment that so far no one has confessed to an overwhelming passion for me. I did expect at least one declaration of undying love, and the nearest I've come to it is Cecil Marmaduke's purple and laurel leaf!"

Elvira's thoughtful expression deepened. "There was that exotic posy from Lord Devern," she pointed out slowly.

"And forget-me-nots from Freddie," her friend countered quickly.

"Not in the same class," declared Elvira. "Oh, Em—Ju would be *so* annoyed!"

This brought up Emma's head. "Your brother is not my guardian now," she said.

"I know—but cannot you care for him in the slightest? It is really very odd, but over this summer I have become quite fond of him, where I used to think him a dead bore. Indeed, I seem to think kindly of most people nowadays."

She paused, her expression far away, her thoughts so obviously elsewhere that Emma could not refrain from asking if Johnnie Gray was included in her kindly thoughts.

"Oh, yes," was the simple reply, accompanied by a sunny smile. "I find him so kind and responsible—of course a soldier would have to be strong and resourceful. One feels so safe in his company. . . . I like a man to be sure of himself and yet gallant."

Emma restrained herself from commenting upon the obvious differences to be found between soldiers and poets, instead, agreeing that she, too, was looking forward to their educational outing.

The day chosen for the expedition was blustery and cold, heralding the arrival of autumn. However, this did not deter the ladies; Elvira happily arraying herself in a new pelisse of apricot velvet, while Emma, having consulted Lady Beauvale upon the conventions attached to the wearing of black, was assured that half-mourning was acceptable and so was wearing a dark gray coat and bonnet with sweeping black ostrich plumes and a paler gray gown.

When the men waited upon them, Johnnie Gray was resplendent in his green regimentals, and Lord Devern sported a blue jacket and yellow buckskins of such magnificent cut that Emma lost all doubts about his wealth, instead acknowledging to herself that they were both handsome enough to make Elvira and herself the envy of other females.

Upon arriving at the exhibition rooms, the group found

themselves amid a crowd of people, some intent upon intellectual stimulus, others wishing both to see and be seen.

"What a squeeze!" exclaimed Elvira, grateful for the protection of Captain Gray's arm.

"Everyone is here," agreed Emma, nodding and smiling to friends and acquaintances. "Even the paragon—but who is her escort?" she asked, indicating the center of the room where Miss Plantagenet was holding court.

Elvira raised herself on tiptoe to view the small man who barely came to Jane Plantagenet's shoulder, but who nevertheless hung avidly on her every word as she read from her brochure and indicated points of especial interest with a knowledgeable finger.

"Why, that's Cecil Marmaduke," she said.

"Well, I take that as very cool!" complained her friend in righteous indignation. "Only a week ago he was sending me flowers, and now I find he has already found himself another lady friend!"

As if aware of their gaze, Miss Plantagenet looked up and, meeting their eyes, bowed gravely before continuing her discourse.

"Are you out of favor?" inquired his lordship, puzzled. "Miss Plantagenet seems rather cool."

"Emma took her to see *Richard the Third*!" Elvira told him, smiling wickedly.

"Bravo!" acknowledged Johnnie Gray.

"So . . . I take it that the expected announcement will not be forthcoming," said Vivian Devern thoughtfully.

"I'd say Marmaduke's ring is as good as on her finger," murmured the rifleman, watching the attentions of the little man.

"Poor Ju," drawled Lord Devern. "Pray give him my sympathies when next you see him."

"I do not think him distraught," Elvira said sharply.

"I think that Lord Devern was teasing," Emma told her softly.

"Shrewd, Miss Beringer," commented his lordship, speaking for her ears alone. "There is a particular statue in the far room which I wish you to see. I daresay the crowd will not be so great there—"

Emma was pleased to find that he was right. The farther room, although smaller, was almost empty of people, and she sank thankfully down on one of the seats provided for weary viewers. Gazing round, she found that the displayed exhibits consisted of rather unexceptional heads and vases.

"Where is the statue?" she asked.

Vivian Devern looked vague. "I think it must have been moved," he told her.

Realizing that the non-existent statue had been a ploy to obtain her company, Emma raised her eyebrows and regarded her companion inquiringly.

"You are right," he confessed at once with engaging candor as he seated himself beside her. "There never was a statue—I merely wished to have you to myself. To say that you have my admiration and respect," he hurried on before she could speak. "And wish above all things that we could be friends."

Rather gratified by this declaration, Emma looked on him kindly and even allowed him to take her gloved hand.

"Sir Julian—" she murmured, thinking of the quarrel between the two men.

"Is no longer your guardian," was the quick response as Lord Devern misunderstood her misgivings.

"No," she agreed, "but he is still a dear friend. And I would do nothing to upset Lady Beauvale."

"I would not ask it," Lord Devern assured her. "I believe that Lady Beauvale can find it in her heart to feel a little kindness for me. And Ju was once my friend. . . . Dear Miss Beringer, you are a favorite with the Leytons, I only ask that you use your influence—our quarrel began years ago. I much regret my youthful misdemeanors and wish them undone . . . or forgiven."

"I believe that lives were altered—and not for the better."

"I see you have already been told the tale. I will add nothing, except to ask you to believe that I was not totally to blame. I was young and in love and thought that nothing else mattered. I thought we could survive the gossip and hostility. . . . I was romantic enough to think that love would conquer all. Eleanor found that she needed approbation. . . ."

Emma reflected that this was not precisely how she had interpreted the story told to her, but said nothing, accepting that everything had various sides to it, depending upon the viewer.

Lord Devern seemed to have finished his plea for aid and turned to other things, remarking lightly upon her state of half-mourning.

"Lady Beauvale thought it quite acceptable—of course I shall still live quietly. I may accept small dinner parties but no balls or routes for a while, yet."

"Do you intend to live in Hodge Hall?"

"I should like to very much, but Lady Beauvale thinks me a little young to live alone—and of course it *is* rather cut off and remote."

"Is it closed up?"

Emma nodded. "My aunt managed with few servants, and those had grown old in her service. Sir Julian paid off all save the housekeeper and a handyman who are looking after the house for me."

Lord Devern smiled at the unconsciously wistful note in her voice. "You need a husband," he pointed out casually.

Emma raised startled eyes to his face but was saved from the need to reply by the arrival of Elvira and her escort.

"There you are! I almost believed you had gone home."

"We would do nothing so reprehensible," answered Vivian Devern, offering her his seat. "When do you return to your regiment?" he asked the soldier.

Only Emma noticed Elvira's quick intake of breath and

the anxious glance she gave to Johnnie Gray as he answered the question.

"I have another four weeks on furlough," he said, his eyes falling as if by accident upon Elvira's downcast face.

"This damned war," Lord Devern emitted lightly.

"Just so," agreed the other man, while Elvira dipped her head even lower and hid beneath the brim of her bonnet.

"It can't go on much longer!" exclaimed her friend. "I cannot remember a time when we weren't at war with Boney."

"He's met his match in General Wellesly," Captain Gray assured her confidently. "Old Nosey is a better man than he is and will show him so, if only a confrontation could be arranged. As it is, we have most of his army over here as prisoners. If it goes on long enough, he'll have no army left."

Vivian Devern straightened abruptly, looking above the rifleman's red head. "I believe the paragon approaches," he said warningly, and with one accord, as if previously arranged, the others rose and made their way out of the other door and back onto the street.

That afternoon was Diana Beauvale's "at home," and knowing she would be busy with her callers, Emma had decided that no better time would present itself for her intended visit to Sergeant Rourk. Knowing that Johnnie Gray had promised to call with the loan of a book, she refused Elvira's half-hearted offer to accompany her and set out mid-afternoon, when her absence would be masked by the influx of Lady Beauvale's many acquaintances.

Her costume had given cause for thought; that of a lady in mourning would give rise to interest, but eventually she had decided that if she wore her dark gray pelisse and removed the black ostrich feathers from her bonnet, she would resemble nothing so much as a respectable governess going about her legitimate business.

And so she was clothed in drab respectability as she made her way to Sadler's Wells Theater. One or two of the more discerning males eyed her with interest as she passed, but in general, few spared her more than a passing glance.

By good fortune she found Sergeant Rourk standing on the steps of the stage door, deep in thought, sucking the top of his silver-knobbed cane, bearing every sign of one in deepest gloom.

"Why, Sergeant," she cried, struck by his attitude, "whatever is the matter?"

Looking up, he gazed at her blankly for a moment, before his face lit up with the dazed expression of one who was confronted by a miracle. "By the Faith, if it isn't Miss Beringer!" he cried, leaping forward to seize her hands. "A gift from the gods—the answer to my prayers!"

Rather taken aback by such an enthusiastic welcome, Emma showed her surprise, and, recovering, Tom Rourk looked at her more closely, taking in her dark clothing.

"Have you lost someone close to you?" he asked contritely. "And me only thinking of my own troubles and how, maybe, you could help out."

"My mother's aunt," Emma told him. "I only met her once, but we were friends, and I'm sorry she is dead." She looked at him more closely, noting the scarcely concealed air of anxiety. "What is troubling you?"

The sergeant clutched his head with a gesture worthy of Edmund Kean himself. "Our benefit is to take place tomorrow night!"

"Yes. I saw the notices—that is what brought me here."

"Oh, merciful providence! Guardian angel, thank you!"

Beginning to have a suspicion of what was coming, Emma looked at him severely. "Sergeant Rourk," she said, "I fail to see why my presence should fill you with such happiness."

Replacing his look of exultation with that of hopeful entreaty, he took her arm. "There is a coffeehouse a few doors along," he said. "Let me offer you a cup of refreshment, and we can talk the while."

Standing her ground, Emma inquired if it was respectable and only on receiving his affirmative allowed herself to be led there. Once inside and seated at a discrete arrangement of high-backed settle and narrow table which presented an area of privacy, she inhaled the pleasant aroma of coffee and chocolate while examining her surroundings.

"Well, Sergeant," she said at last, when he seemed unwilling to speak. "What have you to say to me?"

Tom Rourk looked quickly at her and away again, making a great show of taking his handkerchief from his sleeve to wipe the coffee from his lips.

"A favor, Miss B," he said at last. "I wouldn't ask, but matters are desperate—my Molly has broken her leg. She vows that she'll play the princess come what may—but whoever heard of a princess in plaster? It wouldn't do at all." He looked at her with an expression of entreaty. "Dear, Miss Beringer, *could* you find it in your heart to repay the favor I did you in Portsmouth and play the princess for me? We'll be ruined if we miss this benefit."

# Chapter Fourteen

*E*mma choked into her coffee, and rising to his feet, the sergeant reached over the table to thump her back.

"It isn't a breeches part," he reminded her earnestly. "You wouldn't have to show your legs."

Red-faced and with streaming eyes, Emma stared at him, struggling for breath.

"I wouldn't ask, Miss B, but it's urgent," the actor went on. "We need the benefit—of course Mrs. R is in the full flush of womanhood, but neither of us is getting younger, and with a bit of money, we could set up business. An acting school, we thought, with lodgings for the folk who tread the boards . . . all very tasteful and nicely done. My Molly fancies presiding over a salon, you see."

He looked at Emma so hopefully that she felt called upon to agree. "I am sure she would do it very well—" she began, intending to refuse gently, but was interrupted by the man opposite.

At her words he had brightened, seizing her hand and pumping it enthusiastically up and down. "You'll do it, then?" he cried, totally misunderstanding. "Oh, what a friend! Miss B, you're an angel, that's what you are." Flinging money on the table, he pulled her to her feet, almost pushing her along in his eagerness to leave the coffeehouse. "Come and tell my ladywife yourself, Miss Beringer. She will be overwhelmed, I can tell you."

Somehow, Emma found herself back at the theater and

being urged up a narrow flight of dark, twisting stairs until they arrived at a heavy green-painted door, which bore the signs of many hasty entries, being much chipped and marked.

Sergeant Rourk flung it open with a fine gesture. "My dear," he declaimed, pushing Emma ahead, "look who we have here."

Molly Rourk, who had been lying full-length on a dilapidated sofa bed, raised her head and, recognizing her visitor, moaned faintly, making little shooing movements with her hands. "The silk ear!" she groaned and sank back.

Her husband sent Emma a conciliatory glance. "Miss Emma, my love, has agreed to play the princess for us," he announced, making Emma feel like a bone being offered to a temperamental dog.

Molly Rourk opened her eyes. "Have you asked Doll Harper?" she asked.

The sergeant shook his head. "Not to be found."

"Amelia Bell?"

"She's too old and scrawny—whoever heard of a princess being played by a six-foot beanpole?"

"Sally Buckingham?" Mrs. Rourk persisted.

"Out of town." Tom Rourk answered shortly, growing impatient. "There's no one, I tell you, Molly gal. It's Miss B or no benefit!"

Growing tired of being discussed as if she were not there, Emma made a movement drawing attention to herself. Molly Rourk gazed at her speculatively before giving a brilliant smile and throwing wide her arms in an expansive gesture.

"*Dear* child," she cried thrillingly. "A scepter in our hour of need! A veritable angel of mercy. How kind! How brave! How valiant!"

"I'm really not at all—" Emma murmured, floundering under the flood of adjectives.

"Nonsense!" cried the actress. "You will be magnificent, a veritable Sarah Siddons. Did I not always describe you so?"

Emma was amused. "Well, no, madam, you did not. I believe you described me as a sow's purse when last we met."

Molly Rourk laughed gaily, wagging one finger at her listener. "We actors, you know," she said roguishly. "You must allow us a little license. I remember you as my most promising pupil. If it had not been for that unfortunate little accident with my turban, we would have played to full houses for a week—I know it!"

Emma doubted this, but the old excitement began to fill her, and looking at the two hopeful faces turned to her, she knew that she would not refuse owing, as she did, the return of a favor.

"I'll do it," she said. "Let me take the book home with me. . . . But how can we rehearse? Lady Beauvale, with whom I stay, would never allow me to step on a stage."

Accepting this, Sergeant and Mrs. Rourk put their heads together. "We are booked for the day after tomorrow," she was told. "Can you be word perfect by tomorrow afternoon, and can you contrive to be here then?"

"I don't know. . . ." Emma began, but seeing the despair on their faces, hurriedly agreed.

"Three of the clock—and we will take you through it," the sergeant said, running his fingers through his thinning hair. "Oh Miss B, do not, I beg of you, fail us."

"I won't," Emma vowed and knew that come what may, she would keep her word.

Scurrying across the wide expanse of Covent Garden, she had the uneasy feeling of being watched, but on scrutinizing her surroundings she could see no one she knew, only a group of gentlemen in the far corner, deep in conversation in the entrance to the coffeehouse.

Reaching Cumberland Square in safety, she rang the bell and slipped inside as soon as the door was opened, returning Frobisher's scandalized expression with a brilliant smile and was about to run upstairs when the study door opened and Sir Julian appeared.

"Good afternoon," he said pleasantly, crossing to her side. "It seems so long since I saw you, that I half believed you to have been a figment of my imagination."

"A very solid figment," she could not refrain from pointing out, untying the long strings of her bonnet and removing it.

To her surprise Sir Julian took her chin in his hand and, turning her face to the light, examined it gravely. Standing as patiently as she could, she returned his regard, growing a little pink under his scrutiny.

"You are looking better," he announced. "You have been a little pale lately."

At last her chin was free, but instead of stepping back, she stood still, an expression of blank surprise on her upturned face.

"Miss Beringer—Emma?" There was a puzzled, questioning note in his voice, which brought her back to her surroundings.

She lowered her gaze, blinking rapidly and hoping that her sudden realization had not been noticed. "H-have you been to the Greek exhibition?" she asked quickly to hide her confusion. "Elvira and I vastly enjoyed it."

"So she tells me. I understand that Vivian Devern accompanied you both."

"And Johnnie Gray," she answered, aware of the defensive note in her voice. "You can have no exception, surely?"

"I will not say that it pleases me." Julian Leyton stepped nearer again and took her hand in his. "Have a care, Emma," he said softly. "Devern has hurt one of my family already—oh, yes, I know it was years ago, but I would not have it happen again—especially to you. . . ."

Aware of the growing tumult of emotions that had come with the realization that her feelings for her erstwhile guardian were far from impersonal, Emma became flustered, afraid that he would recognize the symptoms of her unexpected malady. Intensely frightened that he would be amused by her fragile emotions, she hastily assumed a world-weary air.

"La, sir," she said languidly. "I vow that you sound like a bore. Remember, pray, that you no longer have care of me." And at once could have bitten her tongue.

Sir Julian dropped her hand and withdrew a pace, his expression cold and remote. "My apologies," he offered coolly. "I had thought us friends enough to give and accept advice. I see I was mistaken."

With a frosty bow he left her, and Emma, who would have given much to recall her ill-chosen words, retired to her room to calm her shattered equilibrium. Deciding to fill her life with good works rather than contemplate uneasy thoughts, she took a book and went to entertain Maria, who was fast growing impatient of her invalid's life.

"Ooh, miss," she greeted her mistress. "Whatever's wrong? You look as if you'd lost sixpence!" Looking more closely, she saw Emma's pink nose and wet eyelashes. "Here, you're not taking a nasty chill, are you?"

"I'm perfectly all right," Emma assured her, ignoring the disbelieving sniff this information produced. "I've brought a book to read."

Maria seemed unimpressed. "What is it?" she inquired suspiciously. "I don't care for those where nothing happens except folk prosing on."

"You'll like this one," Emma promised, opening the covers of *Northanger Abbey*. "It's about a girl who goes to Bath and likes just the kind of Gothic novel you do."

That night Emma retired early, taking "The Sultan's Slave" with her and when she awoke next morning, despite being heavy-eyed and tired, was fairly confident that she knew her part.

"Can you cover for me?" she asked Elvira over breakfast and quickly made known the reason.

Elvira gazed at her wide-eyed and open-mouthed. "You

*can't!*" she protested as soon as she could speak. "Aunt Diana would never allow it."

"Precisely—that is why I have no wish to make my intentions public," Emma replied.

"Ju would be furious," went on the other girl, sounding torn between fear and relish.

"I know," agreed Emma, hanging her head, "but I must do it—the Rourks were kind to me when I had nothing. I cannot fail them now. The benefit is really important to them—"

"If it got about that you had appeared on the stage, you would be ruined!" stated her friend positively. "And Heaven knows what Julian would say—or do!"

"Don't keep on about your brother," cried Emma, momentarily losing her attempt at calm. "I *know* he will be angry if he finds out. . . . And I shall just have to hope that he does not."

Elvira sighed heavily. "*Just* when I thought things might be going well between you two—with the paragon out of the running, I quite thought that you might become my sis—"

"Elvira!" cried Emma. "How can you say so? The thought has never entered my head."

"Pooh! *I've* seen you both looking at each other when you've thought no one would notice. *And*, don't tell me that you did not arrange that business at the theater, for I will not believe you!"

Flushing, Emma looked away. "I did not *precisely* engineer it," she protested. "I'll agree that I may have pushed things along a little, but purely because I felt her the wrong person for Sir Julian."

"How noble," murmured the other, "and how innocent you look."

The teasing note in Elvira's voice made Emma smile faintly, and under the other's quizzing gaze, she finally gave a little nod. "Well—perhaps it was *partly* for myself—but the truth is that until yesterday I did not realize that I cared

*197*

for him. He took my chin and turned my face up and—suddenly my heart was pounding, and I felt quite faint.''

Elvira nodded in agreement. "Just how I feel every time I see Johnnie," she said with satisfaction.

Emma looked up. "What about Bevis?" she could not forebear asking curiously.

"Bevis?" repeated Elvira, as if she had forgotten the name. "Oh, *Bevis*." She considered before shaking her dark curls decidedly. "No—nothing like. I think I must have been in love with the idea. What a silly girl I was. I can quite see how annoyed Ju must have been—and what a good thing he refused us leave to marry. Imagine, I could have been wed by now. . . . And dear Johnnie would have been denied me, and I him!"

She looked about to cry at the thought, and Emma hastily repeated her original question. "I don't want you to accompany me—indeed, I would rather you did not, for it would distract me," she added candidly. "But if we could leave the house together . . . ?"

Elvira looked thoughtful. "I have a fitting for a new gown," she admitted slowly.

"The very thing!" cried Emma before she could alter her mind. "You could drop me off at the theater, and I'll make my own way back. With luck no one except us will be any the wiser."

"What about tomorrow night? How will you account for your absence for a whole evening?"

"I'll think of something," said Emma, more positively than she felt. "Anyway, it won't matter afterward."

"It will if Ju finds out," her companion muttered darkly. "He will not take kindly to it, you know."

"Then we shall have to hope that he never knows. Once it is over, I will have paid my debt—and that will be an end to it."

In reality she was unhappy at the thought of Sir Julian's reaction to her escapade, knowing that he would not approve and suspecting that he would have little understanding of her agreeing to such an undertaking. While suddenly finding herself wishing for his approbation, she was in the position of having to take a course of action which she knew would do nothing but bring his censure down upon her, and she felt decidedly miserable at the prospect.

With a few moments to spare before luncheon, she ran up to the attic with the intention of amusing Maria but was surprised to hear sounds of laughter coming from the open door. Peering curiously into the room, she was surprised to see Sir Julian sitting on the invalid's bed, while a game of spillikins was the cause of the merriment.

Hearing her entrance, two laughing faces were turned to her, and she was invited to join the game. Not having played since she left school, Emma was somewhat rusty and found herself beaten in acquisition of spillikins by both Maria and Sir Julian, who had a well-developed expertise in the game abetted by a very steady hand. Finding themselves both about to be well and truly trounced, the two girls took to cheating and, by a little judicial nudging and shaking at the appropriate moment, managed to acquire a less shameful score.

The vigorously beaten luncheon gong sounded through the house, and to almost universal disappointment, Hetty arrived bearing the invalid's tray.

"Oh, I enjoyed that ever so! I did, indeed," Maria said earnestly.

"We'll come again," Sir Julian assured her. "But I, for one, am in need of my lunch. And Mrs. Frobisher would never forgive us if you did less than justice to her lamb cutlets and the apple pie."

With a wave and a promise to return, Emma preceded Julian Leyton downstairs and was somewhat surprised to find herself drawn into an inconspicuous corner of the hall and detained in the shadows.

"Miss Beringer—Emma, we must talk," Sir Julian began, retaining her hand and speaking with a hesitancy which was unusual. "I feel—that the fates have conspired against us, making us antagonists when we—when *I*, and I hope you, would rather be on friendly terms."

Emma longed to agree with him but found herself tongue-tied. Taking her silence for consent, Sir Julian went on, "I am aware that I am not the easiest of men, and, to be honest, I have found my term of guardianship onerous—" He gripped her fingers tighter as she turned an indignant gaze upon him. "Not because I disliked the duties or their cause," he hastened to reassure her, "but because as your guardian, I had, of honor bound, to keep proper distance."

Emma was still silent, staring up at him wide-eyed and amazed, her quick breath ruffling the lace of her collar. Emboldened by her stillness and lack of remonstrance, Sir Julian smiled down into her wide blue eyes. "Dearest girl, it is time we became better acquainted," he said, "and with that in mind I have booked a box at the theater tomorrow night. Elvira and Lady Beauvale will accompany us—"

Emma's heart bounded at first with delight and then with dismay. "The theater!" she cried and, in her agitation, could only think of one theater. "Oh, no—I cannot. Do not ask me!"

Turning aside to hide her face, she pulled her hand free, and Sir Julian made no attempt to retain his grip.

"I—see," he said quietly. "I am sorry if I have caused you distress. I had hoped that you returned—" Pulling himself up abruptly, he closed his mouth on the words he had been about to say, instead finishing formally, "My apologies, Miss Beringer, I see I was mistaken."

Emma blinked back the tears that threatened to fall and shook her head. "No—no, do not think, I beg of you . . . It is only that I *cannot*!"

"Pray do not upset yourself. I see that I should not have spoken. Let us forget that this interlude ever happened."

The smile that accompanied this speech nearly broke her resolve, and she was within an ace of confessing all and begging for his help, but, determined to put an end to the embarrassing episode, Sir Julian tucked her hand into his elbow and led her across the hall, and the moment was lost as they joined the others for the midday meal.

"Well, I cannot think of an excuse for tomorrow evening," commented Elvira, sounding quite cross, as they left Cumberland Square that afternoon. "Aunt Diana will think it most odd, especially now that Ju has booked a box at the theater—"

"Not Sadler's Wells?" cried Emma, voicing a fear that had worried her for hours. "*Surely* you are not going there?"

She sounded so panic-stricken that Elvira hastened to re-assure her. "No, no, never fear, we aren't going to be in the audience for your benefit. But, what *are* you going to do, Em?"

"I don't know," admitted the other distractedly. "I can't think of a single valid reason for being absent for the evening. I'll have to arrange to be kidnapped, or something. I don't think pleading a headache would work again."

"No indeed," agreed her friend as they arrived at the dressmaker's establishment. "Shall I call for you?" she asked doubtfully, preparing to descend from the vehicle.

Emma shook her head. "No. I shall make my own way home. . . . And in the meantime I shall be grateful if you would give your mind to finding an excuse for me."

They parted at the door, Elvira to her fitting and Emma to walk the short distance to the theater. Here, she found all in readiness for the rehearsal to begin. Tom and Molly Rourk gave an almost perceptible sigh of relief at her entrance, the sergeant hurrying forward to greet her with exclamations of delight and an extravagant bow.

"I shall prompt from the wings," announced his spouse, hobbling to a sofa which had been placed in readiness and arranging herself in as graceful a pose as her plastered leg would allow along its somewhat drab length. "A still, small voice in the dark, so to speak."

"I think I know my words," said Emma nervously.

"Then—to work. The actors are as before, so there is no need for introductions. So—to work," cried Sergeant Rourk, eager to begin, and he quickly set the scene to refresh her memory.

To her relief Emma found that with the help of aide-mémoire pinned strategically to props and even the scenery and furniture, she could manage creditably. The booming voice of Mrs. Rourk issuing from behind the scenery proved a little distracting, but altogether she felt that she would be able to acquit herself with more than reasonable aplomb, and after several hours of intense work, Tom Rourk called a halt, declaring that he was satisfied.

"Don't you agree, my love?" he inquired anxiously, peering into the wings.

"Indeed I do, Mr. R," his wife called. "A sufficiency would be too much—we must leave it now, while the iron is hot and bring it to the boil tomorrow night."

"How right you are, Molly, my dear," agreed her husband, apparently understanding this confusing speech without difficulty. "Until tomorrow evening then, Miss B."

"Child," called the actress thrillingly from her couch. Obeying the summons, Emma found her with an arm outstretched in a dramatic gesture and allowed her own hand to be taken and clasped to the other's bosom. "Child!" repeated Molly Rourk in even more thrilling tones. "You have a gift—I declare I see another Sarah Siddons in the making. Your princess may even equal mine. I can say no more."

"You have said enough, my love," announced her spouse. "Only a true Thespian could be so generous in praise of another!"

Mrs. Rourk accepted this with a beatific smile and said complacently, "Our little Miss Emma will prove a pupil worthy of me, mark my words, Mr. R. A veritable Queen Midas, I promise you."

"I certainly hope that I have the golden touch, for your

sakes," agreed Emma. "I must own to a degree of nervousness. . . ."

"Without nerves one cannot claim to be an actress," Mrs. Rourk told her grandly, while the sergeant nodded sagely. "A little honest fright will put the edge upon the blade, so to speak, polish your shield to perfection and turn your chrysalis of talent into the beauty of immense achievement!"

Emma blinked under this flow of rhetoric. "I daresay that you are right, Ma'am," she said weakly, and made good her escape before Mrs. Rourk could confuse her further.

The afternoon was far advanced, and dusk had begun to fall with faint gray shadows as she left the theater. Hurrying through the streets, she gave her mind to the problem of an excuse to stay behind the following night and so did not notice the ragamuffin figure following her, until the child suddenly ran past, grabbing at her reticule as he went.

Hanging onto the strings with one hand, Emma fetched the half-grown figure a telling clip over one ear with the other, eliciting a yelp of pain from her would-be assailant. Taken by surprise, the boy clutched his ear and burst into loud sobs.

"Ow, you hurt me, you did!" he accused, glaring balefully at her from out of a dirty face.

"Well, you should not have tried to steal my bag," Emma felt called upon to point out.

"It ain't right—you shouldn't have."

The urchin waxed so indignant and his sobs and howls so loud, that Emma began to feel in the wrong. "Do stop that noise," she urged, as he dragged his tattered sleeve across his wet face. "Look, I'll give you a penny—"

The noise stopped abruptly as he surveyed her across the edge of his arm. Keeping her reticule out of reach, she felt inside and held a penny out invitingly.

"What's your name?" she asked as he shuffled forward, eyes fixed on the coin.

"Joe, missis," he said, making a grab for the money and

biting it quickly before bestowing it somewhere about his person.

"Well, Joe, do you always try to rob ladies?"

"Yes," he admitted. "They're easier than men." Eyeing her, he rubbed his ear reflectively. "I ain't never had one clout me lug'ole, afore!"

"It's what you deserved," Emma told him. "Now go away, you bad child."

Setting off homeward once more, she had gone some way when she became aware of being followed and, turning quickly, found her former assailant close upon her heels.

"What do you want?" she demanded.

Joe stopped a few paces away. "Nothing."

"Well, go away," she said impatiently, setting off again, uneasily aware of the small figure that dogged her footsteps.

Entering the square, she paused and waited for the child to catch up. When he failed to arrive, she turned to find him leaning casually against a railing, staring up at the sky, whistling shrilly.

"Joe," she said sharply, and he started with assumed surprise. "Come here."

"Me, missis?" he asked innocently, having made a play of looking round for the person she was addressing.

"Why are you following me?"

"Me, missis? I wasn't, miss, I was seeing you safe home, miss. There are plenty of bad folk around, y'know. The streets ain't safe."

Uncertain whether to laugh at his cheek or clip his other ear, Emma looked down at him. The cocky grin only reached as far as his mouth, his eyes were watchful and wary, their expression far too old for a child. Although he leaned against the park railing, his hands in his ragged pockets, she could see that he was tense and poised for instant flight. There was something so gallant and yet pathetic in his stance that she was touched and her expression softened.

He scuffed one bare foot in the dust of the pavement. "I—

thanks for the penny, missis," he muttered without looking at her, and made to shuffle off.

"Wait—" she cried before thinking, and he paused, sending her a glance at once wary and hopeful as she rummaged in her reticule. "Here's sixpence," she said, holding it out. "Go home now, and give it to your mama."

"Ain't got no ma," he shouted after her as she hurried off. "Ain't got no pa, neither."

Determined not to look back, she crossed the grassy square and rang the doorbell. Glancing over her shoulder, she was dismayed to see the small figure still watching her and was relieved when Frobisher opened the door and she could slip inside.

The encounter with the urchin had prove beneficial, for upon climbing the stairs, she found a ready-formed plan had arrived in her brain and, having regarded it from all angles, knew that it would suffice as her reason for crying off from Sir Julian's planned theater visit. Accordingly, she continued upstairs to Maria's room in order to enlist her aid and, when she descended to dine with the family a short while later, had only to mention that the invalid seemed a little unwell to begin to put her plan into action.

The next morning, having nothing better to do, the two girls decided to partake of the last of the sunshine and walk in the railed garden belonging to the square. Busy with her own thoughts, the memory of Joe had slipped to the back of her mind, and Emma was somewhat surprised when Elvira suddenly inquired why a dirty little boy was following them.

"Oh, dear." She sighed, recognizing the disreputable figure hovering casually a short distance away. "It's Joe."

Elvira wrinkled her nose in distaste. "Do you know him?" she asked incredulously.

"He tried to steal my reticule," admitted the other, making shooing movements, which the child studiously ignored.

"I shall get one of the footmen to see him off," announced Elvira firmly.

"No—don't do that. He's only a child—and an orphan."

"You shouldn't speak to him—it only encourages them, and if he's a thief, we should really call the beadle," Elvira said severely.

"Pooh, what nonsense! I would not have thought it of you, Elvira! Look how thin he is—I daresay he is hungry, and that is why he steals." Ignoring her companion's scandalized expression, she marched to a seat, sat down, and beckoned imperiously to Joe, who had been listening to this exchange with unabashed interest.

Sidling up, he hovered at one end, while Elvira, with many expressions of distaste, perched herself on the other.

"Now, Joe," began Emma sternly, "what are you doing here? This is a private garden, you know, and not open to the public."

Sniffing and wiping his nose on his sleeve, he shrugged expressively and said nothing.

Emma tried again. "Where do you live?"

He seemed unable to answer, venturing at last that he knew of a nice little alleyway that was all right, as long as it did not rain.

"Surely you don't live in an alley!" exclaimed Emma, shocked.

Joe laughed at her ignorance. "Course not," he assured her cheerfully. "I just *sleeps* there. Old Grumbleguts 'ud kill me if he found me there in the day. Proper old devil *he* is!"

Emma and Elvira exchanged horrified glances. "And—how do you live?" asked Emma soberly.

"Oh, I—" Mindful of his audience, Joe swallowed the words he had been about to say and concluded angelically, "I *finds* things. And some folk gives me things. I manage—sometimes Old Grumbleguts throws out bits of pies and such like. They don't half taste good, I can tell you. He's a good cook and no mistake. People comes from all over London for one of his pies."

In his enthusiasm Joe licked his lips, making hearty smacking sounds to show his appreciation.

"Where are your mother and father?" demanded Elvira indignantly. "Does no one care for you?"

"Me ma and pa are dead, I told *her*." He indicated Emma. "I cares for meself."

"Don't you go to school?"

"A'course not!" He regarded Elvira impatiently and returned his attention to Emma. "You going back to the theater?" he inquired. "Cause if you are, you need someone to see you right. It ain't proper for young ladies to wander about without no one to watch out for them." He looked at Emma meaningly before leaning forward to make his proposal. "I'll look after you, missis—it'll cost you a penny a day, and I can't say fairer than that."

"You are only a little boy," Elvira pointed out.

Hunching a shoulder, he ignored her, speaking to Emma earnestly, his expression intense. "I'm older than what I look, miss—and I knows a lot. I'd see you right and proper, honest, I would."

Emma was touched. "I'm sure you would, Joe," she said kindly, "but I've a better idea. How would you like to live in my house?" Behind her, Elvira was making scandalized squeaks, but Emma ignored her, taking Joe's dirty chin in her hand and turning his face up to hers. "Not here, but in the country. You could be my gardener boy. What do you say?"

# Chapter Fifteen

*J*oe seemed undecided. "I ain't never been in the country," he said doubtfully. "D'you mean with cows and things?"

"Well, there *are* cows in the country, but not in my garden. It would be quite different from here—you'd have new clothes and a bed and enough food, and in return you'd have to be good, do as you're told—"

Joe hesitated no longer. "I'll come, miss," he said and, shuffling his bare feet, appeared ready to start that very minute.

"But first you'll have to live here while matters are arranged," Emma told him, rising to her feet. "Do you think Jem can be persuaded to care for him for a few days?" she asked Elvira.

"I don't think Ju will take kindly to having a waif foisted upon him," was the answer. "Surely you are not intending to bring him into the house? He's really very dirty. Aunt Diana would not care for it, you know."

"Sometimes, Elvira, you have too much sensibility," Emma told her friend. Taking the urchin's hand, she inspected him, noting the grubby skin and tattered, dirty clothes and, reluctantly, had to admit that the other was right. "I shall take him straight to the stables," she announced, "and leave him in Jem's capable hands."

Leaving Elvira at the front steps of the house, she made her way round the side and in at the entrance to the mews.

Here, she found a groom and asked him to send Jem to her, while a bemused Joe clutched her hand and gazed round in awe. She was pleased to notice that his eyes were bright and alert for all his evident nervousness and that he stood straight and upright by her side.

Whatever emotions he was feeling, Jem hid them behind an impassive manner as she made her wishes known. He and Joe eyed each other warily before, apparently recognizing kindred spirits, they walked off together, leaving Emma to go in search of Sir Julian and make her peace with him.

She found him in his study, ensconced behind the pages of a large newspaper, which he lowered at her approach.

"I would like a word with you, if you are not too busy," she began.

He folded the news sheet and dropped it on a nearby table. "I was making sure that all is right with the world," he said lightly. "I see that nothing more amiss than a French prisoner of war escaping has happened."

Emma was momentarily diverted. "From one of the hulks in Portsmouth harbor?" she asked, remembering the rotting ships she had seen when she had arrived at the port.

"From Porchester Castle—I believe that they wander almost at will in the village there—the wonder is that more do not attempt it."

"In general, I suppose, their accent would give them away," she suggested.

"Indeed so. This one has been gone for almost a week, which makes it likely that he has an accomplice, I'd say, to keep him hidden. The report says that soldiers are scouring the area."

"With no great enthusiasm, I'll be bound," Emma said. "They will have a fellow feeling for him." Having exhausted the subject, she fell silent, biting her lip and glancing at Sir Julian from under her eyelashes.

"You wanted to see me?" he prompted at last.

"Y-es. I have need of your help." Raising his eyebrows,

he looked interested, and she hurried on; "I have decided to adopt—well, not adopt exactly, more *foster* a small boy and would be extremely grateful if he could lodge in your stables until I can find a means of sending him down to Hodge Hall."

Sir Julian's expression remained impassive, despite a gleam of amusement in his eyes. "May one inquire what boy, and how this came about?" he asked blandly.

"I met him yesterday when he—when he tried to steal my reticule." Ever honest, Emma's voice nevertheless held a distinctly defiant note.

"One can see how that would encourage a wish to adopt him," he agreed in so reasonable a voice that Emma felt annoyance rising.

"Of *course* it did not," was the withering reply. "At first I was very angry and smacked his head, which startled him, you know."

"It would," remarked Sir Julian agreeably.

Ignoring this, Emma went on. "He was so surprised that he began to talk. . . . And the poor child has *nothing*! He is dressed in rags and seems to live on the remains of pies that some butcher throws out. He sleeps in an alley, which he assures me is nice, unless it rains!"

Her voice broke, and she swallowed convulsively, making Sir Julian regard her closely.

"He seems to have played on your good nature," he said. "Possibly he is a member of a gang, taught to inveigle himself into houses, which are then burgled."

Emma shook her head. "I am certain that he is not," she said emphatically, "but just in case, I have left him in the stables under the care of Jem."

"Very wise. I will have a word with that young man and see what he thinks. Jem is very shrewd."

"And Joe can stay here in the meantime—just until I can make arrangements to send him down to Hodge Hall?"

"You cannot be opening an asylum for all and sundry, you know," Sir Julian pointed out gently.

"I know. . . . But Joe will make a very good gardener's boy, and if one has money, one may as well use it to some purpose, not just for one's own enjoyment."

"I see that you have the makings of a philanthropist," her companion observed, impressed.

"And I see that you intend to tease me. Very well, Sir Julian, laugh if you will, but in this I am serious. Will you allow Joe to stay here until a message can be got to Hodge Hall, notifying them of his arrival?"

"Of course, child." Sir Julian's expression was so kind and indulgent that again Emma had to fight back the urge to confess all. To compensate for such weakness, she straightened her posture and spoke coolly, assuming a remote manner.

"I am most grateful, sir, and will bother you no more."

If Julian Leyton was surprised by her manner, he hid it well, merely informing her that a groom would be sent upon the message and watched her thoughtfully as she escaped from the study.

Late that afternoon, having spent the hours since luncheon with a well-primed Maria, Emma slipped downstairs and presented her excuses to her hostess.

"Poor Maria is not at all well . . . a low fever and headache, nothing to worry about over much, but I really feel I should stay with her, rather than go to the theater this evening," she explained in a suitably disappointed manner, while feeling uncomfortably guilty at her deception.

"Of course you must do as you think best, my dear, but could not Hetty or Hill oblige?"

"Maria is in a restless mood, you know how it is with invalids. She will settle for no one other than me, I am afraid."

"Emma dear, you must learn to control your kindness. Servants will rule *you*, given the chance."

"I shall give in to her just this once. And, indeed, she has

211

not asked me. She seems so low and fretful that I decided to keep her company, out of humanity.''

Lady Beauvale said no more, and when the theater party set off that evening, Emma watched from an upstairs window.

''Sir Ju won't half be mad,'' Maria told her half-fearfully, her eyes round with excitement as she peered over the bedclothes. ''He'll turn me off, I shouldn't wonder and you—''

''Oh, Maria, do be quiet,'' cried her mistress, who did not want to hear her maid's surmisings, having an uncomfortable suspicion that they might be true. ''In a few hours it will be over—we must just hope that nothing goes amiss and that no one is any the wiser.''

She spoke more positively than she felt, having long before that moment wished that she had not agreed to the foolhardy venture.

''*And* what about walking home after midnight?'' went on Maria remorselessly. ''It'll be proper dangerous, 'm, that's what. I'm that worried—''

''Well, there at least you have no need,'' Emma assured her, ''for I sent a note this morning to Captain Gray begging him to escort me home.'' Pleased with her forethought and certain that Johnnie Gray would comply with her request, she beamed at her little maid, who did not appear too impressed.

''Let's hope it works,'' she said, snorting.

''Of course it will. Johnnie Gray is a man to be relied upon. You may rest easy, Maria, in the sure knowledge that I shall be well looked after.''

After making sure that the girl had everything she needed, Emma left the house and made her way to the theater in Covent Garden. Already people were wending their way toward it in the half-light, happy in the thought of an evening's entertainment.

Entering by the stage door, she hurried upstairs and poked her head around the green-room door. Molly Rourk, who was lying on the bed-settee with her leg propped up, brightened and tossed aside the book she had been desultorily reading.

"Dear child!" she cried. "Your shining countenance fills me with joy—I *had* wondered if you would hide your light under a bush, so to speak, and deny us the pleasure of seeing your performance. Now, run along to the dressing room. I have bidden my own dresser to help you. Remember all I have taught you, and you need have no fear. I shall not wish you luck, for we of the theater have a superstition that to do so is unlucky, instead I shall say—bring the house down!"

With the odd request ringing in her ears, Emma went in search of the dressing room, finally finding it after several attempts. An old crone was already ensconced, busily setting out pots of paint in front of a misty, fly-blown mirror.

Looking up as Emma entered, she stared through the curl of smoke rising from the bowl of a clay pipe she held clenched between her teeth. Having examined the girl from head to foot, she gave an unexpected smile, showing blackened stumps and waved her toward a screen in one corner of the room.

"You'll be the New Hope?" she remarked, speaking in the capital letters Emma had come to expect from anyone associated with the theater. "Well, well and a right pretty little piece, too. You'll be the darling of the audience in no time."

Changing into the familiar pink costume which someone had altered into a surprisingly good fit, Emma seated herself in front of the dusty table and allowed the old woman to make up her face. Gradually, under the gnarled, experienced fingers, she saw herself transformed from a genteel, modern lady into a colorful beauty, whose striking looks would have attracted attention in any age. The pink turban was placed on her fair curls an the veil adjusted with delicate precision.

"Well, miss," commented the dresser, stepping back the better to examine her handiwork, "though I say it myself— you could name your price tonight. There's some out there as would set you up in your own establishment if you was so much as to give them a wink!''

Emma blinked and then accepted the comment as the compliment it was intended to be.

"Then I shall be very careful not to wink," she said lightly. "I am doing this performance as a favor to Mr. and Mrs. Rourk, who were very good to me a few months ago."

"Nice couple they are . . . not a bit high-blown for all they are famous. It'ud have been a sad pity if they'd had to lose this benefit. A tidy sum 'ud set them up nicely. And, I've been promised a place in their school of acting."

With a final pat of approval, Emma was whisked from the dressing room and escorted to the stage. Above, the sound of the orchestra tuning up the buzz of the expectant audience could be clearly heard, its murmured anticipation carried to Emma, making her suddenly sick with fear. Sensing her stage fright, the dresser propelled her across the boards to her place in the wings as a jaunty sea shanty was struck up.

With a smile and nod for her alone, Tom Rourk, in full costume, strode past her and slipped between the closed curtains. The clamor that greeted his appearance died down, and he began speaking in his actor's carefully pitched voice.

"My dear friends," he began, "my dear wife, that well-known and loved lady of the theater, has sustained an injury to her lower limb, and to her regret and mine, she is unable to perform tonight." There were loud sighs and groans from the audience. "However," he went on, obviously holding up his hand for silence as the commotion gradually died down. "However, all is not lost—at the last minute someone, who must be nameless, stepped in and saved the day!"

"At short notice a lady of quality, ladies and gentlemen, has agreed to take the part of the Princess of Morocco. Beautiful and talented, for this one night only, she will tread the boards for your edification. Watch carefully, my friends, so that you can tell your children that you saw the one and only appearance of—a lady of fashion!"

To tumultuous applause he returned, nodding triumphantly to Emma. The actor playing the Jolly Jack Tar dashed past as the curtains parted, taking up his place not a moment too soon, and all at once the play was underway, sweeping Emma along in the wake of its excitement.

To her delight the audience took her to its heart, and she experienced the heady excitement of knowing that she held it in thrall. The mystery of her identity was deliberately heightened, the Eastern veil serving to mask her features, and even the final kiss had been contrived so that her face remained hidden.

When the final curtain fell on the lovers' embrace, the applause was thunderous, the audience jumping to its feet and demanding that she should unmask. Acknowledging the applause with a curtsy, she intimated her refusal to lift the veil with a graceful gesture, so appealing that the audience was immediately won over to her side, showering the stage with money and flowers.

After six curtain calls and five speeches of thanks from Sergeant Rourk, the actors were at last allowed to go, and Emma thankfully ran to the dressing room, her arms filled with flowers that she had gathered up from the stage floor.

Going first to the green room, she found Molly Rourk there, a strange expression on her plump face. Knowing that she could not but be aware of the audience's rapture, Emma laid the mass of blooms in her lap.

"These, ma'am, are for you—from a loving, but disappointed, public," she said. "I am merely the messenger."

Mrs. Rourk's expression cleared miraculously, the drooping disappointment disappearing to be replaced by fond smiles. "My dear apprentice!" she cried. "Only a true Thespian could acknowledge a debt with so much grace. I flatter myself that I had no little part in the success of tonight. I shall always think of you as my little pygmy!"

"Pygmalian," corrected the sergeant, entering at that moment. "What a success—due mainly to your talent as a teacher, my love—if Miss B will forgive me for saying so."

"Without Mrs. Rourk's help, I could not have done it," admitted Emma honestly. "But now I must take off my makeup and leave quickly, if I am to get home without discovery."

As she spoke the green room door opened and the other actors streamed in, a noisy and exalted throng, all speaking and laughing at once. Realizing that she had been forgotten, Emma slipped away unnoticed and, having removed all sign of the Princess of Morocco, made her way down the stairs to the stage door, certain that the rifleman would be growing impatient.

To her dismay there was no sign of Johnnie Gray, and when she had waited several minutes, she began to doubt that he was coming. Covent Garden was deserted, playbills and other discarded rubbish blowing across the cobblestones being the only sign of the recent crowd, and she rapidly became uneasy, shivering in the night air.

Suddenly the sound of approaching hooves made her lift her head hopefully, and as a chaise came into view, she sighed with relief, stepping in without question as the door was opened and the steps let down.

"Oh, Johnnie," she cried, settling herself in a corner, "I thought you had let me down."

"I fear the redheaded rifleman has," drawled an unexpected voice from the darkness. "Captain Gray is out of town, so cannot be blamed. How lucky that I should happen along. Will I do in his stead, Miss Beringer?"

Stiff with shock, she could think of nothing to say, and Lord Devern tapped on the roof with his cane. As the driver obeyed the order and started off again, he leaned forward and spoke into the uncomfortable silence.

"Do I detect a hint of greasepaint, Miss Beringer?" he asked delicately. "I had no idea that you had a liking for the theater. The performance was very good, was it not? Especially the lady of fashion who played the lead.''

Emma moved involuntarily, and her companion leaned back against the leather upholstery, a satisfied smile playing around his mouth. With his chin sunk into the folds of his snowy cravat, he watched her from beneath half-closed eyelids.

"It is very odd,'' he went on, "but then, coincidences so often are, don't you find? Some months ago when I was last in Portsmouth, the very same play was being performed— and that very night I had the pleasure of meeting a mysterious lady, who had obviously spent the evening treading upon 'the boards.' You must admit that it is strange—''

"Where are you taking me?'' Emma demanded, recovering her voice.

"To Cumberland Square, of course,'' she was told, as if any other destination were unthought of.

"How does the cab driver know?''

Vivian Devern laughed softly. "I told him before we started across the Garden,'' he said, to her surprise. "My dear Miss Beringer, I must confess . . . I saw you leave the theater the other afternoon. It was easy to put two and two together, once I found out that Molly Rourk was indisposed, and I took it upon myself to make sure that you would reach home safely. Ju really would not care for you roaming the streets alone at night, you know.''

"I am aware of that—and had asked Johnnie Gray to escort me. . . . I cannot understand what has happened. . . .''

"I saw him driving out of town early this morning. Which makes it fortunate that I saw you and guessed what you were about. Indeed, you are doubly lucky, for I am setting off early myself tomorrow morning, intending to sail my yacht in the Solent. . . . So, a day later and you would have found yourself friendless!'' He studied her downcast face for a moment before, leaning forward again, he possessed himself of one of her hands. "Miss Beringer—''

Emma was not to discover what he was about to say, for he broke off as there was a thump against the back of the carriage and an irate driver could be heard, shouting and cracking his whip.

"Whatever is the matter?" cried Emma, startled.

"Some wretched child, jumping up behind to steal a ride."

"I do not consider that so very dreadful—pray tell the driver to stop that at once," Emma commanded as the whip continued to crack and whistle past the window as the cabby redoubled his endeavors to dislodge the unwelcome passenger. "The child will be hurt—and he's doing no harm."

In her agitation she looked ready to jump out of the vehicle, and Lord Devern reached up to knock on the roof again. "Desist, Jones," he said languidly.

"Its all right, my lord, he's fallen off," the driver returned, a note of satisfaction in his voice.

Vivian Devern put out a restraining hand as Emma leaned to peer out of the window.

"Take no heed," he said. "It would take more than a tumble to damage a street urchin."

And, to her relief, Emma saw a small figure climb to its feet and begin to run after the coach. "I'm surprised, Lord Devern, that you are so unfeeling," she said severely.

"I've done it myself," she was told, "and sustained little hurt when whipped off." The silence lengthened again, and Emma was wracking her brains for some safe conversational gambit, when her companion spoke again. "Miss Emma, let us cease to beat about the bush. I am well aware of your activities this evening. Indeed, I am full of admiration for your acting ability and readily admit that you could make a career upon the stage—though, to be honest, I cannot see why you should wish to when you are more than provided for. I take it that, while Julian was aware of your first taste of greasepaint, he is ignorant of your latest peccadillo and that you wish to keep it that way."

"Yes," Emma admitted, shuddering at the thought of Sir

Julian ever learning of her exploit. "It would be a very un-gentlemanly thing to tell him," she pointed out.

"My dear Miss Beringer, your secret is safe with me," his lordship assured her. "I can understand perfectly well your desire to help old friends and applaud you for it. Also I can sympathize with your wish to retain secrecy—Ju, I assure you, would *not* understand."

"No, indeed!" was Emma's heartfelt agreement, and feeling more in sympathy with her companion, she relaxed a little, leaning back against the leather upholstery as the carriage trundled through the quiet streets.

"It was very opportune that you happened by just when you did," she remarked, surveying the man opposite, who bowed silently. "Quite a coincidence, in fact," she went on. "Indeed, I find it quite remarkable."

"There was nothing remarkable about it—as I am sure you are already aware. It came to me in a flash—seeing you with the sergeant, I recognized the actress who had accompanied Julian up the stairs of the George in Portsmouth all those months ago." He eyed her with a slight smile. "You are not easily forgotten, my dear," he pointed out quietly.

"N-no one will believe you," Emma stammered.

"After tonight they would," was the calm response, "but have no fear, I do not intend to make known the identity of the mysterious lady of quality who trod the boards so admirably. To be truthful I find I like the idea of knowing more than the estimable Julian."

To her relief, for she was finding the conversation uncomfortable, the carriage stopped, and Emma saw that they were alongside the steps and portico of Sir Julian's house.

Lord Devern opened the door and, climbing out, lowered the steps himself. With a gallant gesture he held out a hand and, trustingly, Emma bent her head in the low interior and prepared to descent. To her surprise, Vivian Devern placed both hands round her waist and lifted her down, drawing her close and closing her protesting mouth with an unexpected kiss.

Too astonished to release herself, Emma was surprised when her assailant suddenly gave an exclamation of pain and stepped back abruptly.

"You leave her alone, d'you hear!" yelled an indignant voice, and a small figure threw himself at his lordship, furiously kicking his shins and pummeling him with bony, clenched fists.

"Joe!" cried Emma faintly, suddenly realizing who had been the unwanted passenger. Lord Devern seized the small figure by the scruff of the neck and raised a hand. "Don't dare hit him," she exploded, and hung grimly on the upraised arm.

"Street brawling!" drawled a voice behind them. "Not your kind of affair, I'd have thought, Devern."

All three antagonists turned to see Sir Julian surveying them coolly, obviously just returning from some nocturnal activity of his own.

"Ju!" cried Emma gladly, and thankfully ran to his side only to be disconcerted by the cold gaze turned briefly on her.

"Release the boy," he commanded in dangerously quiet tones.

Lord Devern initially hesitated but finally dropped Joe with a gesture of disdain.

The urchin scampered across the pavement to stand beside Sir Julian. "Give him what for," he encouraged loudly, taking swipes at an imaginary enemy with his closed fists.

"Be quiet," murmured Sir Julian, and to Emma's surprise, he fell silent. "Good night, Devern," Julian Leyton said inexorably.

With a harsh, smothered laugh, Lord Devern bowed elaborately and, climbing back into his carriage, ordered the coach to be driven on.

"What are you doing out at this hour, Joe?" demanded the baronet.

"Just making sure that the lady got home safe—I wasn't doing nothing wrong, honest."

"There, I have my doubts. If Jem finds any watches or other valuables in your pockets, he has my permission to do more than bath you—"

"Honest, guvnor. I ain't done nothing—save watch out for the lady. You ought to take better care of her, yourself," he added darkly.

"Enough," said Sir Julian sharply, but his hand briefly brushed the tousled mop of newly washed hair that covered Joe's unusually clean face. "Be off with you."

With a salute which was almost, but not quite, cheeky, Joe took to his heels, running round the corner toward the mews, and Sir Julian turned to Emma.

His dark gaze traveled slowly over her, from her head to the toes of her shoes. His nostrils flared as he caught the familiar but unexpected odor of greasepaint and cheap perfume.

"Now," he said softly, taking her elbow in a painful grip and turning her toward the house, "let us go in, if you please."

Passing the goggle-eyed butler, who had come out to see the cause of the noise, Sir Julian calmly handed him his hat, gloves, and cane. "Go to bed, Frobisher," he ordered gently, in a voice which brooked no argument, and led Emma into the study, closing the door firmly on the retainer's interested gaze.

"Well, miss?" he asked in a tone that made Emma quake. "What have you to say?"

# Chapter Sixteen

$\mathcal{T}$aking a deep breath, she prepared to confess the whole and hope for understanding, but before she could speak, he went on, speaking bitterly, as if unable to wait for the explanation he had demanded.

"I had expected better than to come upon you behaving like a ballet dancer."

Recognizing the euphemism, Emma gasped and, rarely for her, was bereft of speech.

"Thank Heavens that Lady Beauvale is long abed. If she had happened to see such behavior in one whom she has allowed to associate freely with her niece, she would have been shocked beyond comprehension. To have sneaked out like some common thief is bad enough, God knows, but to be found clinging fondly to a man whom you know has done us wrong, goes beyond all reason. And to do so in the middle of the street, in full view of all and that at a time when decent folk are abed—is totally unacceptable!"

Leaning against the door, Sir Julian surveyed her grimly, and Emma was surprised to read the depth of rage in his black eyes.

"Contemptible, miss," he observed. "To deceive us with tales of your goodness in caring for your maid when, in fact, you were creeping out on an assignation with Devern . . . and that, by the perfume you carry, in the lowest den of iniquity you could find."

His scornful tone stung Emma, and where a moment before her conscience had been troubling her, suddenly her guilt was transformed into anger, and lifting her chin, she glared stormily at her accuser.

"You take too much upon yourself, sir," she cried. "I am not answerable to you!"

She was the recipient of a stony gaze. "I had hoped that you might refute the matter."

Emma considered the matter. "Which one?" she inquired sweetly. "The den of iniquity or my wicked assignation?"

The baronet ground his teeth. "You do not deny that the jackanapes was kissing you?"

"No, indeed. How should I? It appears that you saw it all perfectly."

"I saw enough to know that you were enjoying his attentions—"

"La, sir," she cried, lost to all reason, "what is in a kiss?"

"Obviously in your estimation, not a great deal—which is why *I* shall claim my due." Levering his shoulders away from the door, he came purposefully toward her.

For a second Emma watched him, uncertain of his intent, then reading his purpose, she made an ineffectual attempt to evade him. Catching her as she tried to slip past, Sir Julian pulled her roughly into his embrace, twisting his fingers in her hair to subdue her struggles, and closed his hard, angry mouth over hers.

Fury at such treatment consumed Emma, and she struggled with all her strength, kicking against his shins until she was lifted off her feet and then punching with her clenched fists until her hands were pinioned behind her back.

Crushed against the hard, masculine length of him, Emma began to find his overpowering strength exciting, and instead of rage, a pleasurable exhilaration began to flood through her veins. An enjoyable warmth filled her with happy relief as she realized that Sir Julian returned the feelings she had suppressed for weeks, and she relaxed in his arms. Involuntarily her mouth softened under his caress, and when he released his grip, her arms crept upward to clasp around his neck, her fingers playing with his short, black curls.

Surprised by her own passion, Emma shivered with anticipation when Sir Julian raised his head, glanced up from under half-closed eyelids, expecting to see her own emotions mirrored in his face.

Instead, he was regarding her from icy black eyes, his expression cold and grim. Startled, she drew back as if cold water had been dashed in her face and gazed at him, wide-eyed and shocked.

"So, madam," he said, curling his lip. "It is as I thought—anyone will do."

Releasing her so abruptly that she almost fell and had to steady herself against a chair, he shriveled her with a glance of contempt. "Devern, me—who else, if it's not an indelicate question? By the smell of you, a play actor, but then you always did have a *penchant* for the vulgar theater, did you not?"

Supposing herself loved one moment and treated to a cruel tirade the next, Emma gazed at him in bewilderment, growing pale as realization dawned and she understood his accusations. For a second she stared up at him, her heart in her eyes before, drawing her pride around her, she straightened her shoulders and faced him bravely.

"You are wrong," she said with pitiful dignity, speaking in a shaking whisper. "I *did* deceive you, but not for the motive you suppose, and for that deception I apologize. . . ." She made a futile, helpless gesture with one hand. "There—there is nothing more to be s-said." With a brave attempt, she curved her stiff lips into a travesty of a social smile. "So, I will bid you good night," she said and, turning on her heel, left the room without waiting for his reply.

Sir Julian made a half-gesture to restrain her as she passed, but his hand fell to his side, and he watched without comment.

The way to her room seemed endless, the candles left earlier in strategic places were guttering, sinking into a sea of melted wax and throwing huge formless shadows as she passed. Once in her own room, Emma stood against the door, beyond tears, and attempted to take stock of the world that had crashed about her; there seemed nothing left, no hope, only a shattered future.

There appeared only one course open to her, and that was to leave Cumberland Square. Even though the thought filled her with an icy despair and brought a desolate sob to her throat, she knew that there was no other solution. . . . The thought of having to confront Sir Julian again was totally unbearable, and having decided upon her course of action, she at once began to put in into operation. Moving as quietly as possible, so as not to disturb anyone, she packed a few necessities in a small carpetbag and sat down at the table to write notes to Lady Beauvale and Elvira, leaving them propped beside the mirror.

Finally stripping off the evening gown she wore, she dressed again in a plain dove gray dress and pelisse that would not excite comment, tied the strings of an unexceptional bonnet under her chin, picked up the carpetbag, and after a final glance round the room, where she now realized she had been so happy, crept down the stairs.

Dawn was just breaking as she let herself out of the house and set off quickly across the square. Intending to hire a poste-chaise, she headed toward the nearest office. The streets were almost deserted, and she walked swiftly, her mind busy with a turmoil of emotions and so was oblivious of the tilbury which approached from behind and was checked as the driver recognized her.

Her name being called brought her out of her reverie, and she looked up to meet the surprised gaze of Vivian Devern.

"Miss Beringer," he repeated, as if doubting his eyes, "what brings you out at this hour?"

Turning toward the vehicle, Emma hesitated, and in that

moment by silent, but mutual, consent, the events of the previous evening were agreed to be forgotten. Knowing that only the truth would serve as an answer and yet unwilling to make her unhappiness known, she paused before replying.

"I wish to go to my house in Hampshire," she said at last, without elaborating. "And am about to hire a chaise."

To his credit, Lord Devern did not inquire into her reasons, instead insisting that he and his carriage were at her disposal.

"But—you were about your own business," she exclaimed. "I remember you saying you were going to Portsmouth."

"Hodge Hall is not far out of the way," he answered reassuringly, reaching a hand down to help her climb up beside him as if all was arranged, and somewhat to her surprise and certainly to her relief and gratification, Emma shortly found herself bowling out of London without the task of having to hire a public chaise, a feat which she suspected could prove difficult for an unaccompanied female.

"Oh, dear!" she exclaimed suddenly, having correctly identified a member of a group of noisy young gentlemen wending their way home after a night spent in social activity.

Bending her neck, she hid inside the deep brim of her bonnet and hoped that Freddie Melvin would not recognize her as Lord Devern flourished his whip in answer to his kinsman's greeting.

"You are safe now," he said a little later. "I think you need have no fear—it would be a wonder if Freddie recognized anyone after a night spent carousing with his cronies."

"I do hope not—though, why I should worry about it, I do not know. After all, I am of age, and no one can take exception at my driving with whom I please."

"Bravely spoken," drawled her companion, "but Ju is a formidable adversary."

Emma shot him a startled glance. "I had not thought—"

she exclaimed, conscience-stricken. "You do not think he will call you out again?"

"I would not be so foolish as to accept," she was told, and having reached the outskirts of the city, Lord Devern sprang his horse, and the light carriage picked up speed.

Trying to clutch her seat unobtrusively as they swayed and bounced over the dusty road, Emma admitted that while he was a good driver, Vivian Devern's talent was erratic. Where Sir Julian had never presented her with any qualms even while traveling at excessive speeds, she now was troubled with nervousness that made her uncomfortable. Several times they came within a hair's breadth of overturning, and when they scraped by a chairmaker's wagon, causing much of its load to be scattered over the road, she felt called upon to remonstrate.

"The fellow was in the way. When I have overturned you, Miss Beringer, then you may complain," she was told coolly, with no slackening of speed.

Taken aback by such ungentlemanly treatment, Emma found herself at a loss for words, falling quiet for several miles as they clattered through scattered hamlets and dashed past laborers and their families preparing for the new day.

The journey seemed interminable; her face was cold from the rush of chill air, and every muscle in her body had begun to ache with the effort of keeping her seat. The thought of a public poste chaise now began to have its attraction, and she found herself wishing heartily that she was safe inside such a vehicle, rather than perched atop Lord Devern's tilbury, however fashionable and dashing the equipage might be. . . . Besides, she had more than a sneaking suspicion that she had been decidedly foolish in accepting his offer to take her to Hodge Hall. Some instinct told her that his apparent kindness was more for his own good than hers.

Having made the briefest of stops to stretch their legs and water the horse, they started off again, and once back on the road, the remorseless speed was taken up again. A little after noon they paused for a quick luncheon, while the horse was exchanged, and then set off again. Emma was somewhat disturbed to notice that Vivian Devern had acquired a habit of peering over his shoulder and could not forebear to ask if they were being followed.

"This stretch is notorious for highwaymen," she was told curtly as the tilbury was tooled round a bend in the road.

She stared in disbelief. "Surely they do not *overtake* their intended victims—should you not rather be looking ahead for trouble?"

As her companion did not reply, Emma found herself reflecting upon how different this journey was from that undertaken with Sir Julian, and from there her memory dwelt upon the happy moments she had spent with him, which now seemed doubly precious. Tears filled her eyes, and blinking furiously, she loosed her grip on the leather upholstery to discreetly wipe her cheek, hoping that her companion would not notice her distress, which after all she must admit to having brought upon herself.

Turning away, she began to look about her, hoping to find some familiar aspect which would indicate that the long, uncomfortable journey would be near its end. Every bone in her body felt bruised, protesting each time a wheel hit a rut or stone. To her growing puzzlement she could recognize nothing, the countryside seemed much flatter than the rolling Hampshire downs she had admired on her previous journeys. For the first time in that interminable day, she attempted to turn her mind from the thoughts of her problems and the wretched understanding of how upset Elvira and Lady Beauvale must be by her actions. The very thought of Sir Julian and how low his estimation of her must be filled her with such dismay that she had to bite back a sob. Rather than give way to her emotions, she straightened her aching back and looked about. A suspicion, which would have dawned much sooner if she had not been so preoccupied, surfaced gradually, and she fought down a rising unease.

"Pray tell me," she began, speaking calmly. "Where are we?"

"Tired, Miss Beringer?" Lord Devern asked with another of his backward glances, and at that moment the hired horse chose to go lame, breaking his rhythmic trot as he favored his right foreleg.

The curse Lord Devern uttered would have shocked a lesser female, but Emma had heard much the same language many times as she followed her soldier father across the Peninsula, and beyond raising her eyebrows, she merely pointed out that there appeared to be an inn a little further along the road.

Bidding her to hold the reins, he jumped down to examine the animal's leg before, advising her to keep her seat, he led the equipage the short distance to the cluster of buildings. The fact that there was no exchange horse available did nothing for his temper, and his expression had tightened alarmingly as he handed Emma out of the carriage.

"We'll have to spend the night here," he announced, indicating the shadows which had begun to form in the corners of the yard.

The thought that the accident had been organized crossed Emma's mind, but one glance at the swollen fetlock of the horse told her that the injury was genuine. However, she was aware that money had changed hands a few minutes earlier as Vivian Devern spoke with the landlord, and judging by the sidelong glance sent in her direction, she had been the object of their conversation. Unhappily aware of her vulnerability, she decided that it would be wiser to go along with the suggestion for the time being, despite her growing unease. Following the landlord into the small black-and-white-beamed building, she was led upstairs to a room furnished with a table and chairs. Beyond was a bedroom, connected by a door. Here towels, sweet-smelling soap, and fresh water waited invitingly, and she made haste to wash away the signs of travel. Refreshed and invigorated, she returned to the outer room, feeling more herself. The lethargy of the last hours had dissipated, leaving her feeling once more ready to confront the world.

Returning to the outer room, she paused in the doorway, surprised to find Vivian Devern in what she had viewed as her private sitting room. He stood at the window, one hand holding back the curtain as he watched the road below.

He looked up with a smile at her entrance. "I've ordered dinner," he said easily.

Emma raised her eyebrows. "Is there no dining room?" she asked.

"Apparently none," was the cool answer. "Surely you are not averse to a tête à tête?"

Wondering how to reply, for she was definitely having grave misgivings about the wisdom of her action in accepting so readily Lord Devern's escort, Emma was saved from the need to answer by the arrival of the landlady and a junior minion, each bearing a tray loaded with as many dishes as it would hold.

"Evening, m'lord, miss," she said, bobbing a curtsy before proceeding to lay the table. "There's a ham, a pigeon pie, a nice fricassee of chicken, a salad, a fruitcake, and one of my own cheeses." She set each item on the table as she spoke and, going back to the door, brought in a black, stout bottle which she placed beside two glasses. "And a nice bottle of brandy,' she announced triumphantly, "which not so long ago was in the hands of them Frenchies!" Giving them, what Emma could not but feel, was a knowing look, she beamed conspiratorially. "Knowing as how you didn't want to be disturbed, I took it upon myself to bring all the vittles up at once—I hope I done right?"

While Emma was still digesting this, Lord Devern strode forward and dropped something that chinked into her ready palm. "I am sure it couldn't be better," he assured the woman and held the door gallantly as she and her maid left the room. Behind them Vivian Devern locked the door and pocketed the key with a calm assurance. "Come to the table, dear Miss Beringer,'' he invited softly, filling the waiting glasses.

Emma, who had been standing in the shadows, came forward and, having decided upon her course of action, seated herself at the table. "I vow I am starved," she announced calmly, shaking out her napkin.

Lord Devern paused briefly, sending her a thoughtful glance before setting the glass beside her plate. "Let me help you to a little meat," he said, carving a thin, pink slice from the ham.

Prolonging the meal as long as she could, picking at this, toying with that, Emma pushed food round her plate on the principle that no man would attempt to seduce an eating victim, unhappily aware that Vivian Devern was drinking heavily. Eventually, she was forced to set down her knife and fork.

"A little more cheese, Miss Beringer?" Lord Devern offered silkily. "I would not for the world have you leave the table hungry."

Sitting back, she lifted her chin and, knowing that she could dissemble no longer, eyed him steadily. "Well, my lord, what now?" she asked.

"What would you have?" he returned, amused.

"I would like most of all to retire to my room," she replied honestly, "but, I have the feeling that that is not what you have in mind!"

"How engagingly frank, my dear."

Emma leaned forward, resting her elbows on the table. "I do not see why you should suppose yourself able to address me with familiarity, just because you are intent upon seduction," she remarked conversationally. "I am afraid, Lord Devern, that I am not your 'dear,' and find it very unlikely that I ever will be!"

He leaned back, one long arm carelessly stretched across the table, very much at his ease. "Oh, I believe that such terms are quite acceptable among married folk."

She raised her eyebrows. "So—we are to be married! May I ask when this decision took place?"

"As soon as you became the Beringer Heiress, of course," was the easy answer. "Until then, I must confess, I merely had seduction in mind . . . having realized that Ju was more than interested in his ward."

"Of course! Your one idea is vengeance—how admirable!"

He flushed a little at the sting in her voice and deliberately refilled his glass, regarding her with glittering eyes. "I think," he said, "my *dear* Miss Beringer, it would be as well for you to mend your tongue, if we are to deal well together."

Emma considered, her head to one side. "But then, you see, I have no wish to deal with you at all!" His lordship hid his chagrin behind his glass, and after a while, she went on; "Pray sir, answer my curiosity. If, as I suppose, we are on our way to Gretna Green, what then, will happen to your yacht, awaiting you in the Solent?"

Drink had made him indiscreet, and he shook his head, smiling. "By now, it will be snug in Le Havre harbor."

"France!" she exclaimed, genuinely astonished.

"I see you are surprised. When I was so delighted to see you on the road, a happening that rapidly altered all my plans, I was on my way to meet a kinsman, who happened to also be a prisoner of war. It was remarkably easy to arrange, just a little judicial bribery needed to free him from Portchester Castle, find a suitable hiding place, and arrange to bring my yacht into Fareham Creek."

"So—that was what you were doing on all those trips back and forth." Emma looked at him with new interest, thinking that here was possibly one mitigating virtue in his unfortunate character—until he went on reflectively:

"Corruption only cost half the amount sent to me, so I'm in pocket, too."

"Phaw! You really are obnoxious!" she told him roundly.

Her disgust pleased rather than disturbed him, and he smiled at her obvious distaste. "So I have been told. I'm afraid that all my life it has been so—I take what I want. Only once has it been denied me, and now I can make Leyton pay in full for his previous interference." His voice was a little thick, and he stumbled slightly as he stood up. "Come, my heiress, it is time to cease this game—"

"I will not marry you!"

He laughed, swaying a little. "After tonight, you will have no choice!"

Still smiling, he came round the table, hands out toward her, and Emma scrambled to her feet, dodging away from his clutching fingers. Long ago she had fixed upon a weapon for just such an eventuality, and now she slipped round the table, determined to keep it within reach.

Instead of pursuing her, Lord Devern made a sudden grab across the table, his fingers hooking into the neck of her dress as he dragged her roughly toward him.

"Now, my girl—*now*!" he muttered thickly, crushing her against his body, brandy fumes making her head swim.

Behind her, Emma's questing hand found and grasped the brandy bottle, and raising it above her head, she paused for only the faintest moment before bringing it down with all her strength. At the last moment her assailant must have suspected something, for he glanced up and instead of hitting the back of his head as she intended, she struck him above his left eye. For a second nothing happened, and, the bottle having smashed into a thousand pieces, she was looking round for another weapon, when Lord Devern gave a groan and slowly slid downward to lie facedown on the floor at her feet.

Emma gave him a heartless kick, but when he rolled over to reveal a white face and blood welling from a gash on his forehead, she dropped to her knees with an exclamation of dismay.

"Dear God!" she cried. "I've killed him!"

Reaching up to the table, she found a napkin, folded it into a pad, and held it to the wound, wondering the while what her next move could be. Gradually she became aware that for some minutes there had been the sound of a noisy arrival in the yard, voices hurling questions and finally feet pounding up the stairs. Suddenly the locked door was shaken violently.

"Emma—Emma! Are you there?" a familiar voice shouted urgently, and at her glad cry, Sir Julian put his shoulder to the door and burst the lock.

The look of wild anxiety on his face as he charged in dispelled any doubts she had as to his regard for her, and her heart gave a great leap of joy, but recollecting the listeners, she said quite calmly, "Dear Ju, pray help me, for I am afraid that Lord Devern has met with an accident."

Having ascertained that she was unhurt, Sir Julian went down on his knee, taking the unconscious man's wrist between his finger and thumb. After a moment, he reported briefly: "He'll live." Then, his fury getting the better of him, he turned to Emma. "Goddammit, woman," he snarled. "Why did you have to wound the blackguard—now, how can I call him out?"

"I consider it a very good thing that I did, if you are so blood-thirsty," observed the Beringer Heiress, sitting back on her heels, "for only think how I should feel if you were to meet at dawn!"

By now an interested crowd filled the doorway, excited faces and goggling eyes struggling for the best view.

"Joe!" called Julian Leyton, and the little figure wriggled through the legs of the watchers and presented itself, quivering with eagerness. "Put your hand to this pad," he was commanded, and Sir Julian turned his attention to the landlord.

Soon the room was cleared of sightseers, the unconscious lord ensconced on the bed under the ministering attention of the landlady, a doctor had been sent for, and Sir Julian and

Miss Beringer were settled in the innkeeper's own comfortable parlor.

To her annoyance, Emma had suddenly come over "all missish," as Maria would have put it, and had had to be revived with a cup of tea. Sir Julian's arms had been satisfyingly strong as he carried her to the settle, and despite her halfhearted protests she had been firmly treated like an invalid.

"What I do not understand," she admitted, having finished her tea, "is how you found me."

"There you must thank Joe," she was told. "He saw you creep from the house and followed. When he saw that damned fellow take you up in his carriage, he had the sense to hare back and insist upon my being woken." Julian paused and turned her face up to his before going on. "He also made me acquainted with the facts behind the episode at the gate of my house. I am truly sorry for my misunderstanding."

Emma hastened to take upon herself most of the guilt, and for a moment it looked as if an argument would take place, but realizing where it would lead, they both broke off in some enbarrassment.

"Do, pray go on . . . Joe has only just awoken you . . ."

"I thought that you'd gone to Hodge Hall and was about to take the Hampshire road but, upon inquiry, found that no one had seen Devern's rather noticeable outfit, so headed back into town."

Relieving her of the teacup, he possessed himself of her hand and carried it to his lips, an action which Emma found very pleasant, allowing him to kiss each finger before inquiring:

"And, then?"

"*Then*, I happened upon Freddie—slightly bosky, but able to tell me that he had seen you in the tilbury heading for the Great North Road—so I knew what that devil was up to? And the carriage was clearly visible from the road." He gritted his teeth. "To try the same trick twice! And you, my darling, with only a bottle to defend yourself."

"Oh, I had a pistol, too," she told him composedly, "but I'd hidden that under the pillow—as a last resort, so to speak. I decided that to shoot him would cause such a scandal that it was only to be thought of in extremity!"

For a moment he looked at her in wonder before his shoulders shook, and giving a choked laugh, he gathered her into his arms. "By all that's marvelous! My brave girl! I begin to feel a modicum of sympathy for the wretch—he didn't have a chance!"

Emma nodded in agreement. "I did not care for him, you see," she said simply.

A thought struck them both, and for a moment their eyes locked as a wild notion entered both their heads.

"What would you say—what would your answer be . . . if someone else were to . . . ?" He broke off in some confusion, searching her face. Reading the humble uncertainty in the usually self-confident black eyes, Emma let down her own guard and allowed him to see into her heart. A glad smile transformed his face. "Dearest Emma—kitten," he said. "Will you come with me to Gretna?"

"Gladly, sir," she answered, putting up her face for his kiss, "but only think how confused the gossips will be!"

"The gossips, kitten, may go hang," Sir Julian replied.